Praise for Lauraine Snelling

REUNION

"Snelling's previous novels have been popular with readers, and this one, loosely based on her own life, will be no exception." —*Publishers Weekly*

"Inspired by events in Snelling's own life, REUNION is a beautiful story about characters discovering themselves as the foundation of their family comes apart at the seams. Readers may recognize themselves or someone they know within the pages of this book, which belongs on everyone's keeper shelf." —*RT Book Reviews*

"REUNION is a captivating tale that will hook you from the very start...Fans of Christian fiction will love this touching story." —*FreshFiction.com*

WAKE THE DAWN

"Snelling continues to draw fans with her stellar storytelling skills. This time she offers a look at smalltown medical care in a tale that blends healing, love, and a town's recovery... Snelling's description of events at the small clinic during the storm is not to be missed." —*Publishers Weekly*

"This is a strong, believable story." —*RT Book Reviews*

"Lauraine Snelling's newest novel will keep you turning pages and not wanting to put the book down... *Wake the Dawn* is a guaranteed good read for any fiction lover."
—Cristel Phelps, *CBA Retailers and Resources*

ON HUMMINGBIRD WINGS

"Snelling can certainly charm." —*Publishers Weekly*

"Snelling, a wonderful, talented writer, has brought readers a novel with characters who seem more real than fictional."
—*RT Book Reviews*

ONE PERFECT DAY

"Snelling, whose novels have sold more than two million copies, is sure to grab readers from the start of this holiday melodrama...[a] spiritually challenging and emotionally taut story." —*Publishers Weekly*

"Snelling's captivating tale will immediately draw readers in. The grief process is accurately portrayed, and readers will be enthralled by the raw emotion of Jenna's and Nora's accounts." —*RT Book Reviews*

Reunion

Also by Lauraine Snelling

Heaven Sent Rain

Wake the Dawn

On Hummingbird Wings

One Perfect Day

Breaking Free

Available from FaithWords wherever books are sold.

Reunion

A Novel

LAURAINE SNELLING

NEW YORK BOSTON NASHVILLE

Copyright © 2012 by Lauraine Snelling

FaithWords
Hachette Book Group
237 Park Avenue
New York, NY 10017

www.faithwords.com

Printed in the United States of America

RRD-C

First trade edition: July 2012; Reissued: May 2014
First trade special edition: April 2014

10 9 8 7 6 5 4 3 2

FaithWords is a division of Hachette Book Group, Inc.

The FaithWords name and logo are trademarks of Hachette Book Group, Inc.

The Hachette Speakers Bureau provides a wide range of authors for speaking events. To find out more, go to www.hachettespeakersbureau.com or call (866) 376-6591.

The publisher is not responsible for websites (or their content) that are not owned by the publisher.

Library of Congress has cataloged the first trade paperback edition as follows:
Snelling, Lauraine.
   Reunion / Lauraine Snelling.—1st ed.
    p. cm.
   ISBN 978-0-89296-909-8
   I. Title.
   PS3569.N39R48 2012
   813'.54—dc23
              2011047073

ISBN 978-0-89296-909-8 (pbk.)

Reunion

Chapter One

"What's this?"

The tissue-wrapped box on the dining room table failed to answer. Strange, no name on it. No card. Just a square, white box with a curly blue ribbon spilling over its sides.

Curiosity was one of Keira Johnston's failings. Although she'd never opened a present before its time, she'd thought about it a lot. Shaking the box, albeit gently, left her with no more information. Since she and her husband, Bjorn, were the only two people who now lived in this big old house, it had to be for one of them. She pondered the box, then picked it up and sniffed it. Still no clues.

Just as she dug her cell phone out of her purse, she heard the back door open. She called, "I'm in here."

"Where's here?"

"The dining room. Do you know anything about this box on the table?" She turned at her husband's entrance and gave him a welcome-home hug.

"Hmm. Who could have left that?" His blue eyes twinkled. "Who's it for?"

"No card, no name, just a white box with a pretty ribbon." She watched his face to see if he was teasing her. He seemed as confused as she was.

"So open it."

"What if it's for you?"

"Why would someone give me a present? It's not my birthday."

"Nor mine. Our anniversary is still three months away. Who would put a present here on the table?" She looked pointedly from him to the box, swiping a strand of hair behind her ear. Her hair usually swung in the blunt-cut style she'd worn for years, but now it was in need of a cut and probably a highlight session again. Dark blond, it looked naturally sun streaked due to the gray turned silver around her face. "You open it."

"What, you're afraid of a bomb or something?"

"No. I'm just trying to be generous and my curiosity is killing me."

He hefted the box. "Can't be a bomb, too light."

"Bjorn Johnston, just open it." She rolled her eyes when he shook his head. "All right. I'll get the scissors and we'll open it together. Surely there will be a card or something inside." She dug a pair of scissors out of the "stuff drawer" in the kitchen and returned to stand by him.

"Maybe we'd better sit down." Bjorn pulled out an oak chair from the table. "Oh, did you tell Paul about the date for the family reunion? He called and I couldn't remember the exact day." Paul was their elder son, who was twenty-four and married to Laurie. They lived in Houston, Texas.

She rolled her eyes again. "How could you not know? It is on every calendar in the house and the office. The third weekend in June. I'll e-mail him. We're due at Leah's for supper tonight."

"Oh, I forgot that too. Something must be wrong with the calendar on my cell phone. I set the reminder feature but it didn't. Remind me, that is." He picked up the box, propping his elbows on the table. "Okay, cut the ribbon." Together they unwrapped the tissue paper to find a white box, about eight inches square. They set it on the antique dark-oak table. Bjorn shrugged, opened the one flap lid, and handed the box to her.

Using finger and thumb, Keira lifted the layer of tissue paper inside to see some papers fanned out in a circle so they'd fit in the box. She pulled them out and let out a shriek.

"Norway, tickets to Norway!"

"I was listening, you know."

Keira Johnston danced across the room, waving the packet with airline tickets and threw her arms around her husband, nearly toppling him from the chair.

"Easy." He hugged her back, halfway righting himself. "I wasn't sure you really wanted to go."

"You!" She gave him a playful swat on the shoulder. "How could you tease me like this? How could you keep such a straight face, lying through your teeth? You had me really believing you."

"I know. I think I deserve an Oscar for this performance."

"Modesty sure becomes you." Keira checked the box. "That's all, eh? No wonder there was no rattle and no weight. Tickets to Norway." Keira's eyes widened and she hugged him again. "You said we couldn't go this year. That we'd celebrate our twenty-fifth anniversary next year."

"Really? Did I say that?"

She pulled back enough to stand next to him, one hand on his shoulder. "Stop with the teasing. You know you did."

"Well, how could I surprise you if I gave in so easily?"

"True." She leaned her head on his. "Will Leah and Marcus be able to go?" Her brother, Marcus, was pastor of a local church and his wife, Leah, was Keira's best friend.

"They don't know yet." He looked up to search her face. "We could go alone, couldn't we?"

"Sure, but...it's just that we've always talked about all of us going together. Of course we always used to plan on taking Mother with us." After a moment's silence, Keira tucked the rebellious strand of hair behind her ear again. "I think I can't believe this yet." She stared at the picture on the front of the brochure of deep-blue fjords set against snow-crowned mountains. "Wait, what are the dates?"

"August. I know the family reunion is eating up all our time between now and the end of June. By August we'll be more than ready for some away time."

Keira leaned closer and kissed him again. "You are such a good man, Bjorn Johnston." She smoothed a lock of white hair across his widening crown. "Not sure why you love me, but I am grateful that you do."

"Ah, Keira, you promised to stop thinking that. Remember?"

"I know. I don't think about it, or at least not like I used to, but..."

Wrapping an arm around her waist, he pulled her into his lap. "Uffda, good thing this is a sturdy chair."

She nestled against him. "Have you told the boys yet?"

Besides Paul, they had a younger son, Eric, who was still in college and majoring in business.

"Nope, I thought you'd like to do that." He nuzzled her ear. "You know this means finding your birth certificate so you can get a passport. And it needs to be done soon."

Keira bolted upright and stared at him. "Oh, I forgot about that. It does." She scrubbed her fingers through her hair, making it messy again. She glanced at her watch. "Well, I can't go out to Mother's today but I'll get on it. We're due at Leah's for supper in ten minutes and you know Marcus likes his meals on time." She paused. "If only I knew for sure where I was born, I could call the hospital and get another copy. Why didn't I ever ask Mother?"

Bjorn heaved a sigh and himself to his feet. "I'm sure she put it somewhere safe. What are you bringing?"

"The pan of rolls. I'll get my jacket."

"It's raining."

"Drive or umbrella?" she called from the coat closet.

"Get mine, will you please? And you'd better comb your hair."

Keira groaned, slung the two coats over her arm, and grabbed an umbrella from the hall stand. "I'll be right back." She stared into the mirror in the guest bath. "You know better than to just finger comb it." She brushed her hair and grinned at the face in the mirror at the same time. "Norway. We *are* going to Norway after all."

Bjorn honked the car horn from the garage to let her know that he had decided to drive. It wasn't just raining; now the windows ran rivers.

They pulled under the overhang of the garage at the

house three doors down, which was actually a pretty far distance, since the lots were large enough to make it a city block away. Grateful for the breezeway that led to the back door, they hustled inside where Leah held the screen door open for them.

"Good thing you drove or you'd have to have worn scuba flippers."

Keira handed her the foil-wrapped pan. "These are still warm, but you might want to heat them a bit."

"Do you know?" She glanced from Keira to Bjorn, who was standing right behind his wife.

"He gave me the tickets!" Keira threw her arms around her best friend, who was also her sister-in-law. "I am so excited."

"I never would have guessed." Leah gave her a one-armed hug back. "Careful, I might drop the rolls."

Keira's musical laugh danced along in front of her. "Is Marcus already seated at the table?"

"No, he's still in his office. Bjorn, you go right on in and I'll see if I can get Miss Flabbergasted here calmed down."

"Just remind her she has to find her birth certificate. That'll do it." He hooked his jacket on the row of glass cabinet knobs on the board and strode through the kitchen. "Marcus, come help calm your sister down."

"Coming," a deep voice returned from the other end of the house.

Keira heaved a sigh. "I'll start seriously looking tomorrow. Where can it be? I have already torn that house apart, searching for Mother's important papers so I could settle her estate."

"I know you have. I was there, remember? Well, we'll

just have to look for it again and at the same time we'll dig out all the pictures for the memory book for the family reunion. I should have had that at least half finished by now. Reunion will be here in just a few weeks." Leah, a barely five-foot dynamo with short curly hair, smiled up at Keira.

Keira reached up in the cupboard for a basket for the rolls and Leah dumped them in. The two had worked together for so many years that, like a good old married couple, they read each other's minds. "Anything else need doing?"

"Just set the serving dishes on the table."

"Is Kirsten here?" Keira paused and sobered. "Oh, Leah, I so want you both to go. It would be absolutely perfect if all the kids could go too, but I know that's impossible. Remember how the boys always played so well together? The best of friends. There are good reasons for having cousins about the same ages." Her eyebrows rose. "You *are* going, aren't you." It was a statement, not a question.

"We'll see." Leah popped the basket in the microwave. "Fifteen seconds enough time?"

"That should do it."

"I thought you said dinner was all ready?" Marcus called from the dining room.

"Coming." Leah pulled the casserole from the oven and motioned Keira to bring the rolls.

The foursome was seated and grace had been said when the front door opened and Leah and Marcus's daughter, Kirsten, blew in, shouting a good-bye over her shoulder. "Puppies, I should have waited. I thought you'd be done eating by now, so we stopped for a burger."

"And hi to you too," Leah greeted her teenage daughter.

As the youngest and only girl between the two families, her niece held a special place in Keira's heart; she was more like a daughter, really. After her two sons were born, Keira lost two babies in the first trimester and she'd ended up needing a hysterectomy. She'd always dreamed of having a daughter. Although she now had her daughter-in-law, Laurie, she and Paul lived too far away to spend much time together. Sometimes life just wasn't fair.

Tall, blond, and walking like the "princess" her father called her, Kirsten hugged each of those around the table. "Sure smells good in here."

"Get yourself a place setting."

"No, thanks. I'll be back down for dessert. I've got a bunch of calls to return for the committee." Kirsten was heading the decorations committee for her graduation ceremony in a week. "And then I have to prep for my finals. Aunt Keira, did you by any chance bring any cookies to keep my energy up while I study until the wee hours?"

Keira passed her plate to Marcus, who was serving from the pottery dish in front of him. "I'll make sure you have plenty. I thought you were all ready?"

"I thought so too, but lately it's been so crazy, my mind has holes in it. Need to plug up a few."

"Thanks." Keira smiled at her brother, then looked back to her niece. "You heard anything on that application yet?"

Kirsten looked to her mother, who shrugged. "Yes! I got it! The packet came today. The scholarship will cover tuition, books, and fees. I just have to pay for housing." Her eyes sparkled. "I thought for sure Mom would have told you by now."

"I've not seen her until ten minutes ago." Leah winked at Keira. "And we had something else to discuss too."

"You want to go to Norway with us?" Was that a slight flinch she saw on Bjorn's face? Why would he do that?

"You are going? Oh, I'd love to, but..." Kirsten squinted to think better. "It's the last three weeks of August, right?"

"Yes. Three whole weeks in Norway, the land of your forefathers."

"And mothers," Leah added.

"I have to be at school by then. Could you go any earlier?" Kirsten shook her head, setting her straight blond hair to swinging. "But even if you could, it won't work. All my money has to go for school expenses." She turned to her mother. "Are you and Dad going?"

"We'll see."

Kirsten came around the table, draped her arms over her aunt and uncle, and kissed their cheeks. "You deserve a trip like that. I'll go someday." She headed for the stairway and called over her shoulder. "But take Mom and Dad with you."

"Right. Then who's going to help you get ready for school?" Leah raised her voice.

Kirsten called back from three-quarters of the way up the walnut staircase. "That's what July is for." Her laugh made those around the table smile.

"I know I've said this before, but I'll say it again." Keira smiled at her brother and her best friend. "If I ever had a daughter, I would want her to be just like Kirsten. What a kid."

"If only she wouldn't drive herself so hard. Going to end up in bed again the way she's going." Leah's smile took the sting from her words. "But we'll make it through."

"And then she can sleep for as long as she needs."

"Me too." Leah sighed. "I wish."

"As long as you're looking for your birth certificate, maybe you can find mine." Marcus took a roll from the basket and inhaled deeply. "Glad we only needed our baptismal certificates to get our driver's licenses. Being fifteen sure was a long time ago." He chuckled and inhaled again. "Ah, nothing smells as good as freshly baked rolls." He looked toward his sister. "So, where will you start? I know you brought home all the papers from Mother's desk and the file cabinet after her funeral. Where else might she have kept them?" His eyes widened. "You don't suppose she put them away for safekeeping and..."

"And never found them again?" Keira finished his sentence. She nibbled her bottom lip. "Oh, I hope that's not it. Please, Lord, let that not be so." A chuckle skittered around the table. They all knew Dagmar Sorenson and her stash-and-store habits.

Bjorn set his knife precisely on the edge of his plate. "Well, all I have to say is that we all better be praying hard." He smiled. "Otherwise, Keira, you'll be spending all of your time researching to find out for sure if you were even born and you just might miss the passport deadline."

"And I still need to get ready for the family reunion." Keira groaned and huffed out a breath.

"Tomorrow we start looking," Leah said with a firm nod. "Tomorrow morning at eight."

Please, Lord, help me find it and quickly.

Chapter Two

They were halfway out to the farm, just past the Munsford city limits sign, when Keira slowed to a stop on the side of the street. She heaved a sigh and turned to stare at her best friend. "I have to confess that I hate going out there now that Mother is gone. Bjorn took care of all the winterizing and he's the one who's been going out to check on the place. Maybe we ought to sell it or rent it or something. The house needs to be lived in; houses don't do well at all when they're left vacant."

"Well, first we'll have to clean it up, toss out all the stuff Dagmar kept saving, and label all of her 'treasures.'" Using her years of nursing skills, Leah kept her tone even and matter of fact. "Then the sale has to be agreed upon by you and Marcus. I know the kids will go along with whatever you decide."

"What do you think we should do?"

"About selling the house? I don't know. Right now you need to find your and Marcus's birth certificates, and I want the photographs for the memory book." She raised a hand to stop Keira from answering. "I think we can leave any decision for a later time, like after the reunion."

"Thanks, I guess," Keira muttered under her breath. She put the car in gear and pulled back onto the street. Why she

was so hesitant to visit the home place she had no idea—
and no desire to search deep enough within herself to find
an answer.

She parked in the driveway to the separate garage and
stared at the square, two-story white house with the wrap-
around porch across the front and to the side toward the
garage. White sheer curtains crossed in the upper windows,
geraniums no longer graced the kitchen windows, and the
drapes in the living room closed off the sunlight. The lilacs
along the back fence were sprouting but not blooming yet,
and traces of yellow remained of the forsythia that used the
pump house for support. The oak trees wore the fuzz of a
new season and the climbing Paul's Scarlet rose stretched
along the upper edge of the porch, the leaves and sprouting
canes still more red than green. The barn swallows were
dipping and catching flying insects along with building
their mud nests under the eaves of the barn and the garage.
Her father had always chased them away from the garage
eaves, one more sign of change.

Keira got out of the car without paying much attention
to the flora around her and automatically slid her car keys
into the pocket of her jeans. How could this house appear
so normal when normal would never come again? Someone had been out and weeded the flower bed that circled
the house. Guilt stabbed in her heart region. Weeding
the flower beds had been more delight than chore when
she and her mother had done it together. Bjorn had even
offered to help her weed, but she couldn't force herself to
come out and do it. Swallowing the pain and the tears that
threatened, Keira pushed open the peaked picket gate and
stopped at the fading daffodils that bordered the concrete

walk. She should have picked a bouquet and put the flowers on her parents' graves. Her mother had loved daffodils, a sure sign that spring had arrived. A path circled around to the front of the house and another led to the three stairs up to porch level. The door was locked. The door had never been locked in all the years her parents had lived in this house. She dug in her purse for the keys and finally handed them to Leah to open the door. Tears made inserting the key in the lock impossible.

"I thought I was done with this," she whispered as they finally stepped inside the kitchen. She tried not to inhale the musty smell, the this-house-is-not-lived-in odor, but finally gave up, knowing she had to breathe.

"I'm not sure we are ever done with the tears of grieving. Sometimes they just get put on hold until such a time as this." Leah set her purse on the white drop-leaf table in front of the window and turned to hug Keira. "She loved you very much."

"And I her."

"I know." Ever practical, Leah crossed back and reopened the door. "We need to air this place out and let the sunshine in to freshen it up. Then you can show me where I might find the old pictures and I'll let you search for those birth certificates. Then maybe we can spend an hour tossing, starting in the pantry. Have you thought of having a rummage sale?"

"No, but it might be a good idea." Keira pulled a tissue out of the box on the counter, blew her nose, and poured herself a glass of water. "Ugh, the pipes are rusty." She dumped the glass and let the faucet run until the water ran clear, refilled the glass, and drank it all down in one gulp.

"Where do you think the pictures are?"

"Hmm. Let's start with the closet in Mother's original bedroom."

The two friends climbed the dark walnut stairs, which divided the living room in half, and entered the front bedroom on the right. "Remember the year we added a bathroom up here? Even though it took up such a large part of her bedroom, Dagmar was so happy to not have to go downstairs all the time."

"And then we had to move her downstairs into the room behind the kitchen when she grew too weak to climb the stairs." Keira shook her head at the memory. "And she sure fought that." Walking over to the closet, which was stuffed with old clothes, round hatboxes, and stacks of cardboard boxes, she reached in and took out one of the boxes. She peeled back the tape and opened it. "I thought so." She held up an album. "The last few years, Mother put a lot of her pictures into albums. I sure hope she labeled them. Here you go." She was aware that Leah knew all this too, but for some reason she kept babbling.

Several times during the past few years, Dagmar had asked her and Marcus to come out and go through the pictures with her so she could identify the people in the photos for them, especially the older ones. But with two busy lives, they'd never taken the time to do this simple thing that would have made their mother so happy.

Lord, I want out of here. Please, can't I just leave and not come back? Her common sense chided her. After all, it had been a year since Mother went home to the Lord. A whole year. Both the longest and the shortest year of her life. *Remember Norway. Remember Norway.*

"You sure you wouldn't rather help me at first? Working together can sometimes beat the doldrums." Leah turned from opening one of the double-sashed windows.

"No, I'll start searching the rolltop desk again. Maybe I just missed the birth certificates before. Besides I need to locate some labels in case we find anything we think the family would like." Keira blew out a breath and blinked away the tears. "I know I got all the business papers out of there but I didn't have the heart to sort through all the correspondence Mother saved. I think she saved every card any of us ever sent her. If you find a box like that, just put it aside for me."

"Will do." Leah flipped through one of the albums and set it aside. "Too recent." She paused. "You know the birth certificates could be in one of the envelopes."

"I don't think so. I remember flipping through them enough to see if there were any that were official looking."

"Keep in mind, they may not be in anything official. They could be in a plain envelope or just loose. Once I go through the boxes, I'll take the pictures off the walls, okay?"

"Whatever you need to do." Keira made her way back down the stairs, trailing her hand along the rail worn silky smooth by all the years of use. Her father's rolltop desk, inherited from his father, reigned in what they had come to call the television room. She had cleaned out the file drawers when working on the estate business, but had never attacked the cubbyholes and the upper drawers. The shallow center drawer held pens, pencils, stamps, and other odds and ends. She felt like finding a box and just dumping things into it and sorting them at home, but her fingers continued to shuffle through, discarding, saving, and bringing order to the clutter. The desk was to go to Marcus, as the remaining son. In the divided drawer that held cards and stationery she flipped through the envelopes to make sure there were no letters or official documents mixed in.

She paused and glanced at the ceiling when she heard a thump from the floor above. Should she go see if Leah was all right? Instead she raised her voice.

"You all right up there?"

"Yes, just dropped a box. All is well."

Keira pulled a larger envelope from the stack she'd collected and sat down in the oak chair mounted on casters. The photograph inside needed to go in Leah's pile. Her father, Kenneth Sorenson, smiled back at her. His dark hair had gone pearly white, including his eyebrows. Thick hair so like her own. People had always said she not only looked like her father but also had many of his mannerisms too, like the way his smile lit up his eyes or the way he'd cock his head slightly to the side when listening intently. Something he did so well was listening. He'd sit her on his knee and listen to her stories; always asking her questions, oftentimes questions that made her laugh. "Oh, Dad, hard as it was to lose Mother, your death so young was even harder to bear." She shook her head. "Life's just not fair." Rolling her lips together did nothing to stem the drips from her eyes. She held the photograph away from her face so her tears wouldn't mark it. Slipping it back in the envelope, she set it on Leah's stack and wrote herself a sticky note. "Blow this one up and frame."

"Help! I need more hands."

Keira jerked herself back to the farmhouse. "Coming!

Are you all right?" She charged up the stairs and burst into the bedroom just in time to catch the box that the tips of Leah's outstretched fingers kept from crashing down.

"Oh, thank you. I didn't really want that on my head or on the floor either."

"You ever think of a step stool?" Keira lowered the heavy box to the floor.

Leah threw her best friend a grin, turned back to the box, and paused before sending a questioning look over her shoulder. "Okay, what happened?"

"Nothing. We kept the box from killing or at least maiming you." Keira glanced around at the open boxes scattered on every flat surface in the room, including the floor. "My word, but you've been busy."

"If you say so." Leah turned her head slightly to the side, narrowed eyes studying her accomplice in sorting. "What did you find?"

"A picture of Dad, one of the last ones taken before he died. The memories about drowned me." She sniffed and dug out a tissue to blow her nose. "Anything else you want taken down?"

"Just that box on the back of the shelf, and that's the last of it for this room. Your mom must have the older pictures stashed somewhere else." She pointed to the boxes. "I've been labeling them with a marker so we know the time periods of each box. Your mother did a good job of putting a year or so of them in each box. She sure loved photographs."

Keira glanced around the room again. "I thought for sure all the pictures were in here. Have you looked anywhere else yet?"

"Just here. What kinds of things did she keep up in the attic?"

Keira stared at her friend. "I don't know if she stored anything up there. After Dad...Dad put in the pull-down stairway, at her insistence, I don't remember her ever mentioning it again. Funny. I mean a strange kind of funny, don't you think?" So why had her mother been so insistent about the ladder? "I'll check the closet in the sewing room while you go look in Marcus's old room."

"Should I put all of this away first?" She waved her hand at the cardboard boxes strewn around the room.

"Why? No one else will come out here to help unless we do some real arm twisting."

"Or hint at buried treasure," Leah replied.

The two crossed the hall, each going to a different door and pushing it open. Keira entered her favorite room in the house. It used to be her bedroom, but after she was married, Mother had painted the walls sunburst yellow and stained the old wood floor a dark cinnamon. A sewing cabinet sat in front of one of the double-hung windows with a view of the garden and the barn beyond it.

Blindsided by memories, Keira felt an ache begin behind her eyes and sank down in the armless rocker in front of the corner window.

"I didn't find any more pictures." Leah paused in the doorway. "Are you all right?"

Keira shook her head. "Just a headache, I think."

Leah crossed the room and laid the back of her hand against Keira's forehead. "You sure? You never get headaches. Anything else?"

"Queasy stomach."

"You feel up to doing more here?"

"Of course." Keira heaved herself to her feet, wishing the rocker had arms to propel her upward. She turned to the row of louvered bi-fold doors and pushed them open. Boxes and plastic crates lined the shelves, each one labeled RED, GREEN, YELLOW, NEUTRAL, and so on; all of the quilting fabrics categorized by color to make piecing easier. One shelf held batting, another held quilting books, while a box of patterns sat on another. Her mother loved quilting, piecing many tops for the church women to make quilts for the less fortunate. Each of her children and grandchildren had a quilt from Dagmar, all with memories sewn into them.

Keira knelt in front of the daybed and pulled out the tray on rollers that filled the place that used to house the trundle bed. Her mother and father had given her that bed when she was ten and wanted to have girlfriends spend the night. Four girls had a slumber party to celebrate the new bed and giggled the night away. Yarns of all colors, styles, and weights filled the tray. One section held three-ply yarn in soft pastels for baby afghans. "How many babies around here have slept under afghans Mother knitted or crocheted for them?"

"No idea, but lots." Leah turned from inspecting the shelves of boxes on the other wall. "No pictures here."

"I know. What did you find in Marcus's old closet?"

"Old woolen coats, suits, and stuff like that. Not sure what they're used for."

"For rugs. Remember how Mother rolled strips for braiding rugs even when her fingers were so weak she could no longer braid them? I wonder who might want it all now."

"Not me. I have enough projects for the next ten years."

Leah shook her head. "You're looking like the proverbial ghost."

"I think I have a marching band in my head." Keira shoved the tray back in place and stood. The change in altitude made her flinch.

"You take anything for the headache?" They often teased Leah about kicking into nurse mode. She had worked two or three nights a week at a local convalescent center for years.

"No."

"I'll be right back."

Keira followed her friend down the stairs. There was no other place to look for photographs upstairs, so she'd best try the closets below.

"Here." Leah handed her a couple of tablets and a glass of water. "This might help."

"Thanks." The cold water felt good on her desert-dry throat but hit her stomach, making it groan.

"Why don't we head home? I can come back to search for the pictures later."

"Let's check down here first." But none of the boxes on the shelves or closet floors on the main floor contained pictures or photo albums, so they put the boxes all back and closed them up. "The attic. They've got to be in the attic." Keira closed her eyes. The marching now included drums. Might this be what a migraine was like? She'd never had one, but she'd never felt quite like this before either.

"Let me drive you home. I don't like the looks of you at all."

Sometimes having a medical professional in the family was helpful. At the moment Keira didn't want to drive either.

What might be more advantageous, bed, hot bath, or hit the kitchen? Her stomach lurched and twisted. She picked up her purse and handed her keys to Leah. "Be my guest."

Once in the car, Keira tipped her head back and closed her eyes. But the words flashing in neon on the backs of her eyes made her groan. *Birth certificate. Where's my birth certificate?* Why was she getting in such a stew about this? After all, this was the first real day of searching. Surely that picture of her father had not brought this headache on.

"I'll send Marcus over with a plate for Bjorn. He's bringing take-out home tonight."

"We have plenty of leftovers in the fridge."

"And I know how much he likes fixing his own supper. You want anything?"

"No, but thanks."

"If there is anything I can do, you would tell me?"

"Of course." With the car now parked in front of the Johnstons' garage, both women climbed out. Leah handed Keira's keys back and then gathered the bags of pictures she had found. "Call me."

"Will do." Instead of going through the garage, Keira crossed the grass that needed mowing to the wide concrete steps. The steps were edged with pots of tulips, just showing their brilliant red coloring but still tightly clenched. Usually Keira stopped to admire her flowers, but today she marched right on into the house, purposely ignoring the yellow pansies so similar to those Mother had always planted at the farmhouse. Upstairs, she stopped by the bathroom to start the water flowing in the bathtub before continuing to her closet to get undressed. She eyed the bed. Maybe sleep was the answer to this agony in her head. No, a bath was necessary after working in the dust all day. Dithering like this was not like her either. What was going on? Sorting through her mother's things should not bring on something like this.

After dumping her clothes in a pile, as if she were walking in her sleep, Keira entered the now steaming bathroom, turned off the water, and slid into the warmth. She pushed the button for the jets and stared at the rising bubbles. Settling a rolled towel behind her neck, she closed her eyes. Surely she would feel better in a while.

Finished with her last class of the day, Kirsten followed the river of students back to her locker and leaned her head against the shelf inside. Tired didn't begin to describe how she felt, and if her stomach didn't calm down pretty soon… Maybe something worse was wrong, like an ulcer or something. Her mother would insist she see the doctor any day now, but she didn't have time to be sick.

She sensed his presence before he said a word.

José Flores, her best friend and confidant, and also the love of her life, laid a hand on her shoulder. "You all right?"

"I will be."

"You want to go for ice cream or get something to eat before I take you home?"

"Aren't you working?"

"Later. I have a couple of hours before my shift."

"Oh, that sounds perfect. We have a meeting about the graduation decorations, but it's not until five. Just the two of us?" Lockers banged closed around them and people called out to each other. Just the typical end of a school day, but for the seniors, the true end was coming as fast as the finish line of a NASCAR race.

"Unless you want to invite someone else. I'd rather it just be us."

José always considered her wishes, but still she knew what he really wanted. "Good. I don't feel like a group right now."

"Call me when you get home," Lindsey said from right behind her. "Or are you walking?" Lindsey Weaver had been her best female friend since before kindergarten.

"I will. José and I have an errand to run."

"Okay. Later."

Kirsten answered other greetings as she pulled papers and books out of her locker and stuffed them all in her backpack. Cleaning out her locker wasn't a disaster, like it was for some of the students. She never could tolerate a mess and had often been teased about her compulsion for neatness. She dug a lip gloss out of the pocket where she kept her makeup, applied it, and rubbed her lips together. Seeing his face in the mirror, she caught José's gaze. "What?"

"I just like to watch you do that."

"Right." She checked her face and hair in the mirror, decided she was presentable, and shut the door with a click, not slamming it like others did. "Let's go. I feel better already." They strolled out to the car hand in hand, the top of her head a little higher than his shoulder. Tall as she was, she was grateful he was taller. She liked looking up to him in many ways, not just in stature. He opened the car door for her, something that most guys didn't do for their girlfriends. His grandmother had taught him good manners, one of those things her parents appreciated too. No honking the horn and waiting for her in the car. He always came to the door and rang the bell.

"Where do you want to go?" he asked after buckling his seat belt.

"The drive-in. I want a chocolate shake, and they make the best." She leaned her head against the back of the seat. "Finals start in two more days."

"You're not worried, are you?" He backed out of his parking place and drove out onto the street. "You're sure you wouldn't rather go to a sit-down restaurant?"

"Nope. And by the way, I'm buying." She raised her hand, palm out. "Don't argue with me. I've been letting you buy lately and I know you don't have extra money either. I've got my allowance. Been too busy to spend it."

"But I'm the one with a job." His brow wrinkled.

"Oh, for puppies' sake, don't go pulling macho on me. I know you have a job and I'll have one soon. So just order what you want and let me feel useful."

"Puppies' sake?" He tried to keep a straight face. "Puppies' sake?" And failed.

That was one of the things she liked to do, make him laugh. José Flores had the most wonderful male laugh in all of Munsford. She giggled along with him. It worked and got him to quit harping on letting her pay. After all, they had agreed to be partners, and partners shared expenses.

When her milkshake came, she drew in a long swallow. Uh-oh, big mistake. "Oh ugh, brain freeze." She rubbed her forehead and sinuses.

"Press your tongue against the roof of your mouth, it'll stop."

She gave him a funny look but did as he said without arguing. "Hey, it worked. Where did you learn that?"

"Read it online." He sipped his own shake, being careful not to do the same thing.

When they stopped in her driveway, she unbuckled and turned to face him. "You are coming in, aren't you?"

He checked his watch. "Not for long. I need to go home and change." He climbed out and came around the car, where she waited.

She swallowed. The milkshake was not sitting well in her stomach. "You're at the grocery store tonight?" He often filled in for the courtesy clerks at the grocery store, always in the hope that he would get hired on full time for the summer. Once graduation was over he would also be lifeguarding at the pool. They probably wouldn't see a lot of each other this summer.

"What's the matter?"

She couldn't tell him she felt like throwing up, but closing her eyes and letting her head fall forward helped.

"Are you all right?"

"I will be." Sucking in and holding a couple of deep breaths helped too. Surely it couldn't be anything else. Her stomach was just touchy. But what if…?

"Kirsten." He crouched beside the car. "Tell me."

"I said it's nothing, but I'm…I'm just PMSing and it's making me feel icky."

"Oh."

"I feel lots better. The milkshake upset my stomach, I think." *Please God, let it be so.*

He reached for her backpack at her feet, his face concerned.

"All will be well, José, my grandma always said so." She climbed out and kissed him on the chin. "You'll see."

She's never sick, and this came on so suddenly.

Leah swung the plastic bags of pictures she'd found. Her mind continued to dig into the quandary. Keira hadn't wanted to go out to the home place but she was fine, at least it seemed so at first. A few tears, but that was to be expected. Losing her mother had been hard on her, especially the long fight against cancer. Dagmar Sorenson had indeed been a strong woman, but in spite of the prayers of so many people, the cancer had won.

Like so many medical professionals, Leah had to fight against taking death personally. They had done all they could and had prayed that God would do the final healing. He had, just not the way they all wanted. She'd loved Dagmar too, something that was not hard to do. None of the typical joking comments fit her as either a mother or a mother-in-law. Leah pushed open the wrought-iron gate and took the steps to her house in a rush. So much to do in spite of not having to cook supper. Since Kirsten wouldn't be home until later, she could work for a couple of hours on the counted cross-stitch sampler she'd started for her daughter's high school graduation present. It included a favorite Bible verse, date, and place, all surrounded by pansies, Kirsten's favorite flower.

Humming, she strolled through the entry and turned into the south-facing room that had at one time been a bedroom but now had morphed into her hideaway, complete with sign above the door that read LEAH'S LAIR. She put the sacks of pictures on the table where she had the memory book in progress spread out and stared down at one of the pictures she'd been working with: the day Curt, their older son, had been baptized. She and Marcus looked so young and they'd thought they were so mature. She stared at her husband's face, that look of pride and awe and maybe even a bit of fear. After all, they'd promised to rear their baby in the love and fear of the Lord and teach him to follow God's will. Looking back, they'd lived up to their promises of that day, although the way had not been easy. Curt was now in his first year of seminary. Maybe she should enlarge this print and give it to him framed for his future office.

Turning on the stereo, she settled into her chair, clicked on the floor lamp, and picked up her stitchery. The needle flashing in and out was as mesmerizing as the piano playing her favorite classics. She knew better than to dwell on Keira and the other worries, like how Kirsten had been feeling the effects of graduation stresses and how Marcus was still finding it difficult to counsel people suffering from cancer.

"You must be home, the music is on," Marcus called from the kitchen.

"I didn't hear you come in. I'm stitching."

"Be there in a minute."

She thought of getting up to go greet him, but opted instead to put a few more stitches in the remaining two-toned purple pansy. She loved the homecoming time of day with the lowering sun's rays slanting in through the window, sitting in her comfortable chair and working on her favorite—or rather one of her favorite—hobbies. As much as she loved sharing supper with Keira and Bjorn, having just her and Marcus alone together tonight was a special treat. She reminded herself to mark this on the calendar, a gift from God to rejoice over.

"Now this looks like a bit of heaven." Marcus crossed the room and dropped a kiss on the top of her head.

She reached up and patted his cheek. "Feels like it too."

"You want to eat in here?"

"Why yes, what a great idea. You want me to help set up?"

"No, stay where you are. I'll bring in one of those craft tables."

"How come I was so smart?"

He turned from heading out the door. "How so?"

"I married you."

"I thought that was supposed to be my line." He winked at her and continued on his way. Once Marcus started something, he carried through, the sooner the better.

So what had happened with Keira? Pondering this didn't slow down her stitching. And pondering wasn't really worrying, only thinking about an issue. Right? She switched needles for the next color. On a project like the one on her frame she kept extra needles, each threaded with a different color, to speed up the process. She moved the marking magnet down on the pattern on the metal stand and started stitching again, slanted lines marching across the fourteen-count cloth.

"Oh my, but that smells good." She smiled at her husband as he set up the table and placed the sack of carry-out food on it.

"I know. It was all I could do to keep my fingers out of it in the car." He opened the containers and set paper plates on each side. "What do you want to drink?"

Leah shrugged. "Nothing for right now, let's just eat."

Marcus pulled up a wingback chair and settled into it with a sigh.

"Hard day?"

"Somewhat. Let's say grace and I'll tell you about it." He bowed his head and exhaled a deep breath. "Lord God, thank you for this food and our time together. I thank you that you are always beside and in us and you have a plan for all the craziness I see going on around me. Thank you that you promise wisdom and insight. In your son's precious name, Jesus, amen."

They each helped themselves to the chicken and sides and dug in. After a few bites, Marcus wiped his mouth and fingers. "How come we don't do this more often?" He reached for the drumstick on his plate.

"We used to."

"I know." He paused. "So what happened with Keira and Bjorn? You said they'd be joining us tonight."

"Keira got sick out at the home place. It started with a headache, and then her stomach got queasy. Came on so suddenly, but then you know how she treats symptoms, says they'll go away if you ignore them."

"So what happened?"

"She couldn't ignore how bad she felt, so I drove us home. She's either soaking it out in the tub or sleeping it off in bed. I said we'd take a plate over to Bjorn." She peered into the bucket of chicken. "I see you brought lots."

"Leftovers for lunch."

"So how did your day go?"

"Mrs. Updahl asked me to come to the hospital and pray for her husband."

"Cancer."

"Yes, although it seems they might have gotten it in time."

"And you went?"

"Of course. But it felt like my prayers didn't even make it to the ceiling. I was just saying the words." He looked from his plate to his wife. "I know God always hears and I know faith doesn't depend on feelings, but..."

"But you prayed for your mother fervently and for such a long time and she still died."

He nodded as he tipped his head back. "The enemy would have me think I failed."

"Oh, Marcus, you didn't fail. You were obedient and faithful. What more can you be?"

"My faith wasn't strong enough."

"Or God just saw things differently. Your mother was so ready to go home."

"Of course. After the long fight she put up, she was exhausted."

"All the way through, she said, 'God's will be done.' I don't think her faith ever wavered. Dagmar absolutely trusted God to do the best. Remember her saying, 'I don't like the way they are running things here in my country anyway. I'd rather go home where sanity and love reign. Where all will be well.' I remember laughing at the time, because it was so like her. And she got her wish."

"But God let her suffer so terribly."

Leah blinked back the tears and left her seat to kneel beside her husband's knees. "I don't have any answers for that, either. I don't know why, but I sure want to be like her, a warrior to the end. What an example of a daughter of the king."

"You sound more like a pastor than I do." He laid his hand gently on the back of her neck. "What would I ever do without you?"

She turned her head to kiss his wrist. "I wonder the same. You remember that song we heard? The one that goes, 'How will I stand heaven till you get there?' That's us."

"I fight tears every time I hear it." He blew out a breath. "Thank you."

She laid her cheek on his thigh, the soft khaki fabric over a sportsman's muscles. *Lord God, keep him safe and remind him again how much you love him. He loved his mother so very much, and we still miss her every day.* "Being out at the farm is still hard. Are we sure we want to do the reunion out there this year?"

"I think we should. Better to get it over with than dread it for the future. Besides, we need to make some decisions about the place and I'd like everyone's input. I think Keira feels the same."

"I suppose so. We couldn't find the boxes of early pictures. You think Dagmar might have put them up in the attic?"

"Perhaps. I have some phone calls I need to make, so could you fix up a plate for Bjorn and I'll take it over?"

"Of course." Leah rose and started putting lids back on the containers. "The mail is on your desk. Bjorn's plate will be ready in a couple of minutes."

"Just pack it all back in the sack and I'll take the whole thing."

Food in hand, she headed for the kitchen where she divided up the food and put containers of everything back in the plastic bag and others in the fridge. Taking a pad of leaf-shaped sticky notes, she wrote. "Hi, Bjorn. No idea what bug got your wife, but here is supper. Call me if there is any news. We love you. L and M."

Leah cleared off the counter and returned to her stitching. Kirsten had said she'd be home around seven, so she had maybe an hour left. She had a bag ready for hiding the sampler and a decoy piece out to help keep the secret should her daughter walk into the room unexpectedly. As she stitched, one ear kept track of Marcus. He was still on the phone. As soon as he hung up, now wearing running clothes, he breezed by her, blew her a kiss, and exited out through the kitchen. Perhaps Bjorn would run with him, something they used to do together a lot, but too often now Bjorn would rather ride his bicycle. Said his knees were happier that way, ever since he passed the fifty mark.

Her cell phone rang. She clicked on. "You're not even out of the driveway yet."

"I know. What time is Kirsten supposed to get home?"

"She said seven."

"Okay, I should be back by then."

They clicked off and she sat staring at the flat black face. How about that? An evening with no meetings for anyone. How could she stand it? She shook her head at her slight sarcasm and returned to stitching.

Sometime later, when Leah heard a car pull in the driveway, she tucked the sampler down in the bag and picked up the small piece she was doing just to have a quick gift on hand. The garage door opened and closed, and after a few minutes the kitchen door did the same.

"Mom, you here?" Kirsten called.

"In my lair. Have you eaten?" When no answer came

back, Leah put her stitchery down and went looking for her daughter. At five-nine and all bone and muscle, Kirsten took after Marcus's side of the family. She stood staring into the open refrigerator, her long blond hair twisted and caught up in a plastic clip.

"Have you eaten?"

"Not really, I had a milkshake. Nothing sounds good."

"Did you and Keira catch the same bug? She got sick this afternoon too."

"I'm not sick and I don't have a bug." She shut the door with a bit more force than necessary and went to the cupboard to get a glass so she could pour herself some cold water from the spigot on the refrigerator door.

Leah studied her daughter. The teen had lost weight in these last weeks of being overly stressed out about finals and graduation. While Kirsten kept saying everything would be all right once the ceremony was over, something made Leah think it was more than that. Had perfection become an obsession with her daughter? She was sure she'd heard Kirsten throwing up the other night. The girl had not done that for a long, long time. Leah often wondered how she and Marcus, with help from their two older sons, had managed to rear their youngest without spoiling her beyond belief. Besides doing so well in school, Kirsten and José were devout Christians and planning to go on a missions trip to Mexico this summer. Like her mother, Kirsten felt a deep need to help people.

Leah let her thoughts roam. With their number two son in his junior year of college, promising to help Curt out with his seminary expenses, and now Kirsten talking about joining José in med school after college, Leah figured she might be forced to work full time to help pay all the college expenses.

"We had Frankie's chicken. There's still some left. I could warm it up for you."

"Do we have any soup?"

"Cream of tomato in the can, chicken with spaetzel in the freezer, and I think corn chowder in the fridge. I bought it the other day thinking of quick meals for you and Dad while I'm at work."

"How about the chicken soup?"

"Shall I heat it up for you?"

"Thanks. While it heats, I can get a shower."

Why is she not looking at me? "Are you all right?"

"Mom, I'm not sick. Just tired. I'll take a quick one." Kirsten crossed the room, still not looking at her mother, and headed upstairs to her bedroom.

What's up with that? How long has it been since we've had a mother-daughter session? Leah could hear the shower running as she fixed the tray of food. She debated making tea, and then put the teakettle on. Even if Kirsten didn't want any, she did. Herbal tea would be good at this time of night. No caffeine for any of them. Humming as she worked, she wished she had baked cookies or gotten some from Keira. Perhaps gingersnaps would calm Kirsten's stomach. Maybe… She reached up on the spice shelf. Sure enough, there were still some pieces of the candied ginger. She added a small glass bowl to the tray and poured the ginger bits in, taking one herself.

When the oven timer beeped, she stirred the soup, checked to see if it was hot enough, and set it again for another minute. She went to the bottom of the stairs and called up, "Almost ready. It'll be in my lair."

"Coming."

Leah took the tray into her hideaway and set it on the craft table where she and Marcus had eaten earlier. Returning to the kitchen, she poured the boiling water into the teapot with several apple-spice herbal tea bags and carried that into the cozy room. The slap of tired feet on the back deck told her Marcus had returned.

She found Kirsten sitting in the chair her father had used and nibbling on one of the crackers. "Dad's home."

"Good." Kirsten leaned forward and inhaled the steam from the soup bowl. "Thanks, Mom."

"There's a bowl of candied ginger. Might help settle your stomach."

Kirsten muttered something under her breath, the nearest Leah could figure was, "I doubt it."

"You want a cup of tea?" She poured her own and a mug for Marcus, just as he came through the door. She handed him his cup and sat down in her chair. "All three of us for a change. Maybe I should mark it on the calendar."

Marcus held the cup in both hands as he leaned back in the chair. "Bjorn said that Keira was sound asleep when he came home and hasn't moved since. He thanked us for the dinner but declined a run. Said he had work to do."

Leah set her cup on a coaster and picked up her stitchery.

Kirsten was eating another cracker. She picked up a spoon and raised it to her mouth, then set it back in the bowl.

"Is something wrong with the soup?"

"No, Mom. Something is wrong with me." Kirsten turned to face her father and mother. "You know how my stomach gets when I'm stressed. It'll be better when school is over." She tried the soup again, sipping carefully.

"Maybe I should make an appointment with Dr. Young-strom for you."

"No!" Kirsten put her soup spoon carefully down on the tray. "I'll be fine. You know the pattern." She stood and picked up the tray. "Think I'll take this up with me and get back to studying. Thanks."

Leah and Marcus both watched their daughter leave the room, and then looked at each other.

"I think you should call him." Marcus stared at her over the lip of his tea mug.

"Me too."

Chapter Three

$\mathscr{A}$re you sure you feel up to it?" Leah's voice came over the receiver.

"I'm sure. Must have been a fast bug. I have bread rising, but after it comes out of the oven, how about going back out to Mother's?" Keira turned aside to sneeze.

"Bless you. I'll keep sorting what I have here until you call."

"Good. Later." Keira clicked off the phone and went to check the big yellow bowl she always used for rising bread. Most of the time she used the bread machine Bjorn had given her for Mother's Day one year, but today she had felt the need to knead her frustrations out on the dough. After checking the cookies baking in the oven, she returned to the counter.

Where in that house could her mother have put those blasted birth certificates? Was there some reason for not keeping them with the other important papers? As she dropped cookie dough onto another cookie sheet, she tried to think like her mother. A place for everything and everything in its place. How many thousands of times had she heard those words through the years, especially when she left something lying on the dining room table or the kitchen counter. She could hear herself. "But Mother, I was going to take it up to my room the next time I went up." Arguing with her mother was like trying to pull weeds wearing a glove with a hole in it. All she ever got was a blister.

The timer dinged and she pulled the pan of ginger cookies from the oven. After sliding the other sheet in the oven, she dug out the pancake turner and the cooling rack. As she lifted the cookies onto the cooling rack, she realized there were tears meandering down her chin. What she would give for the chance to hear her mother say those words again, or any of Dagmar's pet phrases. Keira sniffed and wiped her eyes with the back of her hand. Grief had a way of broadsiding her at the strangest times. Wasn't there a time limit on tears? There should be.

Scraping the browned bits into the sink, she recalled all the wonderful talking times she and her mother had shared while baking. One heartache in her life was that she'd never had a daughter of her own to share these things with. So instead she taught her boys, telling them that when they married, their wives would be thrilled to know they could cook and bake, do laundry, clean house. In general, take care of themselves. She wasn't sure they'd believed her, but maybe a mother always wondered if her daughters-in-law would appreciate her sons even more for their homemaking skills. She doubted it. Second-guessing seemed more of a contemporary failing than one of the earlier generation.

By the time the bread was out of the pans and cooling on the racks, she'd still not thought of any place the birth certificates might be. She covered the loaves with a clean dish towel and called Leah.

"Let's hit the road. Or do you want to eat lunch first?"

"How about we leave right after I cut a heel off one of those loaves to eat on the way out there?"

"How about I do that and I'll meet you at the car?"

"Good idea."

With slices of bread on a plate between them, they headed for the farm again. "I hope you came up with some more places to look, because I sure as a tornado blows didn't."

"Nope." Leah took a bite of their lunch. "Oh my, there is nothing else in this whole wide world like bread still warm from the oven."

Keira picked up her bread when she stopped at a stop sign. "Just one of those things that you do and it brings great pleasure to yourself and anyone else who partakes."

Leah cocked her head sideways.

"You know what I mean."

"Unfortunately I do." They both laughed.

"I think baking bread is one of the most rewarding activities. It sure brings up memories of my mother."

"I think your bread is even better than hers. However, her pie crust was unparalleled."

"I know. I never get mine quite the same as hers and it is exactly the same recipe. Makes no sense."

Two hours later Keira had flipped through all the books on the bookshelf in one of the bedrooms and in the two boxes stored under the bed. No certificate. "I don't know what else to do. Take the beds apart? There are no more boxes on shelves, or anywhere else that I've not searched, no more drawers to pull out."

"Did you check the undersides of the drawers? I saw a movie where a map was taped to the bottom of a drawer."

The two friends sat on the stairs, eating ginger cookies and leaning against the banisters.

"Good idea. I'll go back and do that. How are you coming along?"

"I've taken all the photographs off the walls upstairs and removed their frames and backing to take out the pictures. Easier than hauling all those frames around and maybe breaking some of the glass. I love the oval one of your father in that cute suit and long curls. Hard to picture Kenneth sitting still that long."

"His mother told me that she'd had to fight tooth and nail to keep Grandpa from cutting her son's hair before she could have the portrait taken. She promised to cut the curls off immediately after the sitting. I remember Dad saying once that his pa was afraid she was turning his son into a pantywaist."

"That's about as far from reality as Jupiter is from the earth."

"If you want that picture, you know you can have it."

"I know, but I thought I'd wait until after the reunion. I mean, it has hung in that same place so long the wallpaper behind it still looks new, not faded like the rest of the walls."

Keira dusted off her hands and folded the plastic bag to save it.

Leah grinned at her.

"What?"

"Just like your mother and father. Save everything."

"I don't save everything, but why waste a perfectly good Ziploc?"

"I rest my case." Leah stood and glanced back up the

stairs. "All those pictures on the stairwell. Think I'll pick and choose which ones to take apart."

"That's the Sorenson family history wall. You better take them all."

Leah groaned. "If I'd realized what a job this family memory book was going to be, I might not have started it."

Keira watched her sister-in-law trudge up the stairs. Since she'd been sorting things as she looked through drawers and boxes, she well understood what Leah was saying. Her knee popped as she stood up. Why hadn't she thought of looking at the undersides of the drawers before putting them all back?

She hauled the plastic garbage bags of junk to the kitchen and started in on the drawers once again. This time she pulled them out and felt under each one and across the back. Other than a splinter, she finished the kitchen with no reward.

Buffet in the dining room—same result.

In her mother's downstairs bedroom, Leah pulled out the small drawer that held her mother's jewelry. Except for her wedding ring, there was nothing of real value but for the memories. Jewelry had never been one of her mother's deepest wants. Keira stopped and felt again, then lifted the drawer up so she could see the bottom. An envelope was taped to the wood. Hope soaring, she slit the aged tape with her fingernail, peeled off the envelope, and shoved the drawer back in place.

"I found something!" Her shriek carried up the stairs.

"I'm coming. Wait." Leah charged down the stairs. "Oh, I hope. I hope. But why would Dagmar hide your birth certificate?"

Keira shrugged.

Although it was a plain envelope, more like the kind one sends personal letters in rather than official documents, it was still long enough to hold a birth certificate or two. Keira glanced up to see Leah staring at the envelope. Carefully, so as not to rip the envelope, she lifted the flap, the glue long gone due to age.

"Here goes. Please Lord, let it be so." But when she pulled out an ordinary piece of paper, her heart seemed to pause. Shaking her head, she unfolded it.

A hundred-dollar savings bond fluttered to the floor. Leah picked it up.

Keira read the letter out loud:

Dear Dagmar,

I am sending you this so that you always have some money to fall back on. I know you are dead set on making it on your own, but city life is far different from life here on the farm. This way, if you ever get in trouble of any kind, you have money to come home on.

Your loving father
Pa
P.S. I did not tell your mother of this. So let's keep this a secret between you and me. I love you.

Keira and Leah stared at each other. "Well, can you beat that?"

"He loved her very much. A hundred dollars was worth a whole lot more back then."

"And obviously she never told her mother, or it would have gone into the bank."

Leah heaved a sigh. "Well, back at it. Or do you want to
return another day?"

"Give me another hour. I'm about ready to go upstairs."
Keira slid the letter back in the envelope and set it in one of
the cubbyholes on the rolltop desk.

"I could sure use a cup of tea and another cookie about
now."

"There's plenty of tea in the cupboard."

"I know. Let's just finish, okay?"

Forty minutes later, Keira had learned there were no
more treasures to be discovered under the drawers, so she
joined Leah in the sewing room. "I'll help." She reached for
one of the early portraits of her and Marcus that hung over
the daybed. They'd not had a lot of formal studio portraits
taken. In this one she was sitting on a chair with Marcus
standing beside her.

"That is the cutest picture." Leah took it over to the
table and turned it over to slit the brown paper. "I'm going
to have to go back and seal all these photographs up again."

"We'll get some of the others to help with that." Keira
brought the two that had flanked the studio picture over to
the table. Taking the scissors, she did the same.

"Keira, look at this." Leah held up an envelope she found
between the picture and the backing. The two stared at
each other. "What do you suppose this is?"

"I have no idea."

"Maybe another treasure." Hope was written all over
their faces. "Here, you open it."

"No, you do it." With a quivering hand, Keira took the
envelope from her friend and, in spite of wanting to rip it
open, followed her careful ritual. She pulled out two very

official-looking papers. Opening the first one, she glanced at it and handed it to Leah. "Marcus's birth certificate." With trembling fingers she unfolded the second. Sure enough. Her birth certificate. "Thank you, Lord! Now I can go to Norway.

"We were right," she said as she scanned the document. "I was born in St. Cloud. I—"

Leah looked up from reading her husband's paper. "What's wrong? Keira, what's wrong?"

Without a word, Keira handed her the paper to read.

"That can't be right." Leah stared at her friend. "But Kenneth is your father." She read it again. "How can it say 'father unknown'? It must be a mistake."

"What if it's not? How can it be? If my father—Kenneth— isn't my father, who is?" She looked up from studying the paper. "Leah, you can't tell Marcus about this, not yet."

"What? Why?"

"I—I need some time. I need to— Just promise me you won't. Please."

"All right. I promise, but only for now."

"Thank you."

"But you're not making any sense, you know."

Keira didn't bother to answer. Nothing made any sense right now. Questions bombarded her mind, ricocheting like popcorn in a popper. Leah suggested they head home. She locked up the house, even offered to drive, but Keira got behind the wheel automatically. She drove carefully, afraid to trust her eyes, which threatened to overflow. She let Leah off with only a weak nod in return for her good-byes and parked in front of her own garage door. The onslaught caught her before she could open the car door. If tears were meant to wash a mind clean, these failed utterly. Instead she could feel the water turning to steam.

How could her mother have ever done such a thing? Keira could understand falling in love and letting passion get away, but to have had a baby—her—and never share that information with her? All those years and not even a hint that Kenneth was not her biological father. Surely there was a mistake somewhere? She dug in her purse for a packet of tissues and mopped her eyes before blowing her nose, then repeated the process as another freshet blew through. *Kenneth is not my father? But of course he is. We looked alike, talked alike, even our sense of humor matched*. Staring at the closed garage door, she blinked and sniffed and mopped again. How could she think clearly in such a time as this?

Why had her mother never told her? What possible excuse could there be? Did she plan on telling her someday and never got around to it? Could she just not bring herself to confess the reality? Did she just—just what? Keira opened the car door to let the fresh air bathe her hot face. Staring at the concrete walk, it looked to be a mile to the front door. *Mother, how could you?* The silent scream ripped her heart in two.

She swiveled and planted her feet on the concrete drive before heaving herself upright. Was she dizzy? She waited to see. No, not dizzy, but her world seemed to be rocking around her. The same question echoed in her mind. If Kenneth wasn't her father, then who was?

It was too much to absorb, and the tears attacked again. She made her way to the door and let herself in, leaning against the entry wall as she dug for more tissues. If Kenneth wasn't her father, then she wasn't a real Sorenson. Most probably adopted, but not a flesh-and-blood Sorenson. What if... She knew better than to allow that futile phrase to take over but it overwhelmed her anyway. What if, when the family learned of this, they chose to cast her out, ignore her, deem her less? What if they didn't see her as really one of them? After all, every one of them bragged about their heritage, their family, and the strong ties that bound them all together. Enough to return to the home place for a reunion every year. Missing the reunion was unheard of unless one was dying or there was a natural disaster, like a flood. *God willing and the creek don't rise* was only a joke among them all.

"Lord, I can't think about this anymore. At least not right now." She left her purse on the entry table and staggered up the stairs, the banister beneath her shaking hand more like a lifeline than a solid piece of wood.

After taking two aspirin, she collapsed on her bed and curled into a fetal position.

Bjorn found her there several hours later. "Keira, are you all right?"

Keira blinked, confused for a moment before the long-buried secret came bursting out. "I am not a Sorenson. My birth certificate says 'father unknown' and now I don't know who I am." The words ran together while he sat down on the bed beside her and gathered her into his arms.

"What do you mean?" he asked, unable to take it in. She took a moment and a deep breath before explaining what she had found in another rush of words.

"Easy, easy. Surely there is some mistake. We can look into this more. Mistakes do happen, you know."

"I know, and I am one!" she wailed into his shoulder.

"Keira, come on, settle down. You are not a mistake. You make mistakes, but that doesn't make you a mistake." His gentle attempt at humor made her cry even more.

"How could she keep this a secret all these years? If she truly loved me, she would have told me. Sometime!"

"You know she loved you and Kenneth adored you. This is not making any sense." He leaned over and pulled a tissue out of the box on the nightstand and handed it to her. "Think on the good side, you know you always tell me that."

She raised her head and gritted her teeth. "There are no good sides to this."

"Sure there are. You found your birth certificate, so now you can get your passport."

"But the people we were going to see really aren't my relatives after all. Why would they want to see me now?"

"We're going to see my family too, remember? I think you're making too much of this. I know it's a shock, but…"

"But you know who your father was, and your grandfather, and so on, six or more generations back. I might not even be Norwegian, besides not a Sorenson." She blew and wiped again, grateful for his hand stroking her back but wanting to yell at him at the same time. Why didn't he get it? She blew out a leaden breath of air and swung her legs over the side of the bed, glancing at the clock at the same time. She'd slept for two hours, an unheard-of occurrence in her daily life.

Another thought struck. "Marcus is only my half brother. I made Leah promise not to tell him, at least not right now."

"Why?"

"You know how he idolizes our mother. She conceived a baby out of wedlock. What kind of woman does that make her?"

"Most likely a very unhappy and terrified woman. She had left the farm, right?"

"Yes, went away to live in a big city, although St. Cloud hardly seems a big city today."

"You could search for your birth certificate in their county files."

"I have my birth certificate now." She bit off the words.

"But it might be wrong, and then you'll know."

Keira glanced around. "I didn't check the dates. I know when their anniversary was. You're right, perhaps there was a mistake." She rose and headed downstairs. Maybe she had been making this a lot worse than it really was.

"Where are you going?"

"For my purse." But when she looked on the desk where she usually left it, it wasn't there. Had she left that at the farm? No, she'd driven home and the keys were always in her purse. Think, Keir, think.

"Here it is," Bjorn called from the entry.

"How did it get there?" She never, ever left anything by the front door, always keeping that perfect since it was the first thing guests would see. Even the boys had learned that early on. The wrath of Mother would descend on whoever dumped his stuff just as he came in the front door. The back door was another matter.

He handed her the leather bag. "What's for supper?"

Ignoring his question, she dug out the paper and scanned the information. The dates did not lie. She must have been conceived more than two months before the wedding. Why had she never questioned that before? Or had her mother lied again? Was her entire life composed of lies? She slid the paper back in the envelope and tucked that into the inner pocket, to have ready when she went to apply for her passport. Like her father, methodical was her middle name. Kenneth had to be her father.

Bjorn opened the door to the refrigerator and studied the ingredients. "We have plenty of leftovers."

"How can you even think about eating at a time like this?"

He leaned in closer to look behind some containers. "Would you rather we go out? I'm hungry. I put in a long day and I didn't have time for lunch." Pulling out a couple of containers, he set them on the counter and peeled back the lids. "Chicken soup or beef stew?"

"I don't care. I don't want anything."

"There's still homemade bread too, right?"

"Yes."

"Good, you cut that while I put this in the microwave. How about we toast the bread? Is there any of that Jell-O salad left?"

How could he think of food when her whole life was falling in shattered pieces around her feet? In spite of herself, she sliced the bread and popped it in the toaster as he suggested. When the meal was ready, they sat down at the table and Bjorn closed his eyes.

"Lord God, to whom nothing that happens is a surprise, we give you the shock that Keira is experiencing. We know that you have a use for everything that happens in our lives and that you will make good come of it. Thank you for this food so lovingly prepared. Amen."

"Amen," she echoed, again by force of habit. How God could work good out of this was beyond her.

Bjorn ate a few bites before smiling at her. "How come some things taste better after a sojourn in the refrigerator?"

She shrugged and took a bite, just to appease him.

"Let's go back to the beginning. What do you know of your early years?"

"Not a lot, come to think of it. Other than that I grew up on the farm in what I have always considered the perfect life. I was Dad's favorite and Mother was partial to Marcus. We didn't care, we just knew that. After all, in the Sorenson clan, the firstborn son always had a special place."

"Did you ever ask for stories about when you were young?"

"I guess. I mean in family get-togethers, they'd all talk about the early years. Kenneth and his brothers got in lots of trouble at times because they loved to pull tricks on people."

"But what about your mother?"

"She didn't laugh a whole lot. And she was determined I would behave as a young lady should. Marcus could do no wrong, no matter what he did."

"Were you jealous?"

She thought a moment. "No. That's just the way it was. If I needed a lap, Dad was always there for me."

"No hint, ever, of a secret?"

Keira heaved a sigh. "I'll have to think on that. I mean, don't all kids think that maybe they were in the wrong family by some mistake?"

"I guess, especially when being punished." He cleaned his plate and pushed it back to rest his elbows on the table.

"It's a shame so many of your family have already left this earth. Who do you ask?"

"Aunt Helga is the only one. There are letters in boxes too. You know my mother saved everything."

"So I guess we start going through them or..."

"Or what?"

"Or you just decide this is no big deal and go on with your life."

"I want to know who he is." That popped out without her considering it. But of course what if her real father was still alive? Perhaps he could answer some of her questions, especially why didn't he marry her mother when he learned she was pregnant? Or what if her mother never told him? This was beginning to sound like a soap opera. She never had liked soap operas, and now she was playing a leading role.

The drum started behind her eyes again. "I'm going to bed. I can't deal with this anymore and the headache is coming back." She wasn't sure what felt worse, the headache or the heartache.

Chapter Four

"It's impossible," Leah muttered at the coffeepot the next morning. "I can't keep a secret like this from Marcus. Keira is just asking too much."

The coffeepot released its first-cup-of-the-morning aroma, signaling the completion of the cycle. She poured herself a cup and, carrying the mug carefully, returned to her favorite chair in her lair and picked up her Bible again. She could hear a shower running and assumed it was Marcus back from his morning run. He'd wanted her to go with him, but she'd begged off. The less she was with him, the less she was tempted to tell. Why on earth had she agreed to such a thing? After all, Dagmar was his mother too. And thankfully his birth certificate confirmed Kenneth was his father, just as everyone believed. She was relieved that when she gave him his certificate, he only asked if they'd found Keira's. She'd said yes, which didn't betray Keira's secret, but still felt like a lie of omission. But what could she do? To tell him more than he asked would be breaking her promise to Keira.

After a sip of coffee, really too hot to drink yet, she tipped her head back and closed her eyes. But even her prayers felt stilted. Like everything else this morning.

Thinking back to the afternoon before, she could still hear the anguish in Keira's voice: "I don't even know who my real father is!" They had gathered up the collected pictures and returned home. They'd not said much else.

She heard Kirsten's alarm and then the water turned off. Marcus must be out of the shower. Flipping to Psalms, she started at the last page. Praising the Lord for all things was easier when she read David's lists of the things God had done for him, such as the list of all the parts of creation and the order to praise the Lord. She took herself in hand and started her own list. "Lord, I praise you for answering our prayer to find the birth certificates. I praise you for the sunrise and the bird songs, for Marcus and Kirsten and Curtis and Thomas, and the privilege of being part of your family. I praise you that I can read your Word, that I have food to feed my family." She stared at her feet in pink-plaid mules. "I praise you that we have a wonderful home, pretty clothes to wear, and songs to sing." A tune floating through her mind brought that one up. "Praise ye the Lord, hallelujah, praise ye the Lord..." She put her Bible on the stand beside her chair, rose, and returned to the kitchen, humming as she went. Amazing how much better she felt already.

God would work out this mess too. After all, He said He would turn tears into joy and in all things work together for good for His children.

She set the water to boiling for one of Marcus's favorite breakfasts, poached eggs.

"Mom, could you please throw my gym clothes in the dryer while I shower?" Kirsten called down the stairs.

"Of course." For someone with such gifts of organization, remembering to have her gym clothes ready the night before eluded her daughter. Whoever thought laundry would be a stumbling block?

His outdoorsy aftershave announcing his presence, Marcus kissed her on the back of her neck. "I need to hurry. I have an appointment in half an hour."

She plunked down the toaster. "Eggs in three minutes."

Just a normal morning in the Sorenson household. All but the painful secret she'd promised not to share. He'd always thought his mother was about as close to perfect as a human could be. How would he handle the news that Dagmar had made a major mistake in her younger years?

As Marcus went out the kitchen door, Kirsten came flying down the stairs. "Mom, where's Dad?"

"He just left."

"Can you take me to school? I have so much stuff to take along." Usually if Kirsten needed a ride to school, Marcus dropped her off on his way to his office at the church.

"Where's José?"

"He had something he had to do, so he went early." Because José lived farther from town and worked at odd jobs as much as he could after school, he had a car and usually picked Kirsten up.

"Sure. There's your yogurt, I'll get your gym clothes, and I poured your orange juice." Kirsten had been on a yogurt kick for the last few months. "Do you want toast?"

"No to the toast and thanks for your help. I'll meet you at the car."

Long before, Leah had given up on reminding her daughter that eating too fast was not good for her and was just grateful the girl ate protein for breakfast. With the schedule Kirsten led, she needed all the high-powered food she could get. At the stop sign, Leah glanced at her daughter. Wasn't she pale this morning? And circles under her eyes in spite of the concealer?

"Are you feeling all right?"

"Yes. No. You know how my stomach reacts when I'm stressed. After graduation, I'll sleep for a week."

"Did you take something for it?"

"I'll be fine. Don't worry! Remember Grandma..."

Leah smiled at the words. "I know. I know. All will be well." She pulled to a stop at the curb in front of the school, accepted the swift kiss on the cheek, and watched her daughter sling her backpack over one shoulder and stride up the concrete walk.

Loose limbed and graceful with an athlete's stride, her blond hair held in place with a tortoiseshell clip, Kirsten looked the typical teen. She would be eighteen three days after graduation. She'd not mentioned anything about wanting a party but eighteen was a big milestone.

Leah put the car in gear, pulled onto the road, and headed for home. Her baby was grown up and going away to college in the fall. What would she do now with the rest of her life? She and Marcus were about to become empty-nesters. She shook her head. As she'd already been thinking, she would most likely have to work full time to pay for all the college tuition.

But maybe they should join Bjorn and Keira on their trip to Norway. Somehow they would work out the finances. *Heavenly Father, give me a clue, please. What is it you want us to do?*

And that brought her back to the problem of the secret. Keira knew how much she hated secrets and yet she'd said it had to be this way. Leah parked the car and headed into the house to change her shoes and put some makeup on, not that she wore a lot but she felt naked without eyebrows, mascara, and a touch of lipstick. Good thing no one had seen her. After all, the pastor's wife did have a certain image to keep up.

Half an hour later with her armor in place, she strode down the walk to Keira's. She'd rather be off running. She'd rather be working in her flowers. Face it, she'd rather be washing windows or scrubbing toilets than going to confront her best friend.

The smell of something burning met her at the door. She did her usual two-tap knock and stepped into the kitchen. Smoke tendrils seeping from the oven made her grab a pair of potholders and jerk open the oven door. She snatched out a cookie sheet covered with circles of charcoal and threw it out the door to land on the grass. "Keira, where are your fans? Keira!" She turned on the fan above the stove, threw open the windows, braced the back door to stay open, and ran to open the front door to get a cross breeze. Concern slid into fear. "Keira, where are you?" She charged up the stairs and called out again. Pausing, she heard the shower running. Pounding on the bathroom door, she yelled again.

"I'm in here."

"You trying to burn the house down? You forgot the cookies in the oven." She rattled the handle. Locked. Well, why not? Nothing else was going right. "Open the door. Are you all right?"

The water shut off. "I'm coming." Half a minute or so later, the latch clicked and Keira stuck her turbaned head out.

"You look terrible!"

"Thanks."

"You let the cookies burn. You could have burned the house down!" Finally aware she was still yelling, not to mention repeating herself, Leah blew out a hard breath. "What is going on?"

"Just go away."

"Nope. Is this about the...?"

Keira held up a hand, the other one clenching the bath towel to her chest. "Don't say anything more."

"Fine. I'll go put the teakettle on. You get dressed and get your body back down to the kitchen. I've never seen you like this."

"I've never learned that I don't know who my real father is, either. I have been living a lie all my life. My mother lied to me."

"I know." Leah softened her tone. "We have a lot to deal with. Just get dressed and come down."

"Did you tell Marcus?" Keira raised her voice as she closed the door.

"No. I told you I wouldn't. And I live up to my word." She didn't realize she'd said that aloud until Keira snorted.

"Glad someone in this family does."

"Keira, this isn't like you." But she knew she was talking to no one when she heard the hair dryer roar into action.

"The tea's ready," Leah said when Keira entered the kitchen. "And I put the last of the cookies in the oven. They'll be out in a couple of minutes." If Keira didn't feel a whole lot better than she looked, tea and cookies were not going to be the usual panacea.

"Did I really burn the cookies?"

"Charcoal crisps. They may have welded to the cookie sheet." Leah studied the woman slumped in a chair on the other side of the table. "Did you sleep at all?"

Keira shrugged. "Bjorn thinks I am going out of my mind."

"The news was a terrible shock. So what are you going to do now?"

"Well, to keep him happy I am going to order my passport. He said I can get the photo done at the drugstore and the forms at City Hall. So that's where I'm going when I leave here." Keira picked up a spoon and after adding sugar, stirred her tea.

"You just put sugar in your tea." The horror in Leah's voice must have caught Keira's attention.

She shrugged and stirred some more. "I can't get over the fact that she lied to me." Keira downed her tea, made a face, and pushed away the mug. "I better get going."

"You better use some more concealer around your eyes and add some blush. You want your passport picture to be the real you, not the ghost I'm sitting across from." Leah paused. "You want me to go with you?"

"No, thanks. I know you want to work on the pictures for the book. How am I going to find out what really happened?"

"Go through all the papers and correspondence from that time. And if I were you, I'd go have a long talk with Aunt Helga. She's the only one who might know anything."

Keira gritted her teeth. "It's just not fair that Mother died and my story died with her." She pushed her chair back when the timer dinged. "I'll get the cookies. You want to take some to Kirsten for tonight's snack?"

"Thanks." She snatched a couple of cookies from the cooling rack. "You might want to just throw the other cookie sheet in the trash. Call me later." Leah let herself out the back door and headed out to the sidewalk. Maple leaves whispered with the breeze above her, inviting her to go for a run. Everything always made more sense after running cleared her brain.

She glanced off to the west. Thunderheads loomed black and menacing somewhere closer than the horizon. The rain would most likely be here before she got inside.

The house was chilly since she'd left the windows and doors open. She rubbed her upper arms and stopped at the front window to see the clouds racing closer. She made her way around the house, both upstairs and down, shutting the windows to keep out the rain. Kirsten's window was already closed and the room was neat as usual, even though the girl had almost been late to school. This thing about order was getting out of hand. Since her father was a bit on the obsessive-compulsive side, their daughter came by it naturally. About time for another talk? Awareness was always the first step for change.

The morning flew by as Leah laid the original photos on the glass platform of the expensive copy machine they had rented just for this project. She scanned the pictures in and filed them according to topic, along with a date and names of the people in the picture. She'd place them on the proper pages and include the history when she compiled the pages. Thankfully she had been doing interviews of family members for the last few years, after she decided the family needed an accurate memory book. Some of the interviews had been by phone, some in person, and many through letters other members of the extended families had written, even back to the turn of the century. She was so thankful for the interviews she'd gotten before the older family members passed on. If only she'd worked on it more consistently...but time had flown by. Looking at the calendar was not a good idea. The days before the reunion were running out rapidly.

Concern that she wouldn't get it done plagued her, especially since everyone knew she always got everything done—and expected it. Working in fits and starts had obviously not been as effective as she had hoped, or she would be farther along by now. On top of that were graduation preparations and she had to do something for Kirsten's eighteenth birthday.

If only shutting off her mind was as easy as closing the windows. She who loved stormy weather did not care for internal storms. Keeping a secret like this from Marcus was giving her a headache. Returning to the kitchen, she poured herself a glass of water at the sink. One, then two drops hit the window. The wind had come up, lashing the maples along the driveway. She drank half of the water and caught a jag of lightning, brilliant against a nearly black cloud. More drops hit the glass and several ran together, joining forces on their way back to the earth. Within two breaths, the water was sheeting down the windowpane, blurring all but the startles of lightning. Thunder crashed but was still some distance away.

I have to tell Marcus. It concerns him as much as Keira. I cannot keep it from him. She turned from the window and reached for the cell phone holster hooked on her belt. Nada. Where had she left it this time? For someone as organized and self-disciplined as she was, how could she misplace her cell phone so often? Instead of looking for it, she headed for the wall phone.

Just as she touched it, the phone rang. Leah hesitated just a second to let her heart return to normal and then picked it up. "Sorensons."

"Leah?"

"Yes?" The voice was vaguely familiar but she couldn't place it. "How can I help you?"

"I have to apologize."

Another thunder roll blurred the voice.

"I'm sorry, what did you say?" Was that crying she heard in the background?

"I—I'm sorry, we won't be able to come by for your graduation open house on Sunday."

"Donna, I'm sorry I didn't recognize your voice. What's wrong?"

"You heard about the accident?"

Accident? What accident? "No, I can't say that I have. Donna, what's happened?"

"The boys rolled the car last night?" She took a moment to blow her nose.

"I haven't heard anything about this. Was anyone injured?"

"Two are in the hospital and my Carl tore some tendons in his knee. But he was released."

Since Donna's voice had settled down, Leah breathed a sigh of relief. "Has anyone called Marcus?"

"Probably not, since the other boys' families aren't members of our church. Carl was driving and he said he swerved because three deer leaped out in front of him. He hit one, and the shoulder was so soft from the rain that the car rolled. At least they all had their seat belts on."

"Another thing to be thankful for. So how can I help you, my friend?"

"Well, I guess I just needed to talk to someone who would calm me down. I've been shaking ever since the phone call. We met the ambulance at the hospital. Carl rode in the police car since he wasn't bleeding and seemed okay."

"Were they speeding?"

"I don't know."

"Carl will be able to graduate, right?"

"He'll be on crutches, but yes."

Lightning flared, thunder rattled the window frames, and the phone went dead.

Sure for a moment that lightning had struck her house, Leah took two deep breaths to calm her heart and glanced over at the clock. No electricity. What about the phone lines? She automatically dialed her cell phone so she could find it and hung up the house phone. She laughed at herself when she heard no dial tone. She did so many things on autopilot. How could she dial her cell when the phone line was out? After that last crack of thunder, the storm rumbled off to the east.

She cocked her head. Sure enough, her cell was ringing. "Keep it up," she ordered, heading for the sound. The flashing red light showed through the dish towel covering it.

Marcus had called. She waited until the voice mail icon showed up, dialed, and listened to him tell her about the accident and that he was on his way to the hospital. One of the other boys had sometimes attended youth group.

Reprieve. She could hardly tell him about the birth certificate fiasco right now.

Since she couldn't scan, she moved a chair in front of the table where the boxes of pictures to be sorted waited for her and dug in. The light from the window brightened as the sun drove off the storm clouds, making it easier to see. Some photos she put in a separate pile because they needed work to repair the ravages of time.

When the power came on again, she kept right on doing what she was doing. If she stopped now, when would she get back to it?

Sometime later she heard Marcus in the kitchen. Before she could shake loose from the stack of pictures in her lap, he walked through the doorway. The look on his face told her there was trouble.

"How bad?"

"Bad enough. It looks like the boys are all going to live. One of them is going back into surgery, the other is in ICU. Carl went home with his folks."

"Donna called, frantic and nearly incoherent."

Marcus sank down in a chair. "You know that has always been one of my nightmares. A phone call from the police or a knock on the door."

"I know. But the kids are going to be okay?"

"Leah, you're a nurse. You know that those kids might have to live with the residual effects of their injuries. Their pastor is with them." He raised his head to stare at his wife. "It could have been Kirsten or any of our children."

"But it wasn't. And it could have been so much worse. We can thank God for His mercy."

"And that's the kind of thing I should be thinking, not looking at the possibilities." He heaved a sigh. "Thank you. As always, you have the right words for me."

She smiled and nodded. "That's why God put us together, you know that." She lifted the stack from her lap and stood. "Have you eaten?"

"No, but I'm not hungry." He stood and wrapped his arms around her. "You know that song, 'You Are My Safe Haven'?"

She nodded and kissed his neck.

"I wish I had written it." He rested his chin on the top of her head. "I'll be in my office. Need to get on the sermon. No calls unless it's an emergency."

"Okay." *Not now. He has too much on his mind. I can't tell him.* Through sheer force of will, Leah took the photos over to the copy machine and started scanning them again. Copying and cropping took more concentration than merely sorting.

When her phone rang some time later, she was surprised to hear Marcus's voice. "You could just come in here, you know," she teased.

"I'm at the church. I left you a note in the kitchen."

"Oh." She must have really been concentrating not to hear him leave. "So when do you want supper?"

"Do you have anything planned?"

"Leftovers."

"I'll bring pizza. You heard from Kirsten?"

"No, why?"

"Guess I'm being overprotective. Maybe you should give her a call."

Leah shook her head. What, did he have a broken finger? But she ignored her smart retort. "Call me when you pick the pizza up."

When the clock ticked past six, she tried phoning Kirsten. When the call went to voice mail, she switched to texting. "Will you be home for supper?"

When half an hour passed with no return message, Leah could feel her stomach clench. After hearing the news about last night, every parent in Munsford was probably checking on their teens. She tried calling again. Texting again. Finally, her phone rang. *Thank you, God.* But it was Marcus, not Kirsten. Where was she?

"I'll be home in ten."

"Okay."

"What's wrong?"

"Nothing. We'll talk when you get here." She clicked off. "Lord, keep her safe. Keep them safe." Surely she was with José. She thumbed in the number for the Flores family, only to get voice mail again. After leaving a message, she stood looking out the kitchen window. She called Marcus. At least he answered.

"Would you swing by the high school and see if José's car is still there?"

"Sure."

Enough, she ordered herself. You trust that God is taking care of them and you don't go off worrying like this. That's what you tell others to do. Living, walking by faith. "Lord, I am trusting you. I know you love these kids even more than I do." She closed her eyes. "I am trusting you. I am trusting you." The slam of a car door sent her to the door. Marcus.

"The school was dark, no cars in the parking lot." He set the pizza box on the counter. "You called her? Texted?" He blew out a breath. "You realize we're worrying only because of the accident last night. Kirsten doesn't always let you know where she is."

"I know. We are going to sit down to eat and trust that God has everything under control." She set plates on the table and silver. "What do you want to drink?"

"Any iced tea?"

She nodded to the refrigerator and handed him two

glasses to fill at the ice dispenser. They sat down, Marcus said grace, and they each managed to eat one slice of pizza before she pushed her plate away. "Did we ever worry about the boys this way?"

"Oh probably, but that was a while ago and we've forgotten." He helped himself to another piece of pizza and set one on her plate too. "You always eat two slices," he said with one eyebrow arched.

"Ah, Marcus, if you only knew."

"Knew what?" he asked around a mouthful.

"Nothing." This was no time to bring up birth certificates and unknown fathers, that was for sure. She made herself eat all but the crust and put the box in the refrigerator. "I'm going back to work."

"You want some help?"

She stopped and stared at him. "Well, uh, I guess. You know how to run a scanner?"

He swatted her on the rear for an answer as they left the kitchen.

A while later, they both looked up at the sound of their daughter's voice saying good-bye. Breathing a sigh of relief, Leah grinned at Marcus. "All that wasted worrying. You'd think I'd know better by now." She raised her voice. "We're working on the book. Pizza is in the fridge."

When there was no answer, she put down the picture she was working on and started for the door. Kirsten met her halfway. Shock stopped her midstep. "Kirsten, darling, are you ill?" She reached to wrap her arms around her daughter.

Kirsten sidestepped her, shaking her head. "No, Mom, not ill. I'm... I'm just pregnant." Bursting into tears, she spun and headed to the stairs, pounding her way up to her room.

Chapter Five

Leah stared after Kirsten. Then she looked toward Marcus, who sat watching at the doorway as if Kirsten still stood there. His mouth slightly open, eyes wide, he wore the classic look of shock.

No, it can't be. Not our Kirsten. God, there has to be some mistake. Leah tried to swallow but her mouth was dust dry. She shook her head. Surely this didn't just happen. Looking at Marcus, who had yet to move, she knew he had heard the same thing she hoped she hadn't.

Pregnant. Leah sank into her chair and stared at the ceiling, willing the rabid thoughts and fears away. This room was her den, her lair, her sanctuary. Such words should never be spoken here. Should she go up and talk to Kirsten? A shudder ran from the top of her head to her toes.

"Surely this is a mistake." She looked to Marcus, hoping for an answer, some sign he didn't believe it either.

They'd had such a nice evening, just the two of them. And then a bombshell.

Her mind slipped back, grateful when she realized Kirsten was home safe. Home all right, but safe? Leah sniffed and felt a tear trickle down to her chin. Do something, she needed to do something. But moving hands and feet, let alone standing up, took more strength than she could commandeer at the moment.

Another tear trickled down, this time closely followed by a second. How long she sat there, with not even enough energy to mop the steady flow, she had no idea. When a flicker of anger ignited in her midsection, she heaved a big sigh and, placing both hands on the arms of the chair, heaved herself to her feet.

Oh God, make this not so. Their so-close-to-perfect daughter. Their princess. And José. They had trusted him. Not sure where she could dredge up the will, Leah went to kneel at her husband's knee to offer comfort, if any comfort could be found. She could feel and hear all their dreams for Kirsten crashing and splintering around their feet.

Slowly Marcus looked down at her, his shoulders sagging under the weight of dying hopes.

"This can't be." His voice sounded ragged, ripped by a chain saw. "Did you know or even suspect?"

"No. I thought her queasiness was all stress related." After a slight pause, she muttered, "And I'm a nurse. Some nurse." She gripped his hand. "Maybe we should go talk with her."

"I can't."

Rage attacked like a twister. How could Kirsten do this to her father? Leah shook her head. She knew about rampaging hormones, all right. How many times had she held the don't-put-yourself-in-temptation's-way conversation with Kirsten? Don't be alone together. All their wisdom and their efforts and now it had come to this. Right at this moment, she didn't dare go talk with Kirsten either. She might…she might…Well, she wasn't sure exactly what she might do, but it wouldn't be very nurturing.

"Maybe she's wrong. Maybe she just thinks...because she hasn't been feeling well..." He nodded. "Surely that's it. A big mistake."

"Marcus..." She started to say something else, then shook her head. "I only wish that could be true."

"But we don't know for sure, just what she said."

"Right."

He shook his head and kept on shaking it as if he had the palsy.

Two days ago everything had been perfect, a piece of heaven, they'd both said. And now, how could she? How could someone so smart be so stupid? But Leah knew the answer. Letting themselves be alone and caught up in the thrill of their love for each other. Leah gritted her teeth. They'd both taken the vow of chastity. Right. *Lord God, I sure wish you would make this not so. Please turn the clock back.*

But the agony she knew her daughter was feeling blew out the internal rage. *Oh my darling baby girl. How do I help you?* She kissed her husband's hand. "I have to go to her."

He nodded but continued to stare into some place only he could see.

Leah used the banister to pull herself up the stairs that normally she ran up. How many girls had she counseled through the years regarding no sex before marriage, or at least safe sex. As if there were any such thing. Kirsten and José had looked so pure and beautiful when they took the sanctity pledge at church. Leah stopped at the closed door. Would that she could go anywhere but in. Instead, she knocked softly. When no answer came, she twisted the handle and peeked inside. Kirsten lay facedown on the Shades of Purple quilt her grandmother had made for her.

Dagmar's calico cat, Patches, whom Kirsten had adopted after her grandmother had died, lay curled around the back of her head, one white paw resting on the blond hair. She blinked at the figure in the doorway.

"May I come in?"

A slight nod. The cat yawned, showing brilliant white teeth and a black patch on her tongue.

Leah crossed the room and sat down on the edge of the bed. With a gentle hand, she smoothed the tear-soaked hair back from her daughter's face. "I love you, my darling daughter." But at that moment all she wanted to do was scream and shake Kirsten until she said it wasn't so.

"How can you?" A hiccup separated the words.

Right now I love you because God is giving me the strength to do so. "I know this feels like the end of the world, but it isn't." What a stupid thing to say. *Oh God, I can't stand this.*

Kirsten shook her head, her hair slapping her cheeks. "Maybe not the end of the world, but it sure is the end of my life."

"I know it seems that way."

"You know?" Kirsten snapped her head up. "No, you don't. You don't ever do anything wrong. I'm going to have a baby and I don't even like babies." She slammed her fists on her thighs. "I hate me, I hate José, and I hate this thing inside of me." Flipping over, she buried her face in her pillow.

"All right, Kirsten, let's calm down. You don't mean those things."

"How do you know?" Her voice swelled to a scream. "Daddy hates me."

"No, but he will need some time." Leah stroked the golden hair, now tangled and disordered like their lives, but

Kirsten pulled away. "How long have you known?" Switching into nurse mode made her role a whole lot easier. Was she sure or was this some made-up nightmare?

"This afternoon. I bought a pregnancy test."

"Have you told José?"

A nod. "He said we should get married right after graduation, or even tomorrow."

"I see."

"He wanted to come with me when I told you, but..." Kirsten flopped back on her pillow. "I can't stand this."

"Has he told his grandmother?" Nurse mode, nurse mode.

"Maybe. I don't know." She raised her head, eyes swollen and nose red. "I don't want to get married, Mom. I'm too young to get married." Her voice rose in a wail. "I don't want to have a baby."

"I know. You're too young to raise a child too, but... There are many decisions that will have to be made."

"I don't want to be pregnant." Kirsten twisted and flung herself into her mother's arms. "Mom, I'm so sorry. I let you and Daddy down and messed up our lives."

In spite of the words boiling in her head, Leah kept silent, all her love coming through her hands as she stroked her daughter's back. Unbidden, a thought flashed through her mind. There was an out. She slammed that door and murmured mother words.

"What is Aunty Keira going to say about this?" Kirsten whispered between sobs.

"We won't tell her. At least not right away." *Secrets. More secrets. I'm no good at keeping secrets. How can I get through this without my best friend?* But Keira had enough to deal with right now, and besides, she did have strong opinions about some things and sometimes she could go on a rant.

Sarcasm used to be her way of life too, but Leah had chosen to let that go. She got tired of going to bed wishing she'd not said something. Keira had said the same, but sometimes the snide still slipped out.

As the sobs eased, Leah shifted to stretch out a cramp in her leg. How she needed a run. The sad thing was, she could not run away from this mess.

"I'm sorry, Mom."

"Yes, I know you are. We all are, but somehow we will get through this. Like Grandma always said, 'All will be well. God will get us through.' After all, this is no surprise to God."

"He should hate me too. I broke my vow."

"Ah, Kirsten, no one hates you, least of all God."

"I do." She studied a ragged cuticle. "And I'm not too happy with José at the moment either." Her jaw clenched. "I thought men were supposed to be the strong ones, take care of those they love."

"Kirsten, there's no sense playing the blame game. One step at a time."

"Easy for you to say."

To stop the words from pouring out of her mouth, Leah sucked in a deep breath and held it.

"Will you tell Curt and Thomas?" Now Kirsten sounded like a little lost girl.

Leah's mother's heart screamed in pain, far beyond the mother hurt of other times. She knew that staying in her nurse persona was mandatory. "Umm. Well, not immediately. But given time, this is one secret that is impossible to keep hidden."

"Is praying for a miscarriage a sin?" Tears brimmed over and rivered down her face. "This is so unreal. How could we be so stupid? One time, Mom, only one time."

Leah chose not to answer that. Kirsten was blaming herself enough as it was. *How did we fail these children of ours?* was her question. *What did I do wrong that she wasn't strong enough to resist the hormone rage? Lord God, forgive me for failing my daughter. We should have been better policemen.*

Kirsten's cell phone beeped, telling her there was a text message. When she didn't pick it up, the phone rang. "It's José, and right now I don't want to talk to him." She pulled away from her mother's arms and swung her feet to the floor. Heaving a sigh, she reached for a tissue from the square box on her nightstand. After blowing her nose and mopping her eyes again, Kirsten propped her chin on her hands, resting her elbows on her thighs. "Four days to graduation."

"Do you know how many periods you missed?"

"Two, I think. For a while I was so erratic, but lately I've been pretty regular again. It's possibly time for a third one."

"Have you spoken about this with anyone?"

Kirsten swung her head from side to side. "Only José. I told him I was late two weeks ago. He said not to panic. A lot he knew. One of the girls at school kept her baby and will be graduating with our class. She should have graduated last year. Two other girls I know of have had abortions. They were talking about it one day, said it was easy. Two days later they were feeling fine. Zip and no more baby, no more problems."

Leah couldn't believe they were sitting in her daughter's bedroom discussing abortions and pregnancies like this, so businesslike. Trapping the torrent of inner screams was getting more difficult by the minute.

74 Lauraine Snelling

The cell phone rang again. They both stared at it. When it went to voice mail, Kirsten turned and propped one bent knee on the edge of the bed. "I thought girls who got pregnant were stupid. And here I am. All I want to do is crawl under the covers and not come out. Not ever."

"Me too."

"I'm going to wash my face and see if I can study. I have two more finals to go, English lit and econ. Concentrating has been impossible and I'm tired all the time."

"You need to eat something. I could warm up the soup I made you."

"No, thanks. If I eat, I'll puke."

"Has that happened a lot?"

"No, but enough that I'm not trusting my stomach." Kirsten had always been the practical one. She'd learned to set goals in a class at school and kept on doing so when the semester was finished. It went along with the organizational gene she'd inherited from her father. When Kirsten stood, Leah did too. "I'll be downstairs. Might go for a run first."

The house phone rang and Leah crossed the hall to the master bedroom to answer it there.

"If it's José, tell him I'll call him later."

Leah picked up the phone and pushed the button. "Sorenson residence."

"Mrs. Sorenson, this is José. Is Kirsten's phone not working?"

"No, it's been ringing. She's in her room and said she would call you back later."

"Ah, okay. Tell her..."

Leah waited, chewing on her lower lip to keep from saying the things she really wanted to say, like "How could you do this to our little girl?" But she knew the consent had been mutual, and Kirsten had said as much. Still, it didn't help her emotions. "Yes?" She knew her tone was stiff, something like her neck.

"Oh, nothing. Thanks."

She heard the click before she shut off her phone and set it oh so gently back in the stand. She changed to shorts and a T-shirt and hauled her running shoes out of the closet. Good thing there were street lights, as dusk had dimmed the day.

Marcus was still sitting where she had left him, staring at the carpet. "I'm going for a run. You want to come?"

Slowly, as if he'd aged twenty years, he raised his head and shook it. Grief had etched deep lines from nose to chin, and she could tell he'd been crying.

"I won't be gone long. Kirsten is in her room and plans on studying. She has two finals tomorrow."

"Just like that. Drop a bomb and the world keeps on turning?"

"Would you rather I stay here?"

"No, go run. I know that's how you process things."

"How we both do."

"I can't."

He'd said that twice tonight. I can't. Words he had banished from his vocabulary years earlier. Can't never did anything. With Christ I can. "All things are possible to those who love the Lord and are called according to His purpose." How often he had quoted that verse. Said it was his life verse. "I'll be back soon."

"Put your vest on."

"Thanks." She stopped at the closet and pulled out a

vest with vertical reflector lines on the front and back, putting it on and tying it in front. "I'm going out to Mulberry." Years ago they had promised each other that they would say where they were planning to run in case of an emergency. By now it was habit.

Leah stretched on the front step and ran in place for thirty seconds before jogging down the walk and out the gate heading west. It might have been wiser to drive over to the high school track but she might meet someone she knew. Right now she didn't want to talk to anyone. Not even Keira. As she ran by the Johnston house she saw the bedroom lights were out, along with the ones in the living room. Bjorn was probably working in his office at the back of the house. Hopefully Keira was asleep. She'd check on her in the morning.

She jogged for a few blocks until she could feel her body warming up and then lengthened her stride. She'd never been a sprinter or a marathoner. But running freed up her mind, so she often worked problems out with her running shoes slapping the concrete until the sidewalk ran out and then pounded the dirt on the running/bicycle path that paralleled the road.

Please, Lord, don't let there be any emergencies tonight, Marcus can't handle anything else right now. Losing his mother, who was so young, was bad enough, but this! What are we going to do? What can we do? Kirsten was basically an adult on May thirty-first. One week after graduation. Three weeks before they were supposed to leave for the missions trip. *Lord God, what do I do? I feel like my hands are tied.* She reached the rail fence of the Peterson place and put one foot up on the top rail to stretch, then the other. Bending over, she fought to catch her breath and walked in a circle before heading back the way she had come. One mile out, one mile back.

Kirsten had mentioned two girls who had abortions. What if they encouraged her to do that? What if she was thinking crazy thoughts? How could she even imagine such a thing in the first place, let alone ponder it at length? But a baby would ruin their young lives, cancel out all their dreams. Unless she put it up for adoption. Gave up the next seven months of her life so the baby might live. Wasn't that what they'd all been teaching? Do not punish the baby for the parents' sin.

Either way, they would never see this grandchild of theirs. The least price to pay. Or was it? *But none of it is our decision.* How would she help Marcus get through this? Kirsten was too young to be married and care for a baby, but not too young to get pregnant. The thought brought on tears again. Leah mopped them away.

Chapter Six

I've got to talk with Leah.

But before Keira won the struggle to open her sleep-sealed eyes—or, more likely, tear-sealed eyes—the memory of yesterday came streaming back. She'd not even talked with Bjorn last night. By the indent in the pillow beside her she knew he'd been to bed. What had happened to her? She never slept that soundly. Turning her head, she zeroed in on the digital clock. Seven thirty, Bjorn shouldn't have left yet. She lay perfectly still, listening for the shower or the telephone. Not a sound.

When she rubbed her eyes to clear the sand away, she made an important discovery—the headache that had returned late yesterday was gone. Further checking told her that the stomach roiling of yesterday was gone too. She picked up the phone and dialed Bjorn's cell number. When he answered, she asked, "Where are you?"

"Down in the kitchen reading the paper. The coffee is hot if you feel like a cup."

"Thanks. I'll be right down."

"You're not still sick?"

"Doesn't feel that way. Bye." She shrugged into her robe, stopped in the bathroom to brush her teeth and comb her hair, then, ignoring the mental reminders of yesterday, made her way downstairs. Pictures of her children growing up and now her two grandchildren lined the wall side of the stairs. What difference, if any, would her discovery make in their lives? Did they need to know about it or was it better to leave their memories of their grandmother intact?

Bjorn looked up from his paper and pointed to the cup of coffee he'd poured for her. "I can fix you some bacon and eggs if you like." He studied her. "You still don't look too good."

"That's encouraging." She kissed his freshly shaven cheek. "Thanks for the offer and yes."

"You didn't wake even when I came to bed." He folded the paper and laid it beside his plate, then rose and headed to the stove.

Keira took her seat and lifted the coffee to inhale the steam. The fragrance of coffee was almost better than the taste until she took the first sip. Just the right temperature to drink, so she took a swallow and set the mug back down on the table. "That was a...surprise yesterday." She paused and waited for him to turn from the stove. "Really more of a terrible shock. Finding the birth certificates behind the picture in the sewing room." He watched her as if waiting for her to respond. "But you can fix breakfast first. Nothing will change the fact that Kenneth is not my biological father." Her voice sounded shaky, hesitant even to her own ears.

He studied her through his clear-framed glasses and then turned to the stove. "Are you sure you're not making more of this than it needs to be?" He laid the bacon strips in the frying pan and fetched the eggs from the refrigerator. "One egg or two?"

"One bacon and two eggs. I think my stomach just

realized it didn't have supper. It's growling at me." She drank more coffee. She decided to ignore his comment. More than it needs to be? Ha. "How was your day?"

"Good. Are you coming in today?"

"Planning on it. Ten okay?" How could they be having such a normal conversation when her whole world had been rocked off its foundation?

"Over easy?"

"Yes." Two could play this game. "Did that check come from the Davidson account?"

"It did. They weren't pulling the check-is-in-the-mail scam. Looks like the post office did indeed lose it, or sent it to Alaska or something." He flipped the eggs, set the bacon on a paper towel to drain, and handed her the toast to butter. When he set her plate in front of her, he paused. "It really doesn't matter, you know."

She decided to ignore that comment too. Maybe it didn't matter to him, but he knew who he was and always had. She spread butter on the toast and bowed her head to say a silent grace. When she looked up, he was studying her. Keeping her attention on her plate, she dipped her bacon in the egg yolk and ate a bite.

"So what is really the point in all this? The bottom line."

"The point is I've been living a lie all these years."

"No, you weren't. They were. You were the innocent child who was well loved and cared for. You couldn't ask for a finer mother and father."

"I know that." She could feel exasperation creeping into her voice. "But now I don't know who I am. How much else of my life has been a lie?"

"Yes, you know who you are. Adoption is legally binding

and the adopted person is part of the family. Your only real need to find your biological father is for his health history." He paused and thought a moment. "So you don't know if Kenneth adopted you or not?"

"I would assume he did, but what do I know?"

"There would have to be adoption papers somewhere. Things were different then regarding if the adoption was closed or not. Or if they had to get your biological father's permission for Kenneth to adopt you."

"What if he didn't?" She stared at him, the thoughts churning.

"Makes no never mind now, with them all gone."

"How could he treat her like that?" Thoughts of her mother being deserted pummeled her mind. She must have been young and trusting, naïve.

"Men do strange things, sad things. If he was that kind of man, you were far better off without him."

"True, but why didn't she ever tell me?"

"Did you ever suspect anything?"

"Never. Well, not really. I mean, I do look like my father's side of the family."

"And not your mother, but you do resemble her sister."

"I know. Even to the same body type, leaning toward the rounded side."

"How is it you never saw your birth certificate before? Surely you needed it at some point?"

She digested his question. "Mom used my baptismal certificate when I got my driver's license because she said she couldn't find the birth certificates, either mine or Marcus's. But strangely enough, she had the death certificates for the children who died." Keira knew the story of her mother giving birth, between her and Marcus, to a little boy, who died minutes after being born and then a little girl dying of pneumonia when she was two, the fourth child. Keira well remembered that. She had adored her baby sister, Lizzy, and her mother had taken a while to recover after that happened.

"I don't want to tell anyone."

"Not even Marcus?"

"Marcus has always thought our mother was perfect, so why disillusion him?"

"So did you." He refilled both their coffee cups. "What is that old saw, never judge a man until you've walked a mile in his moccasins?"

She frowned, staring into her cup.

"So what is bothering you the most?"

"That they never told me. Mother was always so adamant about telling the truth. I remember getting my mouth washed out with soap for telling a fib and yet here was this huge lie." *But is that all?* Her mind fought to take over questioning again.

"She could have given you up for adoption."

Keira heaved a ragged sigh. "She could have. You remember when my cousin Estelle had a baby out of wedlock when she was sixteen?"

"That was before I knew you."

"Well, I was so adamant to Mother that Estelle should give that baby up for adoption. That she was too young to raise a baby. On and on. I got pretty hot under the collar about it, but Mother never said a word." She mopped up the last of the egg with the corner of her toast. "Back to your question, what bothers me the most?"

"Yes." He leaned back in his chair, propping his coffee cup with both hands.

"I can't ask her any questions. My mind is foaming with questions."

"What about her sister, Helga?"

"What if she never knew?"

"How would they keep a secret like that?"

"I know. I want to know the whole story. I am hoping there might be some pictures or letters or something in the boxes that Leah and I haven't found yet."

"Go through the legal papers and check out the dates— of their wedding, when they came back home. Maybe the deed to the house?"

"I was so angry at Mother yesterday." She wagged her head. "I just have so many questions."

"By not telling anyone, you'll not have the chance to find out more information. Who knows what someone might remember." Bjorn checked his watch. "Sorry, I have a client coming in at nine. Since my office manager isn't there, I need to open up." He winked at her, then rose and set his cup in the sink. "Don't hurry. We'll continue this conversation tonight. Let me think on it. I know this is a shock." He came over and put an arm around her shoulders, gave her a hug. And when she turned up her face, he kissed her. "If it even entered your mind that this would make a difference to me, put that right away. You are who you are, and we've been in love for too many years to see this as more than a bump in the road."

Keira leaned against him. "Thank you. How do you always manage to say the right thing?"

"Just a gift, I guess."

She looked up to catch the teasing light in his blue eyes. "I'll see you in a while." She finished her coffee after he left.

Ah, Bjorn, this is more than a bump in the road to me. "But I still don't want to tell anyone. Mother, why didn't you tell me? I know attitudes were different then, but what about when I grew older, had a family of my own? You lied to me."

Keira forced herself to go back upstairs, get dressed, put on makeup, and get her car out of the garage to drive across town. She knew she should call Leah when even the car wanted to turn into the Sorenson driveway.

Once in the office, she flipped through the pink slips to see if she could handle any of the phone calls, checked the answering machine, and went into the kitchen of the old house converted to an insurance office to make the coffee. Carrying two cups, she tapped on Bjorn's office door and then opened it. "You two want some coffee?" At their assent, she entered and handed the men their mugs.

"How you doing, Frank?"

"Pretty good, under the circumstances."

She knew the circumstances he referred to. His wife had died two weeks earlier and he was trying to sort through all the paperwork. Bjorn had offered to help him, since the wife had been the one to take care of all the finances and bookwork.

"That old house is pretty lonely."

"I'm sure it is. Good thing your family lives close by."

"Yeah." He raised his cup. "Thanks for the coffee. I make lousy coffee."

She patted his shoulder and returned to her desk to pick up the ringing phone. Flipping open the spiral-bound desk calendar, she set up an appointment, making sure her voice sounded welcoming. Somewhere she'd heard that if you answered the phone with a smile, the caller could tell. She'd lived by that suggestion ever since.

She wrote herself a reminder to ask Frank to supper one of these nights. Just not tonight. Could an emotional shock cause such tiredness or had that bug come back? At lunchtime she ordered in sandwiches from Swenson's Café and kept working on the financial records. Somewhere there was an error and she would find it before she went home. But thoughts of talking with Leah kept intruding.

Lord, I don't know what's going on, but she hasn't called me either. That's not like her. She greeted the couple that set the door chiming when they entered and buzzed Bjorn to tell him his next appointment was there. Glancing at the appointment sheet, the name didn't look familiar. "Welcome. Are you new in town?"

"No, we live in Uppsala. Our neighbors told us to come here."

"You moved to the area recently?"

"Yes, I came home to take care of my mother." The woman smiled. "We are Jim and June Watkins."

"You can go right in. Bjorn will be glad to meet you."

By five o'clock, she still hadn't solved the accounting dilemma and Bjorn hadn't returned from a house call. She ran the adding-machine tape one more time, shook her head, and went back into the kitchen to find something for the pain that now centered right behind her eyes. Surely she was just missing something. Concentrating had been difficult all day, but now the drummer was making it impossible. So contrary to her normal behavior, which was to have everything tied up in neat little bundles, she shut down the computer, cleared off her desk, and left a message on Bjorn's cell phone that the office was closed.

As she drove down the street to her house, she made a face. She knew why she hadn't called Leah, but why had Leah not called her? Asking her to not tell Marcus, that really wasn't a fair thing to do. Was she angry about that? Keeping secrets always caused a quandary, one reason why the truth was better and easier. And she hadn't thought about the reunion all day. What would it take to cancel it? If they were going to do that, they needed to make a decision soon, before far-flung family members started buying plane tickets. But knowing them, most likely some had already bought theirs. What kind of reason could she give? She'd learned something about herself and didn't want to tell them? *Your grandmother got pregnant out of wedlock and I'm the product of that, that*... Keira shook her head. No, that was no reason to cancel the reunion. She would just have to tough it out. Secrets!

Once in the house, Keira took the Swiss steak dinner she'd frozen from a cooking binge several weeks earlier and popped it into the microwave to thaw before she put it in the oven. Setting the teakettle on the burner, she wandered into the home office and pulled open the file drawer with all of her mother's important papers. Getting them all in order had taken her weeks, in between working and normal living stuff. Life went on. When her dad had died she had helped her mother with the paperwork, so she had an idea what all needed to be done. Notifying Social Security had been at the top of the list. The government required that any pension money paid the month the person died be returned. As if they were trying to bilk the government.

The screaming teakettle took her back to the kitchen to fix her tea and put the supper in the oven.

Back in the office, she flipped through the papers looking for anything she'd not realized was important before. She set the manila envelope in which she'd gathered birth, death, and marriage certificates off to the side. On second thought. She felt like a light bulb had gone off in her head. She laid two documents side by side and read the dates. Sucking in a deep breath, she held it and let it all out, feeling her shoulders exit from the near-permanent place that was adhered to her ears. She read the lines again. Kenneth and Dagmar were married two days after she was born. *So Kenneth is definitely not my real father. But then—who is?*

Maybe tomorrow she and Bjorn could go out to the home place and search the attic for any papers and photographs; any kind of clue as to the man's identity would be helpful.

When Bjorn came home, she asked him if that would be possible.

"Sorry, Marcus and I are helping with the Habitat for Humanity house. Ask Leah."

"That puts more pressure on her, since I asked her not to tell Marcus."

"I've been thinking, and I think you should tell Marcus about your mother. After all, he is your brother. Leah would know the best way to do it."

"Thanks." She knew she failed at keeping the bite from her words when she saw his jaw tighten. Where was the understanding husband of this morning?

"You knew we were going to help with the Habitat house construction. In fact, you talked us into it, remember?"

"I know, but..." But then she hadn't known how

important finding those boxes was going to be. Or that they would need to go up in the attic.

"But what?"

"But she and I didn't find the boxes of the old photos and...never mind." She'd only ever been up to the attic once. It was a long time ago, and all she remembered was how it was dark and closed in and those wobbly stairs, which she didn't care to go up again. Just pulling them down was difficult. The sign on the side said EASY PULL. Easy for whom?

She set supper on the table and sat down, waiting for Bjorn to say grace. How could she be thankful with this hanging over her head?

Chapter Seven

Leah was grateful she'd not called in sick but went ahead and worked her usual night shift at the Munsford Residential Care Facility. They were too understaffed as it was. They'd had a busy night, and that kept her mind occupied. Mr. Alsworth had taken a turn for the worse, insisting that he had to go home and trying to get out the door. The fact that he'd lived at Munsford Care for a year didn't deter him. When he took a swing at one of the nurses, Leah had insisted he be restrained and medicated according to the doctor's written instructions. Sometimes she was glad they had a male nurse working the night shift.

Then a woman went into cardiac arrest, and Leah called the ambulance because the family had not signed a no-resuscitation form. One son got there and was furious they had called 911, and his sister was just as angry that he was causing a disturbance. Taking care of the patients was sometimes far easier than taking care of their families.

Little Mrs. Magnuson had been unable to sleep, so she sat in her wheelchair and, propelled by her feet, patrolled the halls, praying for those she felt led to. Leah wanted to ask her to pray for her family too, but didn't because she didn't want to answer any questions.

By the time she arrived home, Leah was too tired to get out of the car. What would she be facing here? When she left for work, Kirsten had been sleeping with her face on a textbook at her desk. She'd helped her to bed and reminded Marcus of the same need. She hoped he wasn't still sitting in his chair. She'd never seen him react to anything like this. Used to dealing with the crises of his congregation and others in the area, he normally sucked in a deep breath, prayed for God to work His plan, and dealt with whatever was going on. Other than his mother passing away at such a young age. That had been hard on him, but their real crisis was when Kirsten had decided to be born in a hurry and they didn't make it to the hospital in time. Marcus helped bring his daughter into the world, and when that baby wrapped her tiny hand around his finger, he lost his heart. He had called her his princess ever since.

How could anger and love manage to cohabitate in her body, mind, and spirit? Leah understood both of these whom she loved but that didn't make it any easier this time. Sometimes her gift of understanding was more a trial than a blessing. She'd always been able to put herself in someone else's situation.

She braced her forehead against the steering wheel. "Dear God, this is beyond me. Get us through this, please. Give us wisdom and compassion and whatever else we need. Right now I could use the energy to get out of the car and into the house." Heaving a sigh, she picked up her bag and opened the car door, a step in the right direction. When she walked through the door into the laundry room, she could hear a shower running. Someone was up and functioning. She set her bag on the table and took out the empty containers from her meal. The shower turned off.

No one had started the coffee, and she'd forgotten to set the coffeemaker last night. So where was Marcus? Climbing the stairs, she heard the hair dryer come on. Kirsten. Marcus let his hair air dry. At the top, she tapped on the bathroom door.

"I'm home."

"I'm running late. Can you take me to school? I—I've not heard Dad moving around."

"Of course." And where is your father? "What do you want for breakfast?"

"Yogurt and toast."

At least Kirsten felt like eating this morning. Leah walked down the hall to the closed door to the master bedroom. She hesitated before opening it. The bed hadn't been slept in, the bathroom not used. Marcus always left his towel over the shower door. She blew out a tightly held breath and changed out of her basic scrubs uniform of burgundy pants and a coordinating print top with puppies gamboling all over it, and into sweats, stuffing her scrubs into the hamper. She brushed her teeth, made a face at the weary woman looking back at her, and headed back downstairs. Duty called no matter how tired Mom was.

Marcus wasn't in the office or the living room or the family room. Where could he be? All that was left were the boys' rooms. Why would he be there? After Curtis and Thomas left home, she had turned one bedroom into a guest room and the other became a catch-all room. She had dreams of one day turning it into a grandchild's room. She could picture the baby crib with its brightly colored mobile hanging above it. She always thought it would be one of the boys giving her the first grandbaby. The dream had dimmed but not flickered out when Curt and Gwen lost their unborn baby. But she'd never thought it would be Kirsten, not until she was older and married.

Closing her eyes, Leah turned and shut the door behind her. She dug her cell phone out of her pocket and hit the button that automatically dialed his cell. When it switched over to voice mail, she started to get worried. Had he been called out during the night? Downstairs, she returned to the office and inspected his desk. No note. He must have gone to the seven a.m. meeting listed on the calendar and turned his phone off. He'd always said phones ringing during church or meetings were the height of thoughtlessness.

Still, this wasn't like him. Had he slept all night in the chair and rushed out to the meeting without showering? Or had he gone running? She went back upstairs to check in the closet. His running shoes were right where he always put them. She could hear drawers slamming in Kirsten's room.

"How long?" she asked at Kirsten's door.

"Five minutes."

"I'll have your breakfast ready to eat on the way."

"Thanks, Mom."

Leah paused. "I..."

"Don't, Mom."

She could hear the desperation in Kirsten's voice. Her daughter was doing all she could to hold it together and get through. The two of them were alike that way—deal with the emergency and fall apart later.

Back in the kitchen she started the coffeemaker and got

out breakfast for Kirsten. She should call Keira and find out how she was feeling. What if Keira was really sick in bed? Wouldn't she have called if she was? How could she talk with her best friend and not tell her what was going on? Leah stared up at the ceiling, commanding the tears to dry up. Good thing she'd not counted the times she'd done that during the night. Busy had been a blessing, all right.

"I'll be out in the car," she called up the stairs. "I have your breakfast."

Leah reached for an energy drink, remembered the caffeine warnings for pregnant women, and instead grabbed a bottle of water from the fridge. Thank God for nurse's training, she thought as she headed out the door. If she had put on decent clothes she could have stopped by the church to check on Marcus, but sweats and a morning-after-the-night-shift face weren't appropriate.

On a whim, she clicked the garage-door opener. Marcus's car sat in its usual place. So he'd walked to church or someone had picked him up. Was Bjorn on that committee? What committee was meeting? No further notes on the calendar. Fear fought with anger in her head. Fear for him and anger that he'd not let her know. Self-pity edged a toe through the door. Why was she the one who had to deal with everything?

Kirsten opened the door and slid in, setting her backpack on the floor. "Thanks, Mom. I'm starved." Biting into a piece of toast, she dug the spoon into the yogurt.

"I thought water might be easier on your stomach than orange juice or coffee. Energy drinks are on the no-no list for pregnancies. Not good for kids, either." Focusing on practical matters made this easier to deal with.

"Thanks."

Leah checked the dashboard clock. They had five minutes to the warning bell. "Going to be close."

Kirsten's cell blipped the text signal. She clicked it off, stuck it in the outside pocket of her backpack, and took a swallow of her drink.

"Do you have anything after school today?"

"Sleeping."

Leah pulled into the turnaround in front of the school and stopped at the wide walk to the front door of the two-story brick building. "I'll be praying for your finals."

"Thanks." Kirsten set the plate on the console, unsnapped her seat belt, and exited the car, swinging her blue-and-red pack up on one shoulder. The wolverine mascot symbol bounced as she jogged up the walk. The bell rang as she pulled the door open.

"Lord, get us through this. This morning seems so normal; I could so easily pretend last night never happened." She had three choices. Go home and crawl into bed, which was the usual thing for her to do after a night shift, stop to see Keira, or go looking for Marcus despite her appearance.

A worm of resentment wriggled into her mind. He could have left a note. No matter how distraught he was. Or angry. Or disappointed, or maybe a better word was desolate. That's what she had seen last night, absolute despair. A yawn nearly cracked her jaw and with that she headed home. She should have made decaffeinated coffee. Oh well, she didn't need to drink it, just go to bed. Her stomach grumbled. She picked up the extra slice of toast that Kirsten hadn't eaten and ate that on the way home.

Marcus was sitting at the kitchen table when she walked

in, head in his hands, elbows propped on the table. He was still wearing the same clothes he'd had on the day before.

"Marcus."

He stared at her through bloodshot eyes. "You took her to school?"

"Yes."

"Thank you."

"You had a seven o'clock committee meeting this morning. I thought you were there. Where have you been?" Keeping her tone even was the result of years of practice.

"Walking."

"Walking where?"

"Out in the country, past the home place, the back roads. I didn't want anyone to stop and ask me if I wanted a ride."

"Did it help?"

He shrugged. "How was work?"

"Crazy."

"You're lucky."

"How so?"

"You had too much to do to think."

"Sort of true. You want coffee?"

He stared at her as if he couldn't make a decision, and then shook his head. "What will I tell the board?"

"The board?"

"At church."

"Why? I mean, you lost me there." She set a full cup in front of him. "What would you like for breakfast?" What did he mean, tell the board?

"Toast, I guess."

"You need some protein. How about I scramble some

eggs?" She turned to the refrigerator and started taking out eggs and milk. She checked the meat drawer and pulled out the bacon too. Anything to keep the appearance of normalcy going. "Did you call in regarding the meeting?"

He shook his head. "Never entered my mind."

"You want me to call and say you're sick?"

"Wouldn't be a lie." He scrubbed lean fingers through his baseball-cap-smashed hair and blew out a breath. "What are we going to do?"

"Marcus, what do you mean 'we'? We are going to wait and see what Kirsten decides."

"You mean we stand back and let her totally mess up her life?"

She already did that. But Leah kept silent, beating the eggs with a vengeance. When she could restore her tone to neutral, she added, "She is nearly eighteen. At that point she will legally be an adult." After cutting up bacon, she flipped it into the heated frying pan and added cream to the eggs. This morning she had no patience for the healthier food she usually served. The silence stretched, feeling brittle like early frost on a mud puddle. The bacon popped and sizzled, reminding her to turn down the burner. She turned to look at her husband.

Marcus was staring out the window at the bird feeder that needed refilling. Or at least that was what she saw, what he was seeing she had no idea. She drained the bacon, then stirred in the eggs and chopped onion. Grateful she had something to do, she put the bread in the toaster and poured herself a cup of coffee. It didn't look like she'd be going to bed anytime soon.

The ringing phone caught her attention, but if Marcus

heard it, he didn't respond. Leah answered and said, "Good morning."

"Hi, Leah, this is Jim Gustafson, is Pastor okay? He didn't make the meeting and it's not like him not to call." Jim was chairman of the board of elders that assisted the pastor in governing the church.

"I know, Jim, thanks for calling. He's feeling under the weather and must have slept through it. I was about to call Marcia and tell her to cancel his appointments for today."

"Sorry to hear Marcus's sick. Hope it is nothing serious. How about I tell Marcia for you?"

"I'd appreciate that. I'll tell him you called, and he'll get back to you soon."

"Thanks. Hope you have a great day."

She about choked on his blessing. Have a great day. Right. Just getting through today and the next few days would be miraculous. Through it how? Where were the guidelines for an only and far too young daughter announcing an out-of-wedlock pregnancy? Leah clicked off the phone and laid it on the counter. Sprinkling cheese on the scrambled eggs, she covered the pan with a lid and turned off the heat. If only she could turn off the heat in her head. She retrieved the plates and silverware, things Marcus usually did when they fixed a meal together. Surely her feeling of irritability was due to her being tired.

He had yet to move.

"You want some cream in your coffee?" All the mundane things that made up life. Bacon and eggs and coffee and birds wanting to be fed. Speaking of wanting to be fed, where was Patches? Leah dished up the breakfast on two plates, plunked down more bread for toast. "I'll be right back." She headed up the stairs and sure enough, she heard a cry from behind the closed door to Kirsten's room. "You got locked in, eh?" She opened the door and the cat stalked out, glaring at her. "Hey, it's not my fault. I didn't shut the door." She followed the cat back down the stairs.

Tail straight in the air, Patches padded into the kitchen where the kibble waited in her dish. She sniffed it and went to stand in front of the refrigerator, the dispenser of milk and the "wet food" the cat infinitely preferred.

Her toast was only warm but Leah buttered it anyway. "Marcus, please eat."

He broke off his stare and looked down at the plate in front of him as if surprised it had arrived there. Obediently, he lifted his fork and took a bite. He ate mechanically but at least he was eating.

Leah took her place, started to eat, reminded herself to say grace, and after a very abbreviated prayer, forced herself to eat. She took a sip of coffee but put it down and got up to put on the teakettle instead.

Marcus pushed his half-eaten meal away. "Think I'll go to bed now. Hopefully I'm tired enough to sleep."

"Did you sleep at all last night?"

He shook his head. "At least I don't think so." He rubbed his eyes. "I should call Marcia."

"It's all taken care of. Jim will tell Marcia, and she'll cancel your appointments. Is your sermon ready for Sunday?"

He nodded. "What are we going to do?" he asked again.

"We are going to take one day at a time and keep this to ourselves until after graduation. That's only three days away."

"One day at a time? How about an hour, a minute? All these years I've talked about taking every thought captive so worry and fear can't get a foothold. I thought I was good at it."

The teakettle whistled, so she rose to make her tea. "Some things are easier to do than others."

"Until it is your daughter in trouble. My daughter. My Kirsten." He stared at his wife. "How are you able to work and act as if nothing is wrong?"

"Things need to be done. I've been praying for us to deal with this. I've been going over the list of options."

"This is a baby, not an option."

"Some would say it is not a baby yet." Leah couldn't believe she was actually putting her thoughts into words—and speaking them out loud.

He pushed his chair back and stood. "I'm going to shower and take a nap, see if I can get ahold of this."

Guilt made her flinch. All the work she and Marcus had done with antiabortion groups, always taking the stand that life begins at conception. She rinsed the plates and loaded the dishwasher. "Lord, I do believe that. I think. I need to get some sleep too. I'm not thinking straight." She shut the door and leaned against the counter. "But this is my daughter, my honest, reliable, lovely, trusting-in-Jesus daughter, and not some statistic."

Chapter Eight

"You've been avoiding me. I called and texted."

Kirsten hugged her books to her chest. "I know, José, but I have to have time to figure this out." The two of them had left the high school grounds after their last final and now they sat at their favorite table in the city park. Children were playing on the climbing bars and swinging in the swings. Soon the Little League teams would be taking over the ballpark to the north. Dog walkers kept pretty much to the circular path around the park, except for those who used the grassy area to keep their dogs chasing a tennis ball or a Frisbee.

"So how did yours go?" she asked.

"So-so. I had a hard time keeping my mind on mundane questions like name the three branches of the government and who is currently holding those positions. And you?"

"I think I aced lit but econ is iffy. If I get an A it will be a miracle. Makes me realize that economics is not my favorite subject. Too many numbers and charts."

He nodded, staring at an ink blot on his index finger as if it were life threatening.

José looked like he hadn't slept, and there were dark smudges under his eyes. "You said you were figuring out something. What?"

"What I'm going to do."

"Marry me right after graduation, that's what we'll do." His square jaw tightened. "You know I love you and you have always said you love me. But you don't call back or even return my texts." His voice cracked. "This is *our* baby."

"And what about the scholarships you have, a free ride to Northwestern? You'll give all that up?" She held up a hand. "Don't answer that. At least not right now."

"Kirsten, all I care about, all I can think about right now, is you and the baby."

"That's easy to say right now, but what about...?" Kirsten slammed her books down on the table. "I am not ready to have this conversation and that's why I have not returned your calls." She fought the tears that seemed to spring up whenever she let down her guard. *Deep breath.* "Did you tell your grandmother?"

"Of course. I said I would."

That was José, all right. If he said he would do something, he did it. Other than their vow of chastity. What happened there? "What did she say?"

"Not much, but she hugged me hard. I know she is praying for us."

José's grandmother, Betty Flores, was known as a wise woman who listened to God and prayed for so many people. José was the center of her life. He had lived with her since he started kindergarten and his biological mother, her daughter, disappeared into the drug scene. She attended the Munsford Community Church, so José and Kirsten had known each other since Sunday school. They'd been friends all those years and in the youth group at church. And then in high school they started dating, with the group at first. And then...

Kirsten jerked her mind back to the park and José glowering at her. "Take me home, please. I don't feel so good."

"I want to talk with Pastor Marcus and your mother."

"No!" The one word exploded into the spring air.

"Why not? That's the proper way."

"José Flores, there is no *proper way* for the mess we're in." She deliberately put a twist on his words.

"You don't have to yell." His eyes narrowed.

"Yelling beats crying when I might never stop."

He heaved a sigh. "Come on, then. But you can't put me off forever."

"I don't plan to." She picked up her backpack.

He lifted her pack from her, holding it tightly, waiting for her to object. He slung it over his other shoulder as they left the park.

Normal. This must stay normal. She swallowed the anger boiling in her throat. "Are you working today?"

He nodded. "At three."

Good, then he would at least quit calling and texting her. The anger snapped and snarled. This was supposed to be a happy time, one they had looked forward to for years. Graduation and the start of their new lives. Their much-anticipated missions trip was shortly after graduation. José could still go, but she needed to come up with some kind of excuse. How long could they keep this secret? She clamped her lower lip between her teeth, ordering her stomach to behave itself. Uncertain as to whom she resented most at the moment, him or her own body, she strode out, forcing him to walk faster too.

"What's your hurry?"

"If you have to know, I need to use the bathroom."

"Oh, sorry."

Sorry for what? For asking the question, for allowing them to be in this position, or for getting them in this position? One moment she blamed him and the next, she castigated herself.

He stopped when they reached the gate and handed her backpack back to her. "Call me."

"Probably not tonight. You get off at ten, right?"

"And hopefully you'll be asleep by then." He took her hand but it was all she could do to not pull away. "We'll make it through this, Kirsten. I don't know how but I— I love you."

Sure, that's what got us into this fix. "Right."

"Do you believe that God will make something good of this? He promised..."

"I don't know what I believe right now." She turned and swung the gate open, wishing she dared to run away. She waved over her shoulder without turning to look at him again. The wounded look he had given her made her want to scream. He could walk away if he wanted to, after all, she was the one carrying the baby.

Since they had turned in their books after the last final, her backpack clinked on the entry table rather than its usual *thunk*. She glanced in the mirror above the table and grimaced. If she thought José had looked bad, no amount of concealer under her eyes had helped. But then, many of the seniors looked exhausted. Finals did that.

Patches greeted her from the third step up.

"Where is everyone?"

The cat chirped again and stood, arched her back in a typical cat fashion, and padded off toward the kitchen.

"Sure hope Mom fed you. She had to have let you out. Sorry." Kirsten opened the door to the refrigerator first, studying the contents to see if anything looked at all appetizing. She pulled out a couple of things and turned to pet the cat, who now sat on a chair. Glancing over to the dishes on the floor, she saw the remaining kibble. Patches wasn't a hearty eater. Kirsten made her sandwich on one slice of bread, cut off a dab of cheese for the cat, and smiled when Patches daintily nibbled the cheese while holding on to Kirsten's fingers with both front paws. After adding some chips to her plate and putting things away, she headed for her favorite recliner in the family room.

Most likely her mother was still sleeping after working the night before and her father was at the church. Halfway through her sandwich, a yawn caught her, a tidal wave of weariness that swept her back into the safety of the chair. *Someone wake me when this is all over.*

When the cat jumped up in her lap some time later, she could hear her mother in the kitchen. But instead of joining her, Kirsten dragged up the stairs and crawled into bed. At least she didn't have to be at school in the morning.

But when she woke to use the bathroom, the house was silent and the clock flicked the numbers to 2:15. Back in bed, guilt dragged up the memories she'd been trying to ignore. Celebrating the incredible offer from Northwestern, one kiss led to the next one, and neither of them tried to put on the brakes. After all, they truly loved each other and planned on marrying someday. Afterward, the guilt that they'd broken their chastity vows nearly drowned them. And then the fear. Would God continue to bless them after they blew their vows like this?

"But we won't do it again," they promised each other. She returned home praying, *Please, Lord. One time—no one gets pregnant on her first and only time. How could we have been so stupid? Stupid! Stupid!* She sat up in bed and clicked on her light, pulling her journal from the drawer. She'd have to burn this one when she finished it, so no one would ever read it.

After she wrote the date she began, "This can't be happening. It just can't. Not to me. Please, God, please make this go away. You can fix anything. Please, no, no! It can't be. It just can't be." She blotted tear splashes. "I have my whole life to live. This just can't be happening. There has to be a mistake somewhere. Surely the test was wrong. I promise it won't happen again. We learned our lesson. I can't do this!" The exclamation point stuttered across the page. She flopped back on her pillows, grabbed a handful of tissues, wiped her nose and eyes, and picked up her pen again. "It's not fair. Please." She slashed lines under the word. "Please make it all go away. Women lose babies all the time. Not me, please, not me. It just can't be." She stopped writing and rubbed the bridge of her nose where headaches sometimes formed. "I'd rather die than go through this." She threw the pen across the room.

"God, please!"

How am I going to get through this? That pregnancy test yesterday, I took it twice. That should be sufficient, but what if the box was faulty? She dug a new pen out of the drawer and wrote herself a note to buy another test kit. "Oh, Lord, I promise to not do it again. I promise to keep my vow. Oh please."

She lay back and let herself dream of this all being a false alarm. She and José had learned a lesson, that was certain. Maybe she should have waited to tell her parents. She hadn't been planning on telling them right away like that, but the words just jumped out of her mouth. The Bible verse on the page of her journal reminded her, "Ask, and you shall receive. Search, and you will find. Knock, and the door will be opened for you." She read it again, one of those verses she had memorized for Sunday school. "Lord, I sure am asking. Please let me not be pregnant. Let this all be a false alarm. I'm so sorry for not keeping my vow, for not saying no. One of us should have said no. But we didn't. Help us all. In Jesus' name, amen."

She turned out the light and snuggled back down. She felt so ready for more sleep. And she didn't need to set her alarm for school.

In the morning when she finally woke up, the clock read ten. Her stomach explained to her that she'd not eaten supper or breakfast and perhaps she should do something about that. Making her way downstairs, she heard her mother in the laundry room. Kirsten picked Patches up off a chair and, cuddling her under her chin, stopped in the doorway. "Morning."

"Good, you're up. I was beginning to think I needed to check to make sure you were breathing." Leah closed the lid on the washer and turned the dial.

"Guess I was tired. Could I borrow the car? I need to pick up some stuff at Barnett's in McGrath."

"Barnett's? Isn't that a bit far away?"

"I know but Barnett's is the only place that has that special hand lotion that I like." Oh great, now she was lying on top of everything else.

"Fine with me. How about helping me at the home place for a while? I need to find the pictures for the reunion book."

"Can I do that after I get back? I shouldn't be gone long."

"Sure, if you fill my list too."

"Okay." Well, at least something was going right.

"José called."

I told him not to call. Can't he listen? "Thanks for not waking me up." Kirsten turned back to the kitchen.

She stirred her usual yogurt and sat down at the table to eat. "Dad at work?"

"Yes."

She wanted to ask how her dad was doing, but she ate without speaking. Right now she didn't want to think about her father. Actually, she didn't want to think about much of anything. She'd take the pregnancy test again and all would be well.

And what if it isn't? something inside her asked. She tossed the yogurt container in the trash, stuck her spoon in the dishwasher, and headed for her room to get ready to leave. Maybe today her period would start after all. She glanced at the calendar. No, it wasn't due for two more days. And she'd already missed two cycles.

Down in the car, she texted José. "I asked you not to call. I will call you later." Hopefully with good news. The May morning sparkled all green and gold, with flowers blooming and the sky so blue she wished she'd worn a tank top. But a T-shirt and shorts with flip-flops also said that summer was almost here. She parked in the huge parking lot and marked what aisle she was in so she could find the car again. Her mother had forgotten one time and they had walked the whole place looking for it, pushing the full cart.

Inside the store she looked around to be sure no one knew her. She stood in front of the pregnancy kit display and made sure she chose a different brand from the one she had used two days ago. Was that all it had been? Felt more like a week. Crossing items off her mother's list, she put them in a red plastic cart and went to stand in the checkout line. Any other time she would have called Lindsey and asked her to come along. They'd stop at the Burger Barn for lunch. Of course she could do that anyway, but it wasn't as much fun alone. She studied the headlines on the magazines by the checkout. Some Hollywood star was caught cheating on his wife, someone else was dating someone new. Same old, same old.

Two days until graduation. Her new life was about to begin. She knew she was still in the running for several scholarships that would be announced at the ceremony. She needed to press her gown. She and her mom had bought her graduation dress several weeks earlier. Good thing it was lightweight. Could be hot that day. All these thoughts kept dancing through her mind as she set her purchases on the conveyor belt and paid the bill. She took her sunglasses off the top of her head and put them on as she pushed the cart outside.

"I'm back," she called when she got home.

"Okay." Her mother answered from upstairs.

Leaving the other plastic sacks on the table, Kirsten took hers and climbed the stairs to the bathroom. *Here goes*, she thought. *Please, Lord, let it be negative*.

But staring at the stick as it changed color, the weight settled back on her shoulders. Pregnant. She sank down on the closed toilet lid. Three tests said the same thing. There was no doubt, no room for good news. She put her head down on the edge of the sink and let the tears flow.

Chapter Nine

"What are you doing?"

Keira looked up from the computer, realizing that her eyes felt like a dump truck had unloaded sand in them. "Trying to find more information about my early life and hoping there was a mistake on the birth certificate I have."

Bjorn crossed the room to stand behind her. Hands on her shoulders, he began kneading the tight muscles. "You need to relax; you're tight as a drum."

She tipped her head to the side to give him better access to the tender spots. "You have healing hands, you know."

"You've said that before. Maybe I should leave the insurance business and become a massage therapist."

"Well, I could run that office just as well, I guess." She turned to look up at him. "Would you want to do that?"

"Something to think of for when I retire."

"I thought we were going to travel, not start a new business."

He used his thumbs to work on the knots at the base of her skull. "Have you found out anything?"

"I requested another copy of my birth certificate and e-mailed Marcus to ask him to do the same. Of course for mine..." She shrugged. "There have been mistakes made, even in government offices." She hit the save key. "I need to find more boxes, see if there is any evidence of another man."

"What if there aren't any other boxes? What if Dagmar got rid of all the early stuff?"

"My mother get rid of something? Come on, honey, you know better than that. Remember the things we found in the barn? She must have moved those boxes out there after Dad died. He would never have allowed old house stuff in his barn." She thought of the two boxes of empty cottage cheese, sour cream, and other pint and quart plastic containers. Next to that were several boxes of old magazines, which they had donated to the senior center; they sold some of them in their rummage sale and used others for craft projects. The box of what Bjorn called junk—screws and bolts and paint cans and plastic bags and who knew what else—an artist from church took. He used all kinds of odd things in his collages.

Bjorn hit an especially tender spot on her shoulder. "Ouch."

"Sorry." He lightened his fingers. "So, when are you and Leah going back out to the home place to search the attic?"

"I don't know."

"You've not called her?"

"No, and she's not called me."

"For two women who talk on the phone every day at least once, usually more, that's mighty unusual. If I were you, I'd be concerned."

"I'll take time to call tomorrow."

He shrugged. "Graduation is Saturday?"

"Yes."

"And we're invited there for the celebratory supper afterward?"

"Yes." Keira hit the save button, exited the program, and then shut down the computer. "You want a cup of tea? I'm having one."

"Sure." He headed for the door. "I saw Kirsten driving by today. Seemed strange for her to be out of school."

"Her last finals were yesterday." She headed for the kitchen to fix the tea, dishing up lemon bars to go with it. She set out two mugs, not bothering with the china cups and saucers she loved to drink her tea from. She always said tea tasted better from china cups. As a concession to the late evening hour, she used herbal tea, a soothing mix that included chamomile, which was supposed to help her fall asleep quickly. Bjorn was fortunate. He was usually asleep before he could roll over, while she courted sleep and sometimes grew envious of his even breathing. Maybe she should put the lemon bars back; neither one of them needed a sugar high. But one lemon bar wouldn't make a difference—would it? She could hear Leah saying, "If you didn't bake them, you wouldn't be able to eat them."

She put the cups and plate, with napkins, on a tray and carried it into the family room, where Bjorn had turned on the television to watch the ten o'clock news. Their two recliners were side by side, separated by an occasional table with a lamp on it. She set the tray on an ottoman and handed Bjorn his cup. One sip and he rolled his eyes.

"More dried weeds, eh?"

"Drink up, it's good for you." She passed him the plate of treats. "But this isn't."

"One cancels out the other."

"Good thought." A somber male face announced that another wave of tornadoes was tearing up Kansas and Missouri and threatening to swing north, bringing torrential rain. While he talked, pictures of empty lots, piles of rubble, and people digging through the remains scrolled across the screen. A lone dog sniffing at a pile of bricks. Two little girls clutching their mother's legs while she watched men pulling roofing off what was now a pile of broken two-by-fours, split siding, and sodden junk.

"Dear God, take care of those people," Keira whispered. She remembered the horrible roar they'd listened to when a small twister hit the outskirts of Munsford. They'd been down in their tornado cellar, praying for safety. They emerged to find that all was well, though someone had lost a barn and trees. What if they'd come out to find everything gone? She clamped her teeth, ignoring her shaking hands. The horror was beyond her imagining.

At the end of the broadcast, Bjorn clicked the remote. "Those poor people, losing everything like that."

"Did they say how many have died?"

"Ten confirmed, probably more." He set his cup on the tray. "The insurance agents and estimators down there are going to be going crazy. Think I'll call Marcus and ask if the church is planning to send assistance." He picked up the phone and punched the numbers. "Hi, Leah. Is Marcus near the phone? Good, thanks." When he hung up, he stared at the blank television. "They'd not heard the news yet tonight."

"So what are you thinking?"

"I'm thinking we better get our emergency team out right away." The last time the church sent emergency aid, Bjorn had been in charge of the efforts, so this was not new to him. "I can't get the picture of the path of that twister out of my head. Blocks wide and it leveled all it touched. Such a giant of one. Are these getting worse all the time or am I managing to forget how bad it can be in between?"

Keira shuddered. It could have been their town, their area, so easily. "Those poor families, searching through the rubble, not for their house as much as their family members." She rolled her lips together and stared at the ceiling to stop the forming tears. What if it were her son or daughter? She stared at Bjorn. Or her husband. "We have to help them. I'm with you, I think the tornadoes are far worse now than they used to be."

The phone rang and Bjorn answered it. "Marcus," he mouthed.

Keira picked up the tray and returned it to the kitchen. Leave it to Bjorn to immediately think of sending aid. After putting the tray away and the cups in the dishwasher, she shut off the back porch light and headed up to bed. The men were still talking.

She was already in bed with her devotional book in hand, praying not only for her normal list but also for the suffering people in Kansas, when Bjorn entered the room. "So, what will we do?"

"He's calling a meeting for seven a.m., started the telephone tree. You want to go?"

"I need to bake for the graduation dinner. Kirsten didn't want a cake but she asked for my apple pies. I'm also trying to think what we can send to help the victims, besides bottled water. I'm assuming that we'll fill Hansen's truck like we did before and send it down the road?"

"I don't know. Marcus sounded strange and then said

he'd been sick and so had taken today off. Maybe he has the same bug you did."

"If he gets over it as fast as I did, that will be a miracle. Certainly hope he's over it by this weekend. Leah must be going crazy. I'll call her in the morning." She picked up her book and put it down. "Those poor people." *Lord, you know the needs far more than we do. Give our guys wisdom as they figure out how we can help. Protect those who need it and heal the wounded. Comfort those who mourn.* She looked up when Bjorn slid into bed and laid a hand on his arm. "You're a good man, Charlie Brown."

"I sure wish you'd get my name right." He kissed her and rolled over to turn out his light. "You going to read long?"

"Nope." She did the same. "I love you, Bjorn Johnston. There now, did I get it right?"

His chuckle warmed the darkness.

The next morning Keira was up and peeling apples when Bjorn joined her in the kitchen. "You want some breakfast?"

"No, I'm sure there'll be coffee and something at the meeting." He stopped before going out the door. "Call Leah."

Keira stared at her husband. He never gave orders like that. "I was planning on it."

"Good." She heard the car start up and the garage door rise. "Yes, sir!" she muttered and then was glad she'd not been a smart mouth before he left. But he sure caught her by surprise. You'd think after nearly twenty-five years of marriage, she'd understand him better. When the clock hit eight she washed the flour and lard off her hands and picked up the phone. Maybe Leah had gone to the meeting too. But she answered on the second ring.

"Hey, I have a question."

"Shoot."

"I'm making pies. You think Kirsten would like a choco-late cream pie along with the apple ones?"

"She said apple but if you want to bake some other kind too, go for it."

Did Leah's voice have an edge to it? "Okay. I'm thinking we should go out to Mother's and get the extra bedding to send to the tornado victims."

"Good idea."

"You want to go? Or rather, can you take time to go?"

Leah heaved a sigh. "I know I should, but the food for the party has to be ready today."

"I was thinking this afternoon sometime, after I'm done baking pies."

"I have the ham in one oven and the turkey in the other. Check with me later. Besides, we'll have to see what the church committee decides."

"You think Kirsten might like to go along?"

"I doubt it, but I'll ask her. I had planned to go out there yesterday but never made it."

"Okay. Later." Keira clicked off the phone. Had all been as usual? Right now she wished she was as good at reading other people as Leah was. But something didn't feel right. Was it all on her side, in her imagination? Rolling pie crust gave one too much time to think.

She had three pies in the oven by the time Bjorn returned.

"We're going to load the truck today and tomorrow and Hansen will drive down there on Sunday. The call is going out for bedding, sleeping bags, clothing, and we'll buy cases of bottled water and food bars from the emergency fund."

"Who is going with?"

Bjorn shrugged. "Hansen, Grady, and me. We'll switch off driving and go straight through." He pulled his flip notebook from his shirt pocket. "I wish we could leave tomorrow. Those poor people."

"I'll get all I can from Mother's. We don't use our sleeping bags anymore." Her mind took off, sorting through the house, looking for items to help. "Good thing it's not earlier. How quickly can disaster crews get there?"

Bjorn looked up from his list. "Radio said the National Guard is on the way, with water purification units, tents, and so on. The Red Cross is coordinating volunteer efforts. Marcia is making phone calls to see where we should go. The telephone tree will reach everyone in the congregation and a plea for help will be on the radio soon." He wrote some more notes. "I'm going with Hansen down to the grocery parking lot to load all their bottled water, then we'll go to Iverson's." He ticked off something on his list.

"Soon as I finish these pies, I'll go get what I can." She turned on the second oven and rolled out the last of the dough. Setting the timer for forty-five minutes after she slid the last pies in the oven, she went down to the basement to retrieve the four sleeping bags. Upstairs, she stripped the linen closet and started filling garbage bags.

She called Leah back. "I'll be ready to leave in fifteen minutes if anyone wants to go along."

"Kirsten and I are both coming. You think we need to take two cars? You could donate many of Dagmar's kitchen things."

"One car should do it. Bring a box of garbage bags. I've about cleaned ours out."

With the pies cooling on the counters, she left the mess in the sink and hustled out to the car. She backed out on the street. "Lord, give us wisdom." That seemed to be her prayer an awful lot lately.

As Keira stopped the car at the curb in front of the Sorenson house, Leah and Kirsten climbed in. "I say strip the beds, everything but the memory quilts Mother finished for family members. We can replace what we need by reunion time," she said. Kirsten was unusually silent. Sullen was the only way to describe the look on her face. Why did she come along if she didn't want to?

"The youth group members are collecting stuffed animals for the little kids," Leah commented.

Sure that Kirsten was the instigator, Keira glanced in the rearview mirror. "What a great idea, Kirsten. I was thinking about baby things too but we don't have anything like that at our house anymore." Kirsten was staring out the window.

"José and Brandon are hoping to go along with the guys to help distribute things. They'll follow behind in another car," Leah said when Kirsten remained mute.

Keira kept her gaze and her mind on the road. The last of the usually pleasant atmosphere they shared had flown out the window with Kirsten's glare.

"So we can fill that trunk too. Maybe...they better take supplies for themselves along. There won't be anything to buy down there."

"That's what José thought too." Leah again, as if she were interpreting for her daughter.

"What a fine young man. This is almost like a pre-missions trip." Was that a snort she heard from the backseat?

A cell rang and Leah answered. "Okay. Make sure you

let Marcia know. She's keeping track of donations and needs. They've already started a fund at the bank for contributions."

"Guess we learned a lot the last time we did this." Keira turned on her blinker at the driveway to the home place.

"Marcus is wishing the truck could be ready to leave tomorrow afternoon, but so many families are involved in graduation."

"Not a good time, but is there ever a good time for disasters to happen?"

"Yeah, something like accidents," Leah answered.

Keira heard a cough from the backseat. She glanced in the mirror to see Kirsten wiping tears away with the tips of her fingers. What was that all about? Had Kirsten and Leah had another fight? They'd gotten along so well through the years that these later months had been a culture shock to all of them. Kids had to exert their independence and all that, but still...rude was rude. And Kirsten had never been rude like this.

Chapter Ten

"Bring the things to the living room and we can pack them there." Keira marshaled her troops. "You two take the linen closet upstairs and I'll start in the bedrooms. Take the mattress pads too. Just drop the things over the banister rather than carrying them down."

"What about Grammy's really old quilts?" Kirsten asked, her first comment for the day.

"That's a good question." Keira looked to Leah. "If they're antiques...?"

"So what would Dagmar rather we do? That people be kept warm or we hoard the antique quilts?"

"Well, if you put it that way...If there is one that you know is special to someone, let's keep that but otherwise we'll send them." She looked to the others for agreement and when they nodded, she did too. "It's a shame we haven't had time to tie off some of those tops she finished. If I'd gotten them to the ladies at church they would have been ready."

"Yeah, well, 'if' is a great word but not much help. Come on, Kirsten." The two headed upstairs while Keira went to her mother's sick room. She stripped the bed and folded the blankets and sheets. Should they send the pillowcases too? Pillows would take up a lot of space. While the truck looked big in the beginning, she remembered how quickly it had filled up the last time it had been used to deliver disaster-relief supplies.

She pulled a plastic storage box from under the bed only to find more old photographs, perhaps the ones she and Leah had been looking for. How had they missed these? Charging out of the bedroom, she hollered up the stairs. "I found them!"

Leah looked over the banister. "Found what? Move back—a load's coming down."

Keira did as she was told as a stack of linens hit the floor in front of her. "Those early pictures. Mother must have been going through them, because they were under her bed."

"Good, we can sort them on Monday."

"I sure won't wait until Monday," Keira muttered, hauling the picture box out to the car and setting it on the backseat so they wouldn't forget it. Returning to the bedroom, she found another stack of quilts on the shelf in the closet. Two of these had names on them. She put the other two in the give-away pile. What about towels and soap? They really needed two trucks. Maybe the church could send another load down later.

By the time the three of them had finished their assigned stations, the pile of donations was huge. As they filled the black garbage bags, they squeezed the air out so as not to take up so much space. Kirsten and Leah each held loaded bags on their laps on the drive back to the church parking lot, where Hansen's truck now waited, ramp in place, and men of all ages were hauling loads up and dodging each other on their way to get more items.

"Bedding," Leah answered when asked what they had.

She looked up into the truck to see cases of bottled water floor to ceiling for about a third of the space. Someone else drove in with a pickup truck filled with more cases of water. "Where do you want the other things we collected?"

"Off to the side for now. They'll go in last." Bjorn had a clipboard with tally marks on it and pencil in hand. "We're expecting another load of water and then we'll start with the softer things. We can really stuff them in odd places."

"I didn't bring the supplies from my house yet. What about yours?" Leah asked.

"Not yet, let's get them now." Keira headed for the car, noticing all the other cars filled with bedding, clothes, and sleeping bags that pulled up and awaited their turn to be unloaded.

When they returned, Keira and Kirsten brought the load so Leah could stay home to work on the dinner.

"So, are you excited for tomorrow?" Keira asked.

"I guess." Kirsten barely nodded.

"You worked hard for this. Is your speech all ready?"

"I wrote it earlier and have it memorized. I could take notes up there but..."

"I am so proud of you." Keira reached over and hugged her niece. But instead of hugging back like usual, Kirsten stiffened before leaning into the hug. "What's the matter, K-girl?" Keira leaned back to see tears swimming in Kirsten's eyes. "Are you all right?"

Kirsten blinked. "Of course. Just tired, I guess."

"Well, we sure will be clapping and cheering for you when you cross that stage."

Kirsten nodded and turned to open the car door. "I'll get the stuff out."

Keira stepped out of the car too, and together they added their new bags to the growing stack. Bjorn waved to catch her attention, so she went over to him. "What's up?"

"We're getting this loaded so quickly we might head south after the ceremonies tomorrow."

"You won't be here for the dinner?"

"Those people need these supplies."

Keira probed her lower lip with her tongue. "I guess. But what about José?"

"He said he was willing. Both he and his friend Brandon. He's driving Betty's SUV, so we can load the back of that too."

"Make sure you take supplies for yourselves; there won't be anything available down there."

"Marcia is setting up contacts with a pastor there. While the roof of their building is severely damaged, it is still standing. He asked us to bring tarps, so someone is rounding those up." He looked around at the busy people in the parking lot. "Sure makes me grateful for what we have here. It could so easily have been us."

Keira nodded, a lump growing in her throat. She'd not really thought about that. "I'll get food packed for four."

"Thank you." He turned as someone called his name and headed toward the truck.

Keira returned to her car to find Kirsten already seated inside. She'd have thought she would have gone to see José and the other kids who were helping to load the truck. Puzzled, Keira slid behind the wheel.

"I just talked to Lindsey. They've gathered four garbage bags of stuffed animals for the kids."

"What a great idea. Bjorn just said they're talking of leaving right after graduation."

"I know."

"And that doesn't bother you? It would me." Did Kirsten and José break up? she wondered. *Something is going on here. But Keira, just keep your nose out of it. She'll tell you when she's ready.* She reiterated her instructions to herself as she drove into the Sorenson drive. "What else needs doing?"

"I'm not sure, but I know Mom has a list a mile long."

"Since the pies are done, I can help."

"Uh, Auntie Keira…"

Keira waited for more, then glanced in the rearview mirror. Kirsten remained in the backseat, tears streaming down her cheeks. "Sweetheart, what is it?" She started to turn around, but Kirsten shook her head.

"No, uh, please." She closed her eyes and sat stiffly, as if dreading something terrible.

What do I do? Keira sent a prayer heavenward. "You want to come up here so we can talk more easily?"

Kirsten shook her head. "No. I don't know. Uh…"

"Okay, would it be easier if I just sit here and stare straight ahead and you can tell me whatever it is that is bothering you?"

A nod. "Yes."

Keira turned to the front and kept her gaze from drifting back to the mirror. "Do you need a tissue?"

"Yes, please."

Keira fished several tissues from the box on the console and handed them back over the seat. While she waited, she pleaded for wisdom and whatever else she might need. What could be bothering her niece like this? They'd had lots of heart-to-heart talks through the years, so how was this different?

"I-I'm pregnant." The words fell like a rock in a well, taking a long time to hit and splash.

Keira pushed out a breath that almost clogged her throat. Not Kirsten. Not their perfect niece. *Oh dear God... Say something.* She heard the inner command but her mouth refused to cooperate. She sucked in another breath and blinked several times, hoping to catch the torrent before it hit. How could this be? The seconds stretched like hours.

"Please don't hate me."

"Hate you? Kirsten, I could never hate you. I love you, no matter what." She wanted to throw open the doors and gather her girl to her heart. Turn back the clock, the day, the weeks, make things all right again. "Listen to me, please. We will do whatever we can to help you and your whole family get through this. Bjorn and I love you like the daughter we've never had." She blew out a cheek-puffing breath and closed her eyes. Pregnant.

"Will you and José be getting married?"

"No. I mean, we planned it for someday but not yet. We just took the pregnancy test the other day. I think we're all in a state of shock."

"You've told your mom and dad?"

"Yes, but I asked Mom to keep it a secret, to let me tell you. I was going to wait until after graduation but..." Kirsten blew her nose again.

Do I tell her that her grandmother went through the same thing? "This is not the end of the world, you know."

"I know, but right now it sure feels like the end of my world."

They sat in silence for a bit.

Finally Keira asked, "How can I help you?"

"I don't know. I don't think anyone can help me right now. I'll get through graduation and try to figure out what happens next, I guess."

"Have you seen a doctor yet?"

"No. Mom asked the same thing. Guess I have a lot of things to do, huh?"

Oh, poor Leah and Marcus. No wonder they'd been acting strangely. "Your brothers?"

"I'll tell them after tomorrow. They couldn't make it for the graduation but they need to know before the reunion. Besides, I can't keep a secret for very long."

"I know the feeling. And while they'll be really upset, they'd be more upset to learn it from someone else."

"Right."

"Can I tell Bjorn?"

"Yes, please."

"Are you sure I can't help you in any way?"

"I think you already did." Kirsten heaved a sigh. "Let's go see how Mom is doing."

Keira waited until Kirsten came around the car and then wrapped her arms around her. "My mother, your grandmother, used to say 'all will be well.' Some days it is hard to believe that, but God can see the whole picture and He has a plan."

"My head knows that but my insides say that He can't clear up this mess. And we brought it on ourselves."

"Good thing He specializes in messes, or we'd all be up to our necks in swamp water most of the time." She locked her arm through Kirsten's. "Get through tomorrow and let's keep talking. And praying."

"Thanks."

The two walked into the house, inhaling the scent of baking turkey as they entered the kitchen.

"Mom?"

"In my lair."

"Can we come in?" Keira knew that Leah had yet to finish the cross-stitch gift for Kirsten.

"Of course."

Kirsten stopped in the kitchen, but Keira headed on back. She stopped in the doorway. Sunlight cast shadows on the hardwood floor, reminding them that spring had come and the outside wanted to come in. "You done?"

Leah nodded. "Thanks for taking her with you. I just finished it. I'll frame it sometime tonight."

"You want me to do that?"

"Would you?" Leah looked up from her recliner with a smile that didn't quite reach her eyes.

"Bag it all up and I'll take it home with me." Keira studied her closer-than-a-sister friend. "What do you need done around here?"

"We need chairs and tables brought from the church. Marcus was going to do that, but now with this truck to fill and send off, he's all tied up. I was going to ask José but..."

"He's over there helping too. Says he and Brandon are going to drive down with Betty's SUV so they have more help and more supplies." Keira crossed to look out the window. "Your yard looks wonderful."

"Thank God for perennials. I haven't had time to plant any annuals yet. Not even the vegetable garden." Leah stretched and blew out a breath. "I have the tablecloths all ironed, I've ordered centerpieces from the floral shop, and the meat will be cooked in another hour or so. I thought to carve it today but I'll do that in the morning. The potato salad is all made and in the garage refrigerator, and you said the pies are all baked. The ice cream is in the freezer, along with the rolls you made last week. Several other people are bringing salads. Can you think of anything else?"

Keira narrowed her eyes, thinking hard. "You're using paper plates, right?"

"Yes, but not plastic forks and such. Marcus hates those things. Besides, I have enough with the good silverware."

"How many are coming?"

"About fifty, and others will drop by."

"Will it ruin the day for Kirsten if José goes with the truck?"

"Nope, it won't." Kirsten, cheese and crackers in hand, wandered into the room. "You want me to call Ansell? We could use him and his truck to get the tables and chairs."

Keira breathed a secret sigh of relief. Thank God the real Kirsten was back.

"That would be perfect." Leah picked up the pad of paper she kept by her side and checked off one more thing. "When?"

"Right now." Kirsten waved her cell. After a quick conversation, she nodded to her mother. "He'll be right over. Bringing his brother too."

"We should wash the windows. I had that on the list."

Keira shook her head. "Blame it on the tornadoes. You should see the pile of stuff over at the church. It'll take some real packing skill to get it all in." She paused. "I didn't see Marcus there. Is he feeling better?"

Leah nodded. "He's been on the phone all morning. It looks like two other churches in the area are doing the same thing as we are. So more trucks will roll. You know, I've been thinking—"

"Uh-oh."

"I keep thinking about that empty truck coming back here and the empty house out there. What if the men brought back one of the families that needs housing for a few weeks. You know, until the cleanup down there is finished or they could find another place to stay."

"To stay at the home place?" Keira's voice rose on the last word.

"Yes. Some people have lost everything. Houses, cars, businesses. I had nightmares about that happening here in our town. Laid to waste."

"Well . . . I don't know. Having strangers stay at Mother's place. I haven't even sorted all her things."

"Keira, what's going on? You're usually one of the first people to pitch in during a disaster."

"Have you mentioned this to Marcus?"

"Not yet. I thought I should ask you first."

Keira shook her head. "Let me think about it." But everything within her was screaming no. She gritted her teeth. What kind of a Christian was she, turning down a way to help in a disaster? She shook her head again. "Guess we won't need the place until near the end of June. Let me think on it. I don't need to make a decision right this minute, do I?"

"Of course not. It was just an idea." But Leah gave her a questioning look before continuing. "I know you're think-ing about the reunion. Maybe this would be a good reason to cancel, like we talked about that time."

Keira shrugged, her eyebrows arching. Then shook her head. "Maybe this is even a better reason to have it. Keep our family close-knit in case some freaky act of nature tries to rip us apart." Even if it would be so much easier on them to cancel, considering all the secrets they were keeping.

A pickup truck pulled up in front of the house, and Kirsten dashed out to climb in. When the back tires squealed as it took off, Leah shook her head. "Will they never learn?"

"Nope, kids have been doing that since they started driving cars. It's a guy thing."

Leah heaved herself out of the chair. "Come taste the potato salad. Tell me if it needs something else, maybe more salt." She led the way to the kitchen. "Get this crisis over with and we can go back to the other—" Leah cut herself off, turning to straighten a dish towel that didn't need it.

Keira cocked her head. "Leah, Kirsten told me she is pregnant."

Leah sagged against the counter. "Oh, thank God. Keeping secrets is killing me. This one was the worst of all."

"She said she wanted to tell me herself." Keira reached to hug Leah. "We'll get through this too."

"At the moment I'm not sure how, but I am hanging onto trust by my shredding fingernails. Now I can at least talk with you about it. Such a relief. You've always been my sounding board."

"That goes for both of us. I hate to tell Marcus even more so now. Two whammies like this with his family."

"I know, but I think he's going to be upset that we didn't tell him right away."

"I'll tell him so you don't have to. Leaves you off the hook." She hoped so, anyway. What burdens they've all been bearing, but Kirsten's was the heaviest.

Leah sniffed and stepped back. "We better get on with the stuff here. Every time I think I have things under control, something else rears an ugly head."

Keira tasted the potato salad and added more salt and celery seeds. "Good thing you got the chips early. They say the grocery store is out of most party things now."

At least the preparations for the party and the relief truck were distracting them from both Kirsten's pregnancy and her "unknown father" situation. Still, she hoped that the copy of her birth certificate arrived soon. "How about I take the frame and things home now before Kirsten comes back? Then I'll come back and set the tables."

Leah nodded and left to get the cross-stitch.

Keira carried the potato salad back out to the refrigerator in the garage. *Lord, please make this graduation go smoothly and help me find the information. I really need your help. I need to know who my biological father is. After all, it can't hurt my parents any longer. Just me—and Marcus.* She heaved a sigh. It wouldn't hurt anyone else in the family, would it?

Chapter Eleven

$\mathscr{P}$lease, José. I need some time, without you calling me."

"But you haven't called me and we need to talk."

"No, we don't. Not right now." Kirsten glanced at the clock beside her bed. "Look, I'm sorry. I'm really tired and everything can wait until after graduation."

"Your dad didn't even say hi."

"Don't feel bad, he's not said anything to me either. They got all tied up in helping the tornado victims. Anyway, what do you think? That he's happy about this mess we're in?"

José's tone stiffened. "I'll see you at the gymnasium then?"

"I guess. They've moved the ceremony inside?"

"That's what I heard. Rain predicted."

The silence stretched. Kirsten couldn't think of anything she wanted to say to him. Strange, they used to talk for hours. "Night." She clicked off and flopped back on her bed. Patches jumped up immediately and padded to her side, her purr already in full force. Kirsten gathered the cat to her and stared up at the ceiling. She should run through her speech one more time but the effort was too great. Lindsey had said she'd call later, but all Kirsten wanted to do was crawl under the covers. She got into her pj's, stared at her cell phone, and then turned it off. Once she was in bed, Patches curled up beside her, purring enough to shake the bed. With the light off, her mind switched back to her own crisis, but she was too tired to even think on that.

There was no sense in trying to style her hair the next morning. The mortarboard would smash it flat.

"You about ready?" Leah paused at the doorway. "You look lovely."

"Thanks."

"I'll carry your robe so it doesn't get wrinkled."

Kirsten turned, trying to see the dress from the back in the full-length mirror. All these months she'd been dreaming about this day, her open door to freedom, done with high school and on to her real life. And now—now she had no idea what was going to happen next. *Just get through today.*

"Is Dad coming?"

"Of course. Why do you ask?"

"Well, I thought maybe he's so angry he wouldn't even come."

Leah crossed the room and stood in front of her daughter. "It's, well…he just…I know things will work out, but this time 'I'm sorry' just can't repair the damage. We all need time to talk, to think, to pray, so let's just get through today and go on."

"I'm glad José is going with the truck."

"Okay."

"I don't want to fight with him and if he's here, I know a fight will start. Is his grandmother still coming to the party?"

"I hope so. I've not talked with her." Leah glanced at her watch. "We need to leave. We'll let you off under the portico at the gym and go park the car."

Kirsten glanced around her room. "Do I have everything?"

"Notes for your speech? Honor cords."

"I didn't make any notes for the speech, just the presentation. I'll be fine. I do have the list of teachers." She picked up her purse, checked to make sure a brush and lipstick were in it, and took in a deep breath. "And the honor cords are on the hanger under the robe."

Only the beat of the windshield wipers broke the silence in the car on the way to the high school. Marcus stopped at the entrance to the gymnasium and turned toward his daughter. "We'll be praying for your speech to go well."

"Th-thanks, Dad." Her eyes filled with tears as she climbed out of the backseat and took the hanger from her mother, who kissed her cheek.

"Once you start to talk, the butterflies will melt away."

Kirsten nodded.

"Hey, Kirsten, we're waiting for you," Lindsey called from the open door.

"I'm not late."

"Nope."

Kirsten waved once more to her parents and strode to the doorway. If only she could run and hide.

"We're all in the theater. They're still checking the microphones and things in the auditorium. Outside on the field would have been so much nicer." Lindsey flipped her cinnamon hair over her shoulder and lowered her voice. "Did you know José is going south with the truck? He and Brandon?"

"I know." Kirsten focused on her midsection, where

butterflies were doing cartwheels and flutter races. Not telling Lindsey what was happening was really hard. "And it's okay."

Lindsey gave her a funny look but dropped the subject as they joined a group of girls. The guys were gathered on the other side of the room, listening to Coach Latimar give them a pep talk. His wife, Mrs. Latimar, was in charge of the girls.

"Hi, Kirsten. You all ready?"

Besides her salutatorian speech, Kirsten would be presenting the senior gift to the school. The class had chosen to plant a line of flowering cherry trees along the north edge of the parking lot with dedication plaques honoring their teachers. She glanced over to see José looking at her. She forced herself to smile at him and was reminded again how handsome he was when he smiled back.

Her heart did the funny little jig it always did when she saw him. The guys were all wearing white shirts and dark pants, no jeans allowed.

When Coach Latimar gave the order for everyone to suit up, the graduates put their robes on and helped each other with the mortarboards—tassels on the right side now, to be moved to the left when they had their diplomas and walked off the stage. "Someone help Carl over there. We don't want him falling on his crutches. Glad you could make it, son." The rest of the class applauded and someone whistled. While the other two were still in the hospital, Carl was stumping his way with his class, a slightly dazed look on his face but he was there.

Kirsten hung her honor cords around her neck and made sure she had her notes for the presentation tucked in the wristband of her watch. The girls' purses would be left in the locked room. Sure seemed strange not to have her own locker anymore. When the order to line up came, they fell into place alphabetically just like they had practiced, with Mrs. Latimar checking them off down the line.

"Where's Sammy?" she asked his walking partner.

"Don't know. I haven't seen him."

Mrs. Latimar drew her finger down the list and read Sammy's phone number to her husband, who had pulled his cell phone out of his pocket. They could hear it ringing just as Sammy charged into the room, his robe billowing around his tall, skinny body. He skidded into place.

"Sorry, I'm late."

"Well you made it, Samuel Stenerson. I swear you'll be late for your own wedding." Mrs. Latimar grinned at him.

"Naw, for his funeral," one of the boys quipped.

The teachers moved back to the end of the line and when they had checked everyone, they walked up to the front. "Now remember, 'Pomp and Circumstance' is a march, so keep the cadence. Makes it easier for your partner, you know," Coach Latimar reminded them.

Kirsten could hear the school band playing and when the music changed, the Latimars opened the double doors and the class marched in. They filed into the rows and took their assigned seats in the order they were to receive their diplomas. The ceremony began with the Reverend Marcus Sorenson offering the invocation.

"Did you know he was going to do that?" Lindsey whispered.

Kirsten shook her head. They all bowed their heads and silence crept over the crowd.

"Lord God, creator of us all, ruler of the universe, look upon these, your children, with favor as they enter the next phase of their lives. Give them wisdom and guide them along your paths that they may bring glory to your holy name. Teach them and help them to know for absolutely sure how much you love them. Thank you for the privilege of knowing them and watching them grow up. In the name of your precious son, Jesus, we pray." He raised his head and looked down at them. Kirsten noticed his eyes never met hers. "I want you to know how proud I am of each of you." He raised his gaze to the rest of the gathering. "And to all of the families gathered here, well done."

Applause broke out as he turned and walked off the raised stage.

Kirsten blinked and sniffed. Her father always had just the right words to say, except to her since she made her announcement. However, knowing her father, he had most likely cleared his prayer with the school board first. Munsford School District had borne the brunt of complaints regarding religious material before and most likely would again. So far, they stood their ground.

"You have the best dad around," Lindsey whispered.

"Thanks."

When it came time to present the class gift to the school, Kirsten walked to the microphone. "As president of the senior class, it is my privilege to honor the entire Munsford High School faculty with a planting of trees. You have enriched our knowledge and challenged our lives in ways unimaginable." She read all their names from the list, grateful she'd not forgotten any. "Thank you." When she took her seat again, Lindsey congratulated her.

"You looked so calm and at ease up there. I'd be shaking so hard I'd drop the mic."

"You can't see inside me."

After the scholarships were read and presented, the principal called Kirsten's name and read off her list of accomplishments as she walked up the steps again, making sure to not trip on her robe. That had been one of her worries. She raised the mic and looked out across the sea of people, including way up into the upper-tier seats. The only time she'd seen the building this full was when the Harlem Globetrotters had come to town and played against the faculty.

She pushed out a breath, and though her lips wavered a bit, she smiled. "Families, friends, and fellow classmates. Most of us have been together for twelve years, thirteen if you include kindergarten. We've laughed and teased and struggled and cried, but we've all stood together. And now we are finished with this part of our life and ready for the next. We've been dreaming about what we want to do, be it go on to college, go to vocational school, or join the workforce. Some of us are going into the military. Dreams are so important to what we will accomplish in our lives. Think of all the times a teacher said to you, 'Stop daydreaming and get your work done.'" Snickers sprinkled the group before her. "But daydreaming is important, especially when it is a rehearsal for the things we are doing. Choosing to see yourself accomplishing your dream will train your mind and body for the skills needed for life. Coaches teach athletes to do this all the time. Olympic athletes know well the value of practicing their skill in their minds. If it works for them, why not for the rest of us?" She paused and looked over the group, keeping her gaze away from José. She knew if she looked at him she would cry and that would not happen this afternoon. The two of them had rehearsed together and made sure their speeches complemented each other.

She also made sure she didn't look at her family, all lined up in the fourth row.

"I want to share something Mr. Whitaker taught us in the ninth grade." She smiled at the man, who looked surprised. "He taught us to write our goals down and to read them often; daily is the best. I started doing that then and I kept on through my years here. Having straight A's was one of my goals. I got one B, so even though I missed my goal, I never gave up. Being senior class president was another one of my written goals. So you see, it does work. Mr. Whitaker, thank you for teaching me this skill. Thank you, everyone, for all our years together." She stepped back and turned to leave, the applause rolling over her.

Thank you, God, that that is over with. I didn't cry or tear up. Another goal met.

José stepped aside for her to come down the three steps.

"You were wonderful," he said with a smile.

"Thanks." Back in her row, she sank down in her chair, sure that her knees wouldn't hold her any longer. The kids around her gave her high-fives and thumbs-up signs, nodding and whispering their approval.

Lindsey grabbed her hand. "I'm so proud of you I could scream."

"Not now, please."

"You are something else."

Kirsten turned her attention to José, stepping up to the microphone after he was introduced as valedictorian.

"Thank you, Mr. Turnkey and all of you gathered here."

Kirsten couldn't look at him because she knew she would cry. As he continued to talk about setting goals and making them happen, she studied her cuticles, her manicure, anything but looking up at him. She figured he was not looking at her for the same reason. When he said, "Thank you," she looked up and nodded. His smile widened and he received the same response from the class as she had.

When the superintendent and the principal moved the table with the stacks of diplomas to the front of the stage, the first row of students stood and filed toward the steps to the side of the stage.

When the superintendent called her name, she walked across the stage, shook Mr. Turnkey's hand, took her diploma with the other, and paused for the photographer before flipping her tassel to the other side. She smiled and hugged the faux-leather diploma to her. She was now on to the next part of her life. Whatever that would be.

When the principal said they were dismissed and the band broke into a jazzy tune, the graduates threw their mortarboards up in the air and cheered. The level of noise rose as everyone talked and laughed. José made his way through all the well-wishers until he stood beside her. They hugged without a word, but looking at him, she knew he was as close to tears as she was.

She swallowed. "You did great."

"So did you. I was so proud of you I wanted to stand on my chair and applaud."

"I'm glad you didn't." An almost smile touched the corners of her mouth. "We did it."

"We did. We will."

Kirsten clamped her teeth. *Don't say any more.* Order or plea, she turned into her aunt's arms.

"You were magnificent," Keira said, hugging her niece. "I knew you were a good speaker but that was wonderful. You and José stole the show." She gave José a hug too. "See you out at the house."

"Thanks." *I'm just glad it's over.*

After all the pictures were taken, the senior class returned to the theater to leave their robes with Mrs. Latimar, who was folding them to pack in the boxes to return to the rental store.

"Thank you, Kirsten. You gave a wonderful presentation."

"Thanks to you and all your coaching." Kirsten had been on the debate team all through high school with Mrs. Latimar as the debate coach and drama teacher.

"I'm looking forward to seeing where you go with your life. With your talent and will to work, you'll be able to accomplish anything you set out to do."

Kirsten blinked and rolled her lips together. If she only knew. But she would know, the whole world would know. Maybe there was only one way out.

"I'll take you home," José said as he handed in his robe.

Fighting tears, Kirsten turned away. "Okay."

"See you in a while," Lindsey said. "Mom wants some pictures at home and then we'll be over."

The Sorensons had invited the families of Kirsten's closest friends for the buffet and then planned on an open house later in the afternoon. Now if only she and José could get there without getting into an argument. The only way to do that would be to declare the topic of the pregnancy off limits. No discussion. Nothing. Tightening up her resolve, she picked up her purse and in a flurry of hugs and promises to see them later, headed out the door with José. Once in the car she collapsed against the back of the seat. If only she could just go home, crawl into bed, and pretend the world did not exist.

"You were so beautiful up there." José turned to smile at her as he put the key in the ignition.

Kirsten sucked in a deep breath. She had to carry on, that's all there was to it. If she'd ever ordered herself to do something, now was the time. First: breathe. Second: put a smile on your face even if it feels like a mask. Third: you will be polite no matter what—and to everyone, including José. "Thank you. You couldn't tell the butterflies were about to carry me off?"

"Nope, not at all."

She turned to catch him watching her. *Think, say something. Come on, brain.* "Is your grandmother coming to the party?"

"Yes, she's riding over there with the Morgans." He pulled into the line of slow-moving cars as they took turns stopping at the stop sign. "You know we have to talk."

"Yes, but not today. Today is for celebrating our graduation." She knew she sounded formal, not like herself, but who was she now anyway? What would become of all her dreams? Their dreams?

Chapter Twelve

Leah walked through the house, making sure all was ready. The decorations looked lovely, the food smelled delicious, and the buffet table was ready for them to put out the food. She and Marcus had left the gymnasium as soon as they properly could, and he was splitting another bag of ice between the coolers, which were filled with soft drinks. The coffee was perking in the tall coffeemakers that she'd borrowed from the church.

Kirsten had been magnificent. She wished she could have seen her daughter's face when her father gave the invocation. His prayer was perfect too. The whole ceremony had gone so well, no shenanigans like there had been in years past. She heard someone at the back door.

Keira called, "Where do you want these pies?"

"I have a dessert table set up in here so we can set them out." Leah went to help, as both Bjorn and Keira carried in flat boxes filled with pies. "They look beautiful."

Keira set her box down. "Everything does. You've done yourself proud, my friend."

"With a little help from my friends."

"So is the truck all packed?" Marcus asked as he entered the room.

"Yes, and Betty's SUV is too. I told the others to be there at three. Debated whether to wait until morning to leave, but since we can trade off the driving, we should be good."

"I printed out directions for you, down I-35, right through Kansas City. Pastor John is so grateful for every little thing anyone can do."

"In all the turmoil I forgot to mention an idea I had." Leah paused for their attention. "You are coming back empty and we have an empty house that could be a haven for a family. Keira and I talked about it, but the graduation preparations took precedence. You think that could be a possibility?"

"So are you saying we should bring back refugees?" Marcus stared from his wife to his sister.

"Leah, I didn't agree. I said let's think about it. This isn't fair." Keira stammered in her shock.

"Well, we could at least put out the offer," Leah answered.

The two men exchanged looks and then stared at their wives. Marcus shrugged and nodded at the same time. "I'll ask John and make the offer. That way our congregation could help them get back on their feet. When they go home, we could send furniture and housewares with them."

"Wait a minute. I'm being railroaded here. We need to talk this over more."

The front doorbell chimed and Marcus headed for the door to invite their guests in.

Leah gave an apologetic shrug. "Sorry, I didn't realize it bothered you that much. Sure, we'll talk later. We don't have to make a decision today, but I think Mother would be happy someone might be using her house and if it's someone in trouble, so much the better." She started to pat Keira's arm but Keira stepped back, her frown still firmly in place. By the glare in her eyes, Leah realized she'd made a bigger mistake than she thought. Why would this bother Keira so much? She was usually the first one to offer assistance of any kind. "Keira, I really am sorry."

Keira nodded but her jaw stayed firm.

"Besides, we'd have to find bedding and get it all ready." Leah shook her head. "You're right, there is no time to do that now." She stepped forward again. "Keira, I'm sorry."

"Yeah, well, greet your company. We'll talk later."

Leah turned to answer a question and the party swung into high gear.

Someone else took over answering the door as groups of guests congregated in each room. Some of the women gravitated to the kitchen, asking if there was anything they could do. So Leah put them to work setting the food on the buffet table.

She turned to see Betty Flores, José's grandmother, smiling at her. With her dark hair shot with silver and her snapping brown eyes, she radiated warmth. "Oh, Betty, I'm so glad you're here." The two hugged, stepped back, and then gave another hug for good measure.

"We'll make it through this, dear one, never fear," Betty whispered.

Leah nodded, afraid to say anything that might trigger the tears. She'd awakened during the night from a dream where she was lost and crying, only to find that her cheeks and pillow were wet. "José did a wonderful job with his speech."

"They both did. I was so proud of them." Betty's eyes glittered with unshed tears. "What can I do to help?"

Leah motioned to the chattering and busy group. They arranged the food on the table and made room for more salads as they arrived.

When Kirsten and José came in, all those gathered made sure they greeted them with compliments flowing freely. Lindsey and some of the other teenagers arrived, and Marcus repeated over and over where the soft drinks were, motioned to the coffeepot, and invited people to help themselves to the beverage of their choice.

A basket on a card table filled with cards and gifts was watched over carefully by two little boys who kept asking who the presents were for and when would they open them. Leah smiled at their mother, who was trying to explain that this wasn't a birthday party so the gifts would be opened later.

"After the cake?" the older one asked.

"We're having pie for dessert," Leah said.

"Pie?" The two little guys stared at each other and at her. "But you can't put candles in pies."

"Come on, you two." Their mother steered them away. "Let's go wash your hands."

"Can we eat right away so those driving the truck can leave?" Kirsten asked, refusing to meet José's eyes.

"Of course. Go find your father so he can say grace."

Marcus clapped for attention. "Let's have grace and then please come and help yourselves." He waited for some semblance of silence. "Heavenly Father, thank you for this celebration day, for bringing our young people through school and opening doors ahead for them. Thank you for the banquet so lovingly prepared and Lord God, protect our truck and those who will take the supplies south. Show us how we can best serve. In Jesus' name we pray." Everyone joined him with the amen.

"José, Brandon, Bjorn, you all go to the head of the line."

When everyone was served and had found a place to sit, Leah moved from group to group, making sure they all had what they needed, visiting and catching up on the news. Kirsten and José did the same, thanking people for coming. José answered questions about the coming trip, and when someone asked about the missions trip in June, he stopped to chat about that.

Leah watched as Kirsten moved on without him. The missions trip. That had gone completely out of her mind. Surely Kirsten would have to back out. Or did she? Kirsten might be showing a little by then, but barely. The danger would be from the food and water.

"What's up?" Keira stopped beside her.

"Just thinking of the changes that will be coming." At least Keira was speaking to her, that was something to be grateful for.

"You always say live in the moment, not the future."

"Easy to say and sometimes hard to do."

"That's for sure."

"Three kids in college, which could break the bank for sure." Leah turned when someone called her name. "Yes."

"Where is your mop?"

Leah headed for the laundry room and the mop while Keira went for the paper towels. They had set up a children's table in the kitchen with the tile floor. The mother of the two little boys was comforting her son, whose lip stuck out far enough for a bird to perch on it.

"Hey, it's no big deal. We'll get you some more." Keira got the ice cubes and Leah wielded the mop. "See, all gone."

"You two weren't roughhousing, were you?" their mother asked, but both boys shook their heads.

"Cake now?"

"Why yes." Leah patted his shoulder. "Someone brought a cake after all. They must have been thinking of you."

"With candles?"

"Honey, if you want a candle, you most certainly can have a candle."

Keira went into the pantry and brought a package of birthday candles back. "I'll take care of this."

"Make the pieces small, please?" the mother pleaded, beginning to look somewhat frazzled.

"I will." Keira returned with three plates so the little girl could join in the fun. She stuck a candle in each, and Leah lit them and stepped back.

"Now when I count three, you blow them out."

"Going to sing happy birthday?"

The women looked at each other, rolling their eyes and trying to keep from laughing.

"Okay." Leah dragged the word out. "But instead we will sing 'happy grad day.' Just one moment." She went to the kitchen doorway and waved her hand. "José and Kirsten, come here quickly." As soon as the two came into the room, Leah started. "Happy grad day to you." The others joined in and the song swelled.

The three little ones blew hard. One had to blow again, but the candles went out and the kiddies had their cake. The rest of them laughed and applauded.

Bjorn turned to José. "We better get going. Say your good-byes."

José spoke to his grandmother, said a general good-bye and thanks for coming, and returned to the kitchen. He hugged his grandmother and whispered something to Kirsten, who nodded.

"You have everything?" Keira asked her husband.

"I'm sure. You packed enough food for days."

"I know, but there won't be supplies when you get closer." She hugged him. "Call me."

Leah hugged him too and the two women followed the travelers to the back door.

"We'll be praying for you," Marcus said.

Kirsten walked as far as the gate, hugged José and her uncle, and watched them head for the car up the block. When she returned to the porch, Leah put an arm about her waist and they watched as the three men got in the car and drove off to where the truck was parked.

"I think Marcus wants to go too," Keira said as she turned back to the open door.

"I know he does, but he didn't have time to get a guest preacher in. Probably better if he keeps doing the organizational work. I think he must have a raw spot on his ear from being on the phone so much."

By the time the guests had left, some of the women had cleaned up the kitchen and all the food was put away. A pie had only one piece eaten, so Leah looked from Betty to Keira. "I say we brew tea or coffee and have this ourselves." She raised her voice. "Kirsten, we're having pie and if you and your dad want to join us, there's plenty."

"Okay," she answered from the living room.

"I thought maybe you could open your gifts too."

Keira's mouth dropped open. "I have to run home and get her present. I forgot it."

"No problem. We'll get things set up." She grinned at Betty as Keira beat it out the door. "Coffee or tea?"

"Tea sounds nice. Should I start putting the pie on plates?"

"Fine. And you know I have vanilla ice cream in the freezer."

"Apple pie à la mode." Betty heaved a sigh. "I've not had that for ages." She took plates out of the cupboard and set them on the counter. "How are things going here?"

"I take it you are referring to the bomb dropped on us the other night?" Leah filled the teakettle and set it on the burner.

"Yes."

"We decided to not bring it up until after today. Marcus is still in a state of shock, and I'm not much farther beyond that. I just can't seem to get my mind around all the ramifications, but I didn't want to ruin today. Those two are under plenty of pressure already."

Leah could hear Kirsten coming so she shook her head. "Let's set this up on the dining room table. Enjoy the flowers some more."

"Mom, maybe we should wait with opening presents until José comes back."

"If you like."

"Well, we already sang happy grad day. Those two little boys were so funny. Wish Curt and Gwen could have been here."

"It would have been nice. But hopefully everyone will get home for the reunion. Finals will be over and school will be

out by then." She poured the boiling water into the teapot
and set a cozy over it before carrying it into the dining room.

"Dad coming?"

"He said he had to finish a conversation first."

Keira came through the back door carrying a beautifully
wrapped, flat package. "Here you go, K-girl." She set it in
front of Kirsten.

"But I thought we were waiting for José."

"You can open this one." Leah dug the scoop into the ice
cream and plopped it on a piece of pie. "Here, Betty, this
one is for you. You want more?"

"Goodness no, this is wonderful."

When they were all served, Marcus wandered into the
room, still looking at his notes. "Ice cream for me too." So
Leah dished out the last and took the ice cream back to the
freezer. She poured the tea into china cups with saucers
and passed them on around.

"Thank you, Lord, for getting us through this day."

Betty said amen and they dug into the dessert.

"Aunt Keira, you make the best apple pie anywhere.
Thank you for doing this for me."

"You are welcome. I was going to make a chocolate
cream pie too, but we gathered up the supplies for the truck
instead." She glanced at her watch. "They must be south of
Savage by now."

"They are and all is well." Marcus wiped his mouth with
a napkin. "Keira, I second what Kirsten said. Your pies are
every bit as good as Mother's, and that is the highest com-
pliment I can give."

"She taught me how. Hear anything regarding using our
house?"

Leah looked at her, questions all over her face. "But I thought..."

"I know I got angry and said no, but the more I thought about it, the more sensible I figured it was." She turned to her brother. "So?"

"Not yet, but John said surely they would have takers. He'll get back to us. That really was a good idea."

"Thanks to your wife." Keira turned to Betty. "We offered to have them bring a family, or people anyway, back with the truck and they can use Mother's house as long as they need to."

Betty nodded with a big smile. "What a marvelous idea. As soon as we know about them, we can start gathering clothes and groceries. If there are children they could finish school here too, if need be."

"We'll have a lot to do getting it ready."

"Maybe I and some of the others can help with that."

Kirsten touched the gift paper. "I can open this one then, even if I choose to wait with the others?" She looked to Keira.

"It's from your mom and dad. I just did the wrapping."

Kirsten slit the taped places with a fingernail and eased back the paper. "Oh, how beautiful." She looked up at her mother. "How did you manage this?"

"It wasn't easy. Keira had to take it home to frame it because I finished the last stitch yesterday afternoon."

"Pansies. I love pansies." She turned the picture so the others could see. She leaned over and hugged her mother. "Thank you."

Kirsten glanced at her father as he quietly scraped the last bite of pie from his plate.

"It's from both your father and me," Leah said. "Though he never was much for needlework, he cheered me on."

"Thank you, Dad. And I—you always help grow the pansies."

He nodded, his mouth full of pie.

They did a review of the day until Betty said she needed to be getting home to feed her dog. She rose and carried her plate into the kitchen. "Thank you for a lovely afternoon. Let me know what you hear from the travelers and I'll do the same." She kissed Kirsten on the cheek and exchanged hugs with the others. Leah walked her out to the car.

"Driving José's car, eh?"

"Yes, since he has mine. You should have seen how tightly they had it packed. We'll talk soon and you know I'm always here if you need me."

"I know." Leah crossed her arms across her chest. "Turned brisk again, but at least the rain let up for the afternoon." *I'm such a coward.* She waved Betty on her way and turned back to the house. *But no discussions tonight, Lord, please. We are all too tired.* She found Keira in the kitchen loading the dishwasher. "You didn't need to do that."

"I know."

"Where are the others?"

"Kirsten went up to her room after thanking me again and I'm assuming Marcus is in his study. You need anything more?"

"Nope. Not that I can think of. Thanks." She glanced at the clock. "I think I'm going up to bed to read for a while. You want me to walk you home first?"

"No, I got over being afraid of the dark a long time ago. Besides, I left the lights on inside the house." Keira hugged her. "I'm sorry I reacted like that earlier. Just caught me by surprise and all I could think was, 'How will I find any more information then?'"

"We'll rip that house apart in the next couple of days. The odds are slim anyone would come on such short notice anyway." Leah paused. "You know I am going to have to tell Marcus; I can't stand keeping secrets like this."

"I was going to tell him but then I kept thinking about everything else he's already dealing with. I hate to dump another shock on him, and it's been a secret for such a long time already..."

"Still, the sooner the better, for all concerned."

"All right. Tomorrow."

"Good."

"Get some rest, you look done in."

Ah, my dear, if you only knew. Maybe tonight she'd be able to get some real rest without all the nightmares and tears.

Chapter Thirteen

When she got home Keira sat down at the computer. Good a time as any to do a more thorough search of old records, especially wedding licenses. What she really needed to do was go out to the home place and get up in the attic. That reminded her of the plastic box of old photos she found the other day. She shut down the computer and went searching for the storage container Bjorn had brought into the house.

Whatever was it doing in his office, the last place she would have thought to look? She hauled it into the family room and set it on the ottoman near her chair. With a craft table set up to sort pictures, she opened the lid. Many of the pictures she remembered from the times she and her mother looked for something special. But now she put those aside, keeping out ones she thought Leah might want, and dug through the rest. This had to be taken from several boxes, so her mother must have been through them shortly before she died.

She looked at every picture and paper in the box but found nothing about a man in St. Cloud. Her birth certificate confirmed she was born there. When had her parents moved away from there? Marcus was born in Munsford, so it was sometime between their births. Strange that there were no pictures of a different town, only of Munsford. She stared at the sorted piles. There had to be another box.

Unless her mother had destroyed them.

The thought knocked Keira back in her chair. She stared, unseeing, at the stacks of photos. Blinking, she rubbed her eyes. One a.m. It had been a long day. She left the mess the way it was and, turning out the lights, made her way upstairs. At times like this she wished she had a dog. Interesting how big the house seemed when she was the only one in it, especially at night.

Think like Mother. She must have gone through the pictures right before she died or they would still be in the other boxes. Surely if there had been other photos or papers she would not have destroyed them. So there had to be more. Keira undressed, thinking on the day.

And what about bringing a family in to live at the home place for a time? Sure, she had finally agreed because it sounded like a helpful and giving idea, but what if they had small children who might break things in the house? Perhaps they should put the precious things in one room and lock the door, like people did when they rented their houses out as vacation rentals. Maybe she should drive into St. Cloud to buy enough sheets and blankets for all the beds.

The best thing to do was put the treasures in her mother's sewing room and put a lock on that door. Leah should have talked the idea over more with her before blurting it out to the rest of them. That thought made her feel grumpy all over again. The home place needed to be used, yes, but there should be some guidelines. Talk about torn. She heaved a sigh. As usual there were no easy answers, but the people in Kansas had lost everything. Back and forth.

Make up your mind, woman. All right. We open the house to strangers and take what precautions we can. That decided, she crawled into bed and took out her devotional book. She read the page for the day and looked up the Bible verses. Since one of the verses referred to the lilies of the field, her mind jumped to the bag of lily bulbs she'd ordered from the seed catalog. Surely it was time to put them in the ground. "Sorry, Father, my mind is like a frog tonight. Thank you for the beauty of lilies and the reminder to not worry." *I haven't heard from Bjorn.* She picked up the phone and dialed his cell, but it went directly to voice mail.

He was most likely out of reception range. She left a message for him to call in the morning because she was going to sleep now. "Lord God, protect them, please. Put angels around that truck and car and make a way for them, like you said." The song "God Can Make a Way" floated through her mind. She clicked out the light and snuggled down under the sheet and comforter. Had she turned down the thermostat? Or had she even turned it on yesterday morning? *I am not getting up to check on it. One night won't overload the heating bill.*

But while she could identify every sound, she still managed to be awake far too long. A branch scraping on the side of the house. Creaking like tired joints as the house settled for the night. The humming of the refrigerator. More tree scrapes, the wind must have picked up. Her mind went gallivanting off, trying to figure out where the travelers were. Had they stopped for a break? Were they switching drivers so no one got too tired? Would the person not driving be able to sleep?

How were her sons? Neither Eric nor Paul had called lately. But then they had texted, most recently to apologize for not being able to attend Kirsten's graduation. She should be grateful that she had heard from them and for the fact that they would be able to attend the reunion. She smacked her pillow into better shape, flipped over, and tried to take deep breaths and relax again. She should be grateful for a lot of things.

Grateful yes, but what about that man? Who was the man who fathered her? And, like Bjorn kept asking her, why did it bother her so much that she was not a Sorenson by blood? She pounded the pillow again, as if pounding a pillow might release some of her feelings and frustrations. Feelings of what? The oh so simple but oh so big question drifted into her mind again. *Who am I?* And the second, *Why didn't my mother tell me years ago? Why did she live a lie?* Bjorn said the lie was not her own, but her mother's. But why was there a lie at all? *Please, Lord God, I need some answers here.* A verse from the Old Testament came to her mind. "I have called you by name." *But what name? Who am I?*

If Bjorn were here he'd heave a sigh and ask her what was wrong. But then he didn't think this new facet of her life was really that important. If only she could agree with him, then this wouldn't be eating at her. *Lord, I wish he were here.*

The slowest five minutes of her life had passed when she looked at the clock again. Throwing back the covers after the third episode of five minutes, she stuffed her arms in her robe sleeves and made her way back downstairs. The pictures kept calling her name. She sat down in her chair and pulled the craft table closer to her lap.

She turned to the stack of the oldest pictures and started to sort again. Perhaps she had missed something. Halfway through the stack she found a strange photo stuck to the back of another. Someone had cut off part of the picture.

She studied the image of her mother, then moved it closer under the lamp on the end table. Her mother and another couple on her left, the women, or rather girls, were the two in the middle. The photo wasn't ripped but someone was definitely carefully cut out. She dug the magnifying glass out of the drawer. Sure enough, that was a man's hand resting on her mother's left shoulder. She turned the picture over and searched for a date. This had to be one of the earliest pictures. Where was it taken? Why had the man been cut out? Was this a clue? Was that her biological father's hand on Dagmar's shoulder?

Keira carefully inserted the picture in an envelope and, flipping all the other pictures over, searched for any other clues. Nothing.

At three a.m. she tucked the picture into the table drawer with the magnifying glass and set the table of photos off to the side so she could get up. One clue.

Back upstairs, she crawled into bed and yawned enough to spring her jaw. After snuggling down, the sense of being alone took her breath away. Her hand found Bjorn's pillow and his empty side of the bed. *Bring them home safe, oh Lord. And please help me go to sleep.*

The phone woke her and a glance at the clock made her clear her throat so she wouldn't sound like she just woke up. "Hello."

"We made it and all is well." Bjorn paused. "Are you all right?"

"Of course, I just haven't talked much yet. You found the church and everything?"

"Yes, but I can't begin to describe the devastation. It looks like a bomb went off."

Keira shuddered. "Worse than what we saw on the news?"

"Yes, it's a cumulative effect. We're waiting for Pastor John to get here to show us where to unload the supplies. I'm thinking we should send a construction crew down as soon as they can get building supplies in."

Keira couldn't help but smile, she was so proud of her husband. "You have enough to eat?"

"More than enough. Don't worry about us, okay?"

"Trying not to."

"Here he comes. He's riding a bike. I wonder if his car was too damaged to drive. Bye."

Keira hit the off button. So many more things she wanted to ask him but that would wait. She dialed her brother's cell. "Good morning. Bjorn just called."

"Good, he just called me too."

"He said Pastor John was riding his bike to meet them. Did he ever mention that his car was too damaged to drive?"

"No, he never said a thing about it."

Keira kept from yawning, but barely. "Bjorn said we should send a construction crew down there. Maybe they could work on the church."

"I'm sure that man of yours will come back with plenty of good ideas for ways we can help. Did you sleep all right in that big house all by yourself?"

"Once I got to sleep. Sure made me aware how much I depend on him. Since he doesn't travel so much anymore, I've gotten spoiled."

"I hear you. I need to head over to the church. See you in a while."

"Right." Keira hung up. *I forgot it's Sunday.* She flew down the stairs to start the coffee and then back up them to get ready. *Thank you, Lord, for the phone call or who knows when I would have woken up.*

Sitting by herself in church made her aware again how much she and Bjorn did together. If this was a taste of widowhood, she wanted none of it. Marcus thanked the congregation for the swift reply to their call for bedding and supplies for the folks in Missouri. "They made it there safely and in good time, thanks for your prayers too. Bjorn mentioned that we should send a construction crew down there, so please be thinking about that." He looked around at the people gathered. "I have to tell you how proud I am to serve a congregation that responds so quickly and with such generosity when we hear of a need. Please continue to pray that God will show us what needs to be done and how best to do it."

After the service, Leah invited her over for dinner. "There's plenty of food left."

"Not surprising, since you always plan enough to feed a swarm of locusts." In Leah's book, running out of food at any event was close kin to disaster. "Thanks. Shame there's no pie left. I have some other dessert in the freezer; do you want me to bring it?"

"Sure, we all need more sugar. Why don't you bring over that box of pictures? Among the three of us, perhaps we can identify a few more people. I thought I'd work on the memory book this afternoon."

The urge to tell her about the cut-out part of the picture was tempting, but there was no time now. "I have something to show you when we get home."

"What?"

"I found it about two thirty, as in a.m."

"Keira, that's not fair."

"I know, so let's hurry."

Keira dropped her car off at home, grabbed the picture to put in her purse, and then bagged up the others she knew Leah would want. But before leaving, she pulled out the envelope and studied the picture again. *"Curiouser and curiouser."* The quote from *Alice in Wonderland* floated through her mind. This was becoming a mystery for sure.

She walked on over to the Sorensons'. "By the way, where is Kirsten?" Keira asked when she greeted Leah in the kitchen.

"Sleeping. She said she didn't sleep well last night and did we mind if she missed church." Leah planted her hands on her hips. "Okay, what gives?"

Keira took the envelope out of her purse and handed it to her. "I sure understand the not-sleeping-well thing. Last night I was wishing we had a dog again." She watched Leah's face for a response. The space between her eyebrows furrowed. "Is this what I think it is?"

"Found it stuck to the back of another picture. Someone was cut out. Look at that curvy line. And see a man's hand on Mother's shoulder? I even got out the magnifier to look better. Definitely a man. But who is the other couple? I don't remember seeing any other pictures of them."

"There might be more in those I have. We'll look after dinner."

After they ate, Marcus excused himself to work in his study. When they were done cleaning the kitchen, the two women headed for Leah's lair to go through the photos Keira had brought over.

"I was looking through them last night and pulled out

some I thought you'd like to use." Keira handed over the plastic bag of photos.

"This must be Dagmar's confirmation picture," Leah said, handing back a gray cardboard piece to Keira. She folded back the top and stared at the picture of three girls in white dresses and four boys in shirts and ties. One of the boys wore a vest. The Lutheran pastor, in his robes, stood behind them.

"Shame that these were all hidden away. Think I'll frame some of them and put them up on the staircase wall."

The doorbell rang and Leah showed two men from the congregation into the study.

When they heard Kirsten in the kitchen, Keira glanced at the clock. Had her niece really been asleep this long? "Is she all right, pregnancy notwithstanding?"

"Of course. She's catching up from all the nights of studying and getting ready for graduation. She really didn't get much sleep."

"Sounds familiar. I still think there must be more boxes in the attic."

"You want to go out there and look? We could go now."

Before Keira could answer her cell phone rang. She checked the incoming number before answering. "Hey, Bjorn."

"Everything's all unloaded, thanks to these two strong young backs we have along. John invited us to stay for supper, but I think we'll head on back. We might find a motel in Kansas City if we get too tired. Once we're out of the tornado zone, we'll stop to eat for sure."

"Well, be careful. I'm at Leah's so I'll pass the news on."

"Thanks. You might call Betty too. José's cell phone is on the fritz."

"I will. Love you. Bye."

She relayed the message to Leah. "Should I go tell Marcus?"

"Yes, that's what the men are talking about in there."

Keira did as she said, and then stopped in the kitchen. "Kirsten, Bjorn passed on a message from José. His cell phone isn't working. They're heading back."

Kirsten turned from fixing a sandwich. "Thanks."

"So how does it feel to be a high school graduate?"

"Tired, good. Never dreamed I'd sleep most of the day away."

"Your mom and I are going out to the home place. You want to come?"

"No thanks. You two have fun."

The home place looked the same as the other day. The grass was going to need mowing again soon. "I was thinking maybe we should plant a garden in case someone needs to live here. They might enjoy that."

"I need to get mine planted first. One of the jobs for this week." Leah opened the door and entered. The unlived-in smell was back. "Where would I find cinnamon sticks?"

"Whatever for?"

"To simmer on the stove and drive out that musty smell."

"Good idea." Keira went to the pantry and returned with a pint jar that held cinnamon sticks. "Mother always kept them to make fruit soup. After a year, should we toss most of the spices?"

"Nah, lots of mine are older than that." Leah filled a small kettle with water, added two cinnamon sticks, and set it on a burner. "They tell Realtors now to bake bread or chocolate chip cookies when they're showing a house. Makes people feel at home."

"That reminds me, I think I'll bake bread tomorrow." Keira headed for the stairway. "Might as well get on with it, monsters or no." She called from about halfway up the stairs. "Bring a stool, will you please?"

Leah answered from the kitchen. "Coming right up."

They set the step stool under the handle for the recessed stairs. Leah looked from the stool to the ring used to lower the staircase. "They didn't figure on the high ceilings. I know I can't reach it. Can you?"

Keira stepped on the first step. "Let me brace on your shoulder."

"This doesn't look like a good idea."

"We're here now." She stepped up to the next step. "Have I ever mentioned how I hate ladders?"

"Once or twice."

Hand on Leah's shoulder, Keira stepped on the top step with one foot and then slowly brought the other one to join it. Still slightly crouched, she stared at the ring. "You think there might be a taller stool out in the barn or garage? I can't reach this even if I stand on my tiptoes."

"And you can't do that. Get down and we'll go look."

Keira climbed down as gingerly as she climbed up. "How come I never minded climbing trees but ladders really get me?"

"I hope that's a rhetorical question." Leah folded the stool back up. "We could just wait for one of the guys."

"How did Dad expect Mom to open that?"

"He probably figured he'd be the one doing it."

They found a six-step ladder out in the garage and together hauled it into the house and up the stairs.

"I'll go up this time. This one should be tall enough."

"If you say so. There just better be more boxes up there after all this work."

"Is there a light up there?"

Together they set up the ladder. "I don't know. I don't do attics."

"Not even when you were a kid?"

"Nope. Attics are notoriously dark places. Every book I ever read that mentioned attics, something bad happened there. I always told the boys that I never went in attics because there were monsters there."

"And you are how old now?"

"I'll get a flashlight." She went back downstairs, dug the flashlight out of the drawer, checked to see if it still worked, and then, realizing she'd dawdled as long as possible, went back up the stairs to find no Leah. "Leah? Where'd you go?"

"To the bathroom. No monster came and grabbed me." Leah climbed the ladder and pulled on the ring. When nothing happened, she pulled again, harder. They heard creaking and groaning as the end of the trap door started to come down.

"Hear the creepy music?"

"Keira, you keep this up and you'll have me scared. We have to move the ladder."

"Which means you have to come down."

"And what if it goes back up?"

"Let's just move the ladder and see."

"I'm warning you." Leah came down the ladder and sure enough, the thing started to close.

"I'm not one to say I told you so, but..."

"Okay, plan B. I'll get something out of the sewing room to tie through that ring and then when you come down, you can hang on to that."

"This all started out so simple."

Keira located a piece of cording and handed it to her friend. "Here you go."

"It'll probably come down so fast it'll crack me on the head."

"Oh, that's a great picture. Don't be so negative."

Leah followed plan B and soon the ladder, with cable hand rails, lowered to the floor.

"Fancy that."

"I'll let you go first, since I climbed the higher ladder."

Keira made a face. "I don't think so. See, I told you, it's dark up there."

"Give me the flashlight. And it had better work."

"I tested it." Keira followed Leah up the stairs, hanging on to the cable on both sides. Open stairs like this were nearly as bad as ladders.

Leah stood on the top step so she could see as she shined the flashlight around. "There's all kinds of stuff up here. A big trunk, boxes, a chair, even a bed." She climbed the rest of the way up and stepped into the attic. "This is a treasure store."

"I'm coming." Keira climbed slowly but made it into the attic without mishap. "Where did all this come from?"

"Just accumulated over the years, I'm sure. Shame we don't have two flashlights." She shone the beam up, looking for electric lights. A single bulb hung above them. "It has a push-in switch."

Keira reached up and, lo and behold, they had light. Not a lot and there were still a plethora of shadows but at least they could see ahead of them. "Look, there's a crib. I think all of us had our turn in it. If the family that stays here has a baby, we're all set." They opened the trunk to find old clothes and some small boxes. One contained a music box. No pictures, so they shut the trunk and continued past an oak chair with a broken leg, a side table, a chest of empty drawers, and boxes of jars, baby clothes, letters.

"This one I'll take home with me." Keira quickly closed the cardboard lid on the box of letters and carried it over to the stairs before dusting off her hands. They should have worn jeans and work shirts.

"Why did she keep this junk?" Leah wondered while digging into another box.

"Who knows? She must have planned a use for it."

Under two other boxes, the women found and opened a third. "Bingo." Leah peeled back the newspaper that covered the top. "Pictures, letters, all manner of things."

"Great. We don't have time right now, so let's take them home to look through."

"Good idea. The light is pretty poor up here." She set that carton to the side and opened the next. More of the same. "Remember when you said Dagmar probably had every card any of us gave her? Well, looks like you were right."

"How could I spend all my years in this house and never know about these things?"

"Because you don't do attics and there wasn't an easy way to get up here." Leah stood and swung the light around the room. "I think we've found everything on this side. Let's put these boxes by the opening and search the other side."

"You know, if someone installed dormers, this space is plenty big enough to finish. Put a real stairway up to it and I can see having a sewing or craft room up here. If someone wanted to get really fancy, they could even put in a bathroom."

Leah flashed the light on the ribs of the roof. "Insulation and wall board. I wonder if they ever thought about that?"

Keira sneezed. "This dust is getting to me. Let's take our loot and leave. Now that we know how, we can come back later."

"We need to tell the kids about this; there might be some things they would like to keep."

"That cinnamon sure smells good," Keira said when they finally had all the cartons moved downstairs and the pull-down ladder sent back up to fit snugly in the ceiling. She glanced at her watch. "Five o'clock. Time flies when you're having fun. I could do with a cup of tea and some lemon bars, how about you?"

Back at her house, with the tea made and the boxes dusted and opened, they sat at the table to decide how to do this.

Leah's cell rang. "Where are you?" Marcus's voice could be heard across the table.

"At Keira's having a cup of tea. I'll be home in a little bit."

"No rush, but there was no note or anything."

"Kirsten knew where we were going."

"Well, she's up in her room and I didn't want to disturb her."

"We found treasures up in the attic at the home place. You're welcome to join us."

"There goes the phone again. See you when you get here."

"Did he sound a mite belligerent at first?" Keira asked, arching an eyebrow. She knew how impatient her brother could be and how he'd worked to curb that tendency for years. She studied her friend. "Is something wrong with Marcus? He wasn't quite himself at church today either."

"What with Kirsten and this emergency, he has a lot on his mind." She paused. "But you know, I cannot keep this secret from him much longer. He is going to be livid when he finds out that he wasn't told right away. You said you would tell him today."

"When have I had a chance?"

Leah gave her one of those looks.

Keira heaved a sigh. "This is for his own good. I hate to destroy his reverence for his mother."

"I think he needs to be the one to make that choice." Leah picked up the cut-out picture and stared at it again. "This has to be him. Why else would he be cut out?"

"She was playing paper dolls?" Keira rolled her eyes. "I know, flippant never helps but I keep thinking of him as *That Man*. I want to know who he is. I have to learn as much as I can."

"I understand that, I guess, but it can't be at Marcus's expense." Leah shrugged. "Let's at least start. We can each take a box." She opened the flaps on the one nearest her. Cards, all sorts of greeting cards. She dug down a ways. "This will take time. What about yours?"

"Packets, bigger envelopes of..." She opened one and found old receipts, papers. She checked the dates. "Back in the forties and fifties. Some earlier, I think." She set the envelope back in the box. "Who knows what we'll find here." *Please, Lord, let there be some clues for me. What if That Man is still alive?*

Chapter Fourteen

What am I going to do?

Kirsten stared at the sampler she'd hung on the wall last night. Pansies, like the ones in the quilt covering her. Like the ones she'd helped her grandmother plant out at the home place. Kirsten had managed not to think about her situation—at least as well as she could—putting it off until after graduation. She wished she could keep putting it off. She wished someone could just tell her what she should do. What would Grandma say to do? She had never said much regarding the abortion issue. For several years the entire family was involved in fighting legislation to legalize abortion. Her father preached against it, they all marched against it, sent out letters. She heaved a sigh.

And here she was in that same predicament they had fought against. Like Tandy, who'd had an abortion, said, over and done with and her life could go on. It sounded so easy.

Unless you believed that was really a baby inside you. She laid a hand on her abdomen. Believing there was really a new life growing inside of her was so difficult. But she hardly thought of anything else. She should never have told her parents. Then if she'd had the abortion, they would never have known, and it would have saved them a lot of heartache. They would have thought she had the flu or something. But the Bible said God knew, He watched over His children even in the mother's womb.

Thou shall not kill.

But scraping a few cells out, that's all it was. Just a mass of cells so far. She'd read that more than once, and that was what Tandy said. Just cells. You wouldn't even be able to see them, really.

But God already had a name for this child. *So why did you let me get pregnant? You could have stopped it.* Right. Like it was God's fault she and José got carried away. For two people who were so smart, how could they be so stupid as to think it wouldn't happen to them? So stupid, so very stupid. She mopped tears that burst forth like they'd been dammed up. She'd awakened crying during the night too. One time. Other girls slept around and they didn't get pregnant. Because most of them were on the pill.

She'd been proud that she wasn't on the pill. Pride, another one of those downfall things. "Pride goes before a fall." Well, they had fallen all right. Big time with forever consequences.

We broke our vow. I broke my vow. A vow of chastity, that I would remain a virgin until my wedding night. She blew her nose, the pile of tissues on the floor growing. She should have moved her wastebasket closer.

She scrubbed at the tears that were leaking into her ears, one hand stroking Patches. Finally she reached over and picked up her goals notebook, with the pen in the binding. Scooting up against the pillows at the headboard, she sniffed and blew again. Flipping to the last used page, she posted the date. Goal one: get as much information as possible. So under that she wrote, "go to the pregnancy counseling center." She wanted to talk to someone who wasn't her family, someone who didn't get hurt from what she asked or said. She deserved any hurt she received.

What about José? That was another question deviling her. As the father, shouldn't he be included in the—in the process?

The men and the truck might be home already. But if they were, he would have called.

Her mind spiraled backward again. He didn't get it when she asked him not to call. She didn't get it either but that's the way she felt. She'd asked herself if she was blaming him, and yes, she was, but not any more than she was blaming herself. Life would be so much easier if she could blame someone else.

At least she'd had Saturday and Sunday without a mention from anyone. Except the monster inside screaming at her that her life was ruined. Back to her goal book. Goal two: make a decision. One decision she'd already made. She was not telling José what she planned to do today. Not José or anyone else.

"Well, Patches, I need to get up." She threw back the covers and headed for the bathroom.

Sometime later, walking into the kitchen, she found her mother with her head in the refrigerator. "Morning."

"I know there was a jar of relish in here and now I can't find it." Leah stepped back and closed the door. "You ready for some breakfast?"

Kirsten nodded. "Where's Dad?" Monday was usually his day off, but she didn't want to talk to him right now anyway.

"There's a group meeting at the church regarding the relief efforts our church can do. They're talking about sending a construction crew down there to help out." She turned the heat on under the teakettle. "There's coffee but it's a couple hours old. I can make new. Oh, but the caffeine isn't good for..."

"Tea sounds better anyway. I'll just make some toast."

While her mother was making breakfast, Kirsten sat down at the table. Step one. "May I use your car today?"

"Sure." Leah set the plates in front of them both.

"Thanks. Do you need anything from the store?"

"I'll make a list." When the teakettle screamed, she poured the boiling water into two mugs and set them on the table, shoving the basket of tea bags over.

Kirsten bowed her head. To her regular grace, she added, *Please help me, Lord. Amen.* She broke off a piece of her toast. "Lindsey said that she might be getting a summer job in Mayfield at the nursery." Anything to keep this sounding as normal as possible. Especially since all she wanted to do was throw herself in her mother's arms and scream and cry and do whatever it took to get the demon off her shoulders.

"Good for her. Is she planning on college in the fall?"

"Community college, probably. She's hoping to go to State, but she still has no idea what she wants to do yet." Kirsten stirred her tea and removed the tea bag.

"What is José planning?"

"Well, after the missions trip, he'll be lifeguarding at the pool again. They gave him a break." Kirsten stared at her mother. "Do you think I can still go on the missions trip?"

Leah kept silent for a long minute before looking up. "I don't know, Kirsten. I think we should talk to the doctor

about that. There are a lot of parasites in the food and water
down there. Have you scheduled an appointment with Dr.
Youngstrom?"

"Not yet. Pretty soon everyone is going to know."
Kirsten pushed her plate away. "Thanks for the breakfast.
I'll brush my teeth and then I'm ready to leave, if that's
okay." She clamped her teeth hard, turning away before the
tears could explode.

"I'll get the list made."

Maybe an abortion would be the best route, Kirsten
thought as she stood in the bathroom. *Kirsten Marie Sorenson, how can you even think such a thing?*

Back downstairs, Kirsten kissed her mother's cheek and
picked up the list. "How about Rocky Road?"

"If you like. We have some vanilla left." Ice cream was a
favorite evening snack for the whole family. In the summer
they made their own with an electric motor–driven freezer
out on the back porch. They used to have a crank one but
when the boys moved out, Dad found the electric one at a
rummage sale.

"I'm going to plant the garden today and could sure use
some help."

"I'll hurry." Once in the car, Kirsten entered the address
in the GPS and headed east. Following the female voice's
instructions, she parked in the parking lot of the Pregnancy
Counseling Center and took in a few deep breaths, hoping
that courage would come with them. Thankful there were
no other cars in the lot, she hurried inside and up to the
reception window.

"I'd like to see a counselor, please," she told the woman
after the greetings.

"Well, you came to the right place. If you would fill this out, I'll go see who is available."

Kirsten took the clipboard and sat down. Did she really want to give them all this information? She printed her name, address, and phone number and read on through the remainder of the questions. Some she didn't know the answers to, some she didn't want to answer. She took the clipboard back to the window. "Do I have to fill this all out?"

"No, not right now. They'll be calling for you any minute."

Kirsten picked up a magazine, without even looking at the cover. Her shaking hand made the pages rattle. *I don't belong here. This can't be happening to me.*

"Kirsten?"

"Yes." She stood and tried to smile but her mouth didn't work right. She followed the woman to the door she indicated.

"Your counselor today is Mrs. Nimitz. She'll be right with you."

At least it wasn't an examining room but an office. Kirsten took one of the chairs beside the desk and glanced around the room. Scenic pictures on the walls, a half-filled bookshelf with a carved wooden dolphin leaping from the water on one shelf, pictures of a family on another.

"Hello, Kirsten. I'm Sharon Nimitz." The woman held out her hand, so Kirsten shook it. "You mind if I sit right here?"

A shrug was all she managed. At least Mrs. Nimitz wasn't wearing scrubs or a lab coat. Instead she wore Dockers, a crewneck cotton sweater, and a smile that set Kirsten more at ease. After all, she was only here for information.

"I see you didn't fill in all the blanks. Do you mind if I ask you a few more questions?"

"No."

"How old are you, Kirsten? That is the way to pronounce your name, right?"

"Yes, and I will be eighteen this month, the thirty-first."

"And I take it you are sexually active?"

"Well...yes, but only once."

"Yes, in this instance. You think you are pregnant?"

"I did the test three times, they all said I am."

"How long since your period?"

"Well, I...I mean we..." Kirsten swallowed hard to clear her throat. "I had a hard time figuring it out. I've not been regular, you see."

"You're an athlete?"

Kirsten nodded. "This happens a lot, I mean irregular periods. And besides, maybe stress and I—um—was bulimic for a while." She blew out a breath. How to keep going. "So I think two but possibly three."

"I see. So you don't keep a record?"

"Not usually. I didn't have any reason to keep a record before—before this."

"And do your parents know?"

"I told them after I took the test."

"Do they know you are here?"

Kirsten shook her head. "I came for some information."

"You'll be a senior next year?"

"No, I graduated two days ago."

"Good for you. What are your plans?"

"I'm planning college and pre-med."

"Having a baby could really make that difficult, couldn't it?"

Kirsten nodded. Her foot twitched like it was just itching to leave the room.

"You understand that what you are carrying right now is not a baby—yet."

"Then what is it?"

"It's a cluster of nonviable cells. You've had a sex education class, right? So you understand the sperm and the egg."

"Yes. But I want to know what happens here."

"The nonviable cell mass is removed and you go on about your life. You might have some mild cramping afterward but no worse than menstrual cramps. We could take care of this tomorrow. If you choose to carry the fetus to term, you will have to choose whether to raise the child yourself or give it up for adoption."

"If I choose to—to, uh, do my parents have to sign for this?"

"You do not have to tell your parents, or anyone else, for that matter. Not if you wait until you are eighteen." Sharon leaned forward.

"And if I can't do this?"

"Then come December, you will have a baby. By then, as I said, you will need to decide whether to keep it or put it up for adoption."

"A girl at school said she had an abortion. It was no big deal."

"We make things as easy as possible for you. Shall I set up an appointment for an examination?"

"Well, I think I'm going to have to think about this. I..." Kirsten swallowed, trying to ease the dryness in her throat. It felt like someone had turned up the heater. Or set one right in front of her. She stood and headed for the door, sure that if she didn't get outside, she would most likely vomit. In the parking lot she sucked in air as if she'd been under-water. *We make things easy for you.* She could still hear the woman speaking, a gentle voice that stayed in her mind.

Kirsten got back in the car and stared at the sign on the door. Pregnancy Counseling Center. Was that just another name for an abortion center? She should have asked more questions about the other options. Her head fell forward, too heavy to be held up. This sounded so easy. No more worries, no more fear, no angry parents. Who would know? She didn't need to tell anyone. Girls lost babies all the time, didn't they? How would she get here? Would Lindsey bring her? That meant she'd have to tell her. Could Lindsey keep a secret? Not usually. How many times had Lindsey said, "Now, I'm not supposed to tell anyone, but…" José? No, he would never agree. Even if she could go through with it in spite of that, she could hardly ask him to be part of it. There was no way to do this alone, someone would have to know.

I know, Father, you are watching over me. I've believed that all my life. But is there some way I can hide this, even from you? She started the car and drove back to the main road. She parked in the lot at the grocery store on her way home, picked up the things on her mother's list, and turned into the Lotta Burgers for a cold drink to stop the urge to cough. Or was it gag? After a couple of long sips, she put the car in gear and drove home to sit in the car in the driveway.

If my brothers knew I was contemplating an abortion, they would kill me. But won't it be just as bad if they knew I got pregnant? If I went back to the clinic, they'd never need to know. It would be like it never happened. She stared at the trellis where the wisteria was spreading tendrils and green leaves on its dead-looking branches. *But I'd know.* If she told her mother where she had been, what would she say? If her announced pregnancy affected her father so badly, what would this do? *But I am not them and they are not me. I don't want to give up my life to have this baby.*

Chapter Fifteen

Marcus, we really need to talk."

"I know, but we have another meeting tonight and before then, I need to talk to John. He said he found a family willing to come up here, but they weren't ready when our truck left. They will send them on a truck from one of the other churches."

Leah watched her husband shuffling papers on his home desk. Was he throwing himself into the relief work so he didn't have to think about or act on things at home? This wasn't like him, but then he'd never faced such a situation before. "Supper is nearly ready."

"Good."

But she could tell his mind was off, running in ten or more different directions. Returning to the kitchen, she turned the burner down on the potatoes and checked the pork chops. She stretched her back, with her fists in the middle at the waist, rubbing the sore places out. The early days of gardening did that. Good thing she'd had Kirsten helping her; it went so much faster. She'd gotten the peas in earlier in the year like she planned, and now they needed stringing. The bush pea pods were already branching out. The thought of fresh peas made her mouth water.

At least she could now talk this problem with Kirsten over with Keira, especially since her other sounding board was keeping as busy as possible and to himself. The only bad thing about planting a garden was all the thinking time available. What would they do? What was Kirsten thinking? How much easier life would be if she didn't have the beliefs she did. Well, that was a stupid thought, life without God would be intolerable.

But sometimes…an abortion would be the quick solution. *Don't even go there*, she ordered her mind. How strange, her dream of being a grandmother was not coming about the way she had thought. She wanted to be overjoyed at expecting their first grandchild. Instead she was allowing horrible thoughts to stay in her head and she knew better. *Lord, I need your wisdom so desperately, and right now I feel like you've turned your back. I know in my head that you promised to always, always be with me, but what do I do?* She could feel a wail wanting to erupt. She forced herself to concentrate on fixing their supper. Anything to shut off the voices arguing in her head.

José had called while Kirsten was out on her errands and said his phone was fixed so she could call him at any time. While she'd passed the message on, she'd not heard them talking. She turned the pork chops to low and set the bowl of applesauce out on the table. Maybe she should have invited him over for supper, but that might have really set off the fireworks here.

"Supper's ready." She called up the stairs and again at the office door. No answer from either of them. She could hear Marcus on the phone, so she stuck her head in the door and waved to get his attention. "How long?"

He flashed five fingers.

She climbed the stairs to check on Kirsten and found her sound asleep with Patches keeping vigilance. After draining the potatoes, she turned the burner to the lowest, same for the pork chops; the corn in the microwave would reheat just fine.

She dialed Keira on her cell phone as she headed for her chair. "Hi, you got a minute? What all did Bjorn have to say about the trip?"

"He was tired, so he took a nap. Said it seemed like the trip back took forever. They stopped to sleep in Kansas City and then came on home. He said it looks like a war zone down there."

"Is he coming to the meeting?"

"I guess so. He said they're talking about taking another truckload down. The Red Cross is in place now so there are cots for people to sleep in but they have to go to the next town over to find buildings intact. School buses are hauling people around."

Leah heard Marcus moving around. "I need to go get supper on the table. Talk later."

After grace, Marcus ate quickly without volunteering anything.

The questions Leah asked received one-word replies. Yes, no, and a shrug. On one hand she understood his pre-occupation, but on the other . . . She cut her pork chop with unnecessary force.

Marcus wiped his mouth with his napkin and rose. "I might be late."

"You're welcome."

But if he heard her, he gave no sign and, grabbing his jacket off the row of pegs by the door, left.

Leah dished up some more applesauce and finished her

supper. This wasn't the first meal she'd eaten alone and it most likely wouldn't be her last. Maybe this crisis right now was a really good thing for him. Gave him time to step back from their family situation and gain some perspective. And maybe not. She fixed a plate for Kirsten, covered it with plastic wrap, and put it along with the leftovers in the refrigerator. Fixing a pot of tea, she took that into her room and, settling in her chair, picked up the stitchery she'd been working on. With oldies but goodies on the stereo she located her place on the pattern and counted the number of stitches of the medium tan on her needle. She knew she should be working on the pictures but tonight she couldn't force herself to do that. At least cross-stitching was mindless.

All the things that she and Marcus should be discussing came tromping into her head. What if Kirsten kept the baby? What would that mean to the two of them? Did God want them to rear the child? Give Kirsten a chance at the life she dreamed of? School without mother responsibilities? Med school, if that is what she continued to want? *But I'm too old to be a mother again. I thought we were done with that. Grandparenting sounds great, but raising another child? Please, we were looking forward to an empty nest. It's not fair.* She caught herself, not fair is right but whoever said life was fair—one of her trademark comments when one of her kids had wailed that. And what did Marcus think of all this? After all, he still had not talked with his daughter, let alone discussed having a baby in the house full time. True, Leah loved babies, loved little kids and big kids, but they'd already done all that. Visions of ball teams and Scouts—either Brownies or Cub Scouts—Sunday school and fevers in the night. Teething and teaching a two-year-old to share.

"I don't want to do all that again. I want to cheer my children on while they do the parenting!" She stabbed her needle into the fabric. "Ouch!" She stuck her finger into her mouth. Even rounded needles could puncture when used with enough force.

Sometime later, Kirsten stood in the doorway, yawning widely. "I missed supper."

"I called but when I checked on you, you were out and Patches warned me off. I fixed you a plate."

"I'll bring it in here, okay?"

"Okay." When her daughter was seated, Leah poured herself some tea and laid her stitching in her lap. Closing her eyes, she let her mind wander with the soaring trumpet.

"I'll call to schedule a doctor's appointment."

"Good. Do you want me to go along or not?"

"I don't know. Mom, Dad still isn't talking to me, other than in the car before graduation."

"He's not really talking to me either. Perhaps an oversight. He's totally involved in the relief effort, coordinating with other churches in our area. This will let up soon."

"I sure hope you're right. I can't stand this silent treatment. Yell at me, scream, whatever, but..." She leaned over, twitched a tissue out of the box, and blew her nose. After a deep breath in and out, she sniffed and continued. "I start work in Uncle Bjorn's office tomorrow. Only two days a week. Wish I could find something else too."

"Have you thought about posting a house-sitting and/or pet-sitting business? Or yard work?"

"No, but those are good ideas. Where?"

"Oh, at the senior center, the grocery store, wherever you see bulletin boards. Tell as many people as you can that you are looking for work. Babysitting doesn't pay enough to help you out, but that might be better than nothing."

"All things I could plan around working for Uncle Bjorn."

"Right." *Dear daughter, how far ahead are you thinking? Just this summer.*

Kirsten set her plate on the floor. "Life isn't very fair, is it?"

"No, God never promised fair. He promised to stay with us no matter what we have to go through." *Here I am telling her what I most need to hear. Thank you, Lord, for the reminder.*

"He could have prevented the pregnancy." Kirsten huddled back in the chair, as if needing the comfort of the wings around her.

"So could you have. Our actions always have consequences, good or bad."

Kirsten made a face. "Don't I know it. I'd give anything if I could live that night over again and come straight home after. We had such a nice dinner, celebrating José's awards." Her voice took on a wistful tone, like a little girl lost.

"There are a lot of things we wish like that. Staying away from the edge of a cliff is the best way to keep from falling over." Leah stitched in the silence. She looked up when she heard a sniff.

"Mom, what am I going to do?" Kirsten's voice was soggy with tears.

"There are no easy answers, that's for sure." Leah prayed again as she followed her thinking. Wisdom, compassion, love, she needed them all. "On one hand you give the baby up for adoption. Yes, you've spent nine months of your life but you saved a life." How could this be her, sounding so clinical as if this were any baby, not her first grandchild.

"But is that the best for the baby?"

"Only God knows the future for sure, not me. But with life, there is hope. Always there is hope."

"Right."

But the look Leah caught screamed hopeless.

Kirsten studied her cuticles for a short eternity before continuing. "If I do decide to give the baby up, how can I get José to agree?"

"Two questions with hard answers." The silence was broken by sniffs from both chairs. "He called, you know."

"I know. I just don't want to talk to him right now." She rushed into the next sentence. "Is the fetus really just a bunch of cells right now? A nonviable bunch of cells?"

Wisdom! Wisdom! "Well, that's what the books say and it's true it cannot live on its own, out of the womb. But God knows each baby and gives it a soul, and a name, right from the beginning." *Take it easy*, Leah ordered herself. *Act as if this were not your daughter talking but someone else's.*

"How can we know that for absolutely sure? I read all the stuff we worked with. I've seen the pictures and the videos. But how do we know that for sure?" She reached for a tissue. "It would be over and I wouldn't have to—to be afraid and have Dad hating me." The last words came out in a rush.

"He doesn't hate you. He doesn't like what you did, but he doesn't hate you." *Please, Lord, pour out the wisdom here.*

"But I don't want to be pregnant!" The cry turned into a wail. "I want to be me and have fun this summer with my friends and go on the missions trip and—and I hate this." Kirsten flung herself out of the chair and staggered up the stairs.

"So do I. So do I. I never thought to be in this kind of a

mess either." Tipping her head against the chair cushion, Leah ached for her daughter. "Lord, I hate this too and I'm sure you're not real happy with it either. Please help us. If she decides to go with the abortion, we have no legal way to stop her. She doesn't even have to tell us. Thank you that she is talking with me. How I wish I could take the burden."

A baby. This time next year they would have a grand-child. But not if she put the baby up for adoption. God, what was right? What was best?

She heard Marcus drive into the garage and open the back door. He let Patches out, telling her to hurry up and get her business done. In a bit he opened the door again. The normal sounds of any of hundreds of evenings in their house. Only it wasn't a normal evening.

Marcus came into her room and sank into the other wingback chair that Kirsten had vacated only a few minutes before. He saw the plate on the floor and picked it up, shaking his head.

"How did it go?"

"Well. The committee is pretty much taking over the project. Bjorn will be in contact with John so I can step back. That's as it should be." He tipped his head from side to side.

"Headache?"

"A bit. Just tension, I think. A good night's sleep would help."

"I can sure relate to that." She watched her husband, seeing the deeper lines in his face, the sadness in his eyes. Was the congregation seeing how he looked and wonder-ing if something was wrong? Or was she the only one who could see it?

"I thought you were working tonight."

"Tomorrow night and Thursday. Marcus, we have to talk."

"I know, but I am not thinking clearly—too tired."

"Kirsten is convinced you hate her." There, she'd said the words, painful to be sure.

"Oh, for crying out loud. I don't hate her." He frowned and tipped his head against the cushions. "But every time I look at her, I want to scream. José too. I get so deep-down angry."

"I see." But she didn't, not really. Disappointed, heartbroken, sad, but for her the anger had dissipated. These two young people and that baby they shared were all that mattered now. Children, that's what they really were, caught in an adult situation they were not prepared for.

"You've got to talk with her."

"I know." He kept his eyes closed. "All these years, since she was little, all she's talked about is being a doctor, making people better. Remember when she'd bandage up all her dolls and the dog? This missions trip—she plans to help in the clinic like she did before." He shook his head slowly from side to side. "There's no way she can do that if she has a baby to care for, provide for." He opened his eyes and stared at his wife. "What are we going to do? I thought of us raising the baby and my whole mind and body went into revolt. We raised our children, there are things we want to do now." His groan came from the depths of his being. "God help me, I've even thought about abortion."

"So have I and so has she. The easy way out for now but with a lifetime of repercussions. Remember all the work we

did against abortion? We were so sure of ourselves, so com-
mitted, so pious."

"You surely aren't thinking of suggesting to her that she
go through with such a thing?"

"All I'm telling you is that the thought has crossed my
mind. You need to understand that this is her decision,
according to law now."

"No one need ever know."

The weariness in his voice and face tore at her heart.
She'd never seen him like this, not even after his mother
died.

"That's what they tout. But you know it will get out
somehow. And even if it doesn't...we'll know."

"I keep ordering Satan to take his lies and stories elsewhere and leave my family alone but..." Leah's head shook
of its own accord.

"He comes roaring back—I know well. What if we
encouraged her? Then we are accomplices." He stared at
the ceiling as if hoping to find answers there. "I want this
all over with as badly as anyone. Have you thought about
what the elders will say when they learn of this? I can be let
go because I can't control my own family; so according to
scripture, I am no longer fit to lead the church. This congregation, my church."

Chapter Sixteen

"Aren't you getting a bit carried away with all this?" Bjorn asked at the breakfast table in the morning. "What time did you come to bed last night? It was past midnight when I left you still sorting through those boxes."

Keira turned from the griddle where she was turning french toast; sausages were already draining, waiting for the plates. "Bjorn, I have to know."

"But what if you never find out anything more?"

"Then that is as it is. But I have to give it my best shot." She set the plates on the table and brought the coffeepot over to refill Bjorn's cup and her own.

"What difference is it going to make?" He spread butter on the hot slices and poured on the warmed syrup. "In the long run, you know?"

She sat down and stared at him. He still didn't get it, this need within her to know, to find out all that she could. "I don't know, but it is necessary. For me, it is."

"I mean, think on it. How has finding that birth certificate changed one thing about your life today?"

"Other than eating up hours on research?" She knew she sounded sarcastic but at the moment she didn't much care. How could he not understand how important this was to her?

"Come on, Keira. Think it through. You're getting carried away with this search."

"And what's so bad with carried away? I'm not hurting anyone or costing us any money. Why can't you encourage me rather than attack me?"

He shoved his chair back. "Oh for Pete's sake. Try to have a reasonable discussion and you get all emotional about it. I'll see you at the office." The last line he threw over his shoulder as he left the room.

"Maybe not."

"You have to be there to train Kirsten. She starts today, remember?"

No, she didn't remember. She woke up thinking she'd start reading through the letters she found last night. Years ago she had learned that hurt feelings led to anger and right now, she knew that for sure. The nerve of him. And as usual, he'd get her riled up and then walk out of the room. She finished her french toast and drank her coffee. It would be so easy to call Kirsten and tell her to start tomorrow, but she knew that wasn't fair.

"How can men be so obtuse?" she muttered as she loaded the dishwasher. "If it was his family, he'd want to know some answers." She pulled the short ribs from the meat compartment and dumped them into the Crock-Pot, then added the rest of the ingredients and set the timer for eight hours. The stew would be ready for dumplings when she got home.

She hit the number for Leah. "There are stacks of pictures here if you want to come and get them. Or go through them here. I'm working today."

"What's the matter?"

"Oh, Bjorn thinks I'm overreacting and wasting my time on this search. Ticked me off."

"Did you find anything else about *That Man?*"

"No, nothing new. Nothing helpful." She heard the front door click shut. "I better run and get ready. I can give Kirsten a ride if she wants."

"I'll tell her. Maybe we'll find something in the letters."

Keira clicked off and headed for the shower.

Kirsten was waiting by the car when Keira went out. "Hey, K-girl, how does it feel to be out of school?"

"Good. Thanks for the ride." The two climbed into the car and headed across town to the office.

"I thought I'd start you on data. I have a bunch of stuff that needs inputting. How are your typing skills?"

"Not the greatest. I topped at sixty words a minute but I'm accurate."

"Good. The computer is all set up and so is the stack of documents. I scan them in, then go over them to make sure there are no errors."

"Okay."

"Not very creative, but necessary. If you have any questions, ask."

With Kirsten settled in the back room, Keira sat down at her desk and flipped through the message slips. Mostly for Bjorn. As if she wanted to even go into his office. Putting them in order of importance, she waited until he was on the phone and then set them on his desk, no smile, no word, and left.

She heard Kirsten's cell phone ringing and her answering it. They needed to discuss the rule of no cell phone calls during office hours other than lunch. But she didn't stay on long and Keira worked on the stack of correspondence.

She decided she'd have Kirsten prepare the cards for the June birthdays, have Bjorn sign them, and then she would. Making a list of tasks needing to be caught up on took a few minutes. With so much of their work on the computer now, there weren't so many files and other menial things for a beginner.

They left the office at four. "So how does it feel to be a working woman?"

"Tired. I don't usually spend that much time in front of a screen with a keyboard. I have my laptop, but we used a PC in the lab at school."

"Make sure you get up and move around, do some stretches, especially your neck and shoulders."

"I did. Moving to the copy machine and back. Thanks for the ride."

Keira watched her stride up the walk, then continued home. She'd not said a word to Bjorn since breakfast. Why didn't she feel victorious for that, rather than down in the dumps? She hated fighting.

The bags of pictures she'd set out for Leah were gone so she knew she'd been there. The box where she'd been tossing letters waited for her on the floor. At least she'd been so busy at work she'd not had time to think about this, other than stewing over Bjorn's reaction. It wasn't like her to not let the anger go by now, but this was really important. To her anyway. She wasn't who she thought she was. None of her dad's relatives were really her relatives, not by blood. She paused. That was it. Who she was. She no longer knew who she was. Half of her genes were unknown. If she wasn't a Sorenson, who was she? Everyone had that innate need to know who they were.

She knew she was her mother's daughter and that side of

the family history, but she wasn't part of Kenneth's, and his whole family's, history—his relatives, the ones who were still around and alive and cared about family reunions. There hadn't been a Jenson family reunion ever, at least not that she could remember. But then all of them but Helga had already left this earth. Of course she must have cousins somewhere, but they'd not kept in touch.

She sank into her chair and forced her mind to gather these thoughts together, then wrote them down so the next time Bjorn made a comment about her obsessiveness, she could give him some concrete answers.

What difference does this really make? Bjorn's question kept fueling her anger. She gritted her teeth and returned to the kitchen to start the dumplings. She checked the cupboard and then the pantry. No biscuit mix.

Well, jellybeans. That had been her favorite swear word ever since Paul had said it one time when he was little. Where had he come up with jellybeans for an expletive? They never knew, but it had worked for her ever since. Jellybeans, jellybeans, jellybeans! Okay, she'd go to the store and buy mix or get out the recipe book and make them from scratch or—no dumplings.

But Bjorn really liked dumplings with his stew.

Who cared what Bjorn wanted right now?

Grow up, Keira Sorenson Johnston. Using her full name when yelling at herself was a mark of desperation. *Woman, you are fifty years old. If you haven't grown up by now, will you ever? But he's the one who started this. Right, and so you will finish it? Get real, you know this isn't bothering him at all, but here you are yelling and swearing at yourself.*

Winning a battle when you were the one on both sides was really a no-win situation.

Jerking out the cooking oil, flour, baking powder, and salt, she set them on the counter and retrieved the egg and milk from the refrigerator. Her mind jerked to a standstill. Could she still include the Sorenson in her name? Of course she could. Even if she wasn't a Sorenson by blood, adoption and legalities counted. Heaving a sigh of frustration, she flipped through recipe books until she found one with a dumpling recipe in it. The page looked well used, as it had the waffle recipe on it too. She glared at the instructions and started measuring. This was crazy. All over a name. She could feel an inner smile tug at her mouth. What was she, some kind of crazy woman? Thank God she'd gone ahead with the dumplings. *Lord, why can't I stay mad at him? Or at the situation? Or life in general? Other people can stay mad.* Did she hear a heavenly chuckle as the verse her mother used to say floated through her mind, "Do not let the sun go down on your anger." *Father, forgive me for being so stubborn.* Keira dropped spoonfuls of dough into the Crock-Pot and set the lid back in place. At least the kitchen smelled good.

She started to head for the stack of memorabilia but turned back. What sounded good for dessert? They hadn't had gingerbread for a long time. With that in the oven, the timer set, and the kitchen in order again, she picked up the box of letters and pulled the craft table closer. She could start by sorting them, but according to year or according to family member?

By the time the timer went off, she had piles of letters clear back to 1958, the year her mother graduated from high school. She'd just taken the gingerbread out of the oven when Bjorn came in the back door.

"Sure smells good in here," he said, sniffing the air.

She set the cake pan on the wire rack on the counter and turned to smile at him.

He held up a hand, traffic-cop style. "Before you say anything, I have to say something."

She could feel her eyebrows rise. Now what?

"I'm sorry for this morning. I do think this is important, but only because it is important to you."

Keira swallowed her tears, tears that leaped to her eyes. She knew how hard it was for him to admit he'd made a mistake. "Thank you. Apology accepted." She stepped into the circle of his arms and kissed him. "Me too."

He rested his cheek against her hair. "What's for supper?"

"Stew with dumplings." She smiled into his shoulder. *Thank you, God, for this man. And thank you that I went ahead and made the dumplings.* "How was your day?"

"You should know, you were there."

"Not really. I was too busy being mad and trying to keep up with the to-do pile and coaching Kirsten to hear or see what was happening."

"Marcus called another meeting tonight. They're talking about sending another truckload this weekend if we can get the word out and have it filled by then."

Keira lifted the lid on the Crock-Pot. "Looks done."

He went to the cupboard and took out the plates. "Good, I'm hungry. I didn't stop for dinner."

She knew that but didn't comment, instead lifting the crock from the outside and setting it on the table on a trivet while he put out the silverware. "What would you like to drink?" All the mundane things of their life together, and so much to be thankful for. "Will you go again?"

"I don't know. We'll see if anyone else volunteers."

After he left for the meeting, Keira returned to her stacks of letters. Amazing how much more she could concentrate when she wasn't focusing on being mad. When her phone rang, she answered with a smile.

"You sound happy," Leah said.

"I am. I'm going through the letters."

"You want some company?"

"Sure. I'll put the tea water on."

A bit later, with both of them settled with mugs of tea and a plate of small pieces of gingerbread to dip in applesauce between them, Keira smiled.

"So how did Kirsten like her first day on the job?"

"She's exhausted. Said she's more tired than after a game of volleyball."

"I wasn't a slave driver, you know."

"No, she said it was the sitting and concentrating to not make mistakes." Leah sipped her tea. "I got through most of the pictures, chose the ones to put in the book. I did find one that was interesting." Leah handed her a photo. "I didn't recognize him. On the back it says, 'Arthur, 1906.' I thought maybe."

"Arthur was my mother's cousin. I think he must have been born in 1906, but he died before I was born, I think he was killed in action during World War II. You should definitely add this to the memory book. I don't think I've ever seen a photo of him before." Keira reached for a piece of gingerbread and dunked it in the applesauce, cupping her other hand under it as a safeguard.

Leah took the photo back. "I will. And we'll keep look-ing. There have to be answers somewhere."

"Kirsten, I'm glad you finally answered. I have to talk with you."

But I don't want to talk with you. Kirsten glared at her cell phone and put it back to her ear. "All you want to do is yell at me. Everyone is yelling at me. This isn't just my fault, you know."

A silence before his voice came back. "Kirsten, when have I ever really yelled at you?" When only a sniff answered his question, he continued. "I know it is not all your fault and I want to make this right."

"Well, two wrongs don't make a right."

"You're not making any sense."

"I don't have to make sense. I'm pregnant, remember? You can go about your life just fine but I will get bigger and bigger and everyone will know." She sucked in a breath. She was screaming into the phone. Screaming was never appro-priate in this house.

The pause stretched. She pictured the look of puzzlement he always wore when he was trying to figure her out. His voice was gentle. "Kirsten, we have to talk this over, face to face."

The gentleness irritated her again. "I'm sorry. I'm really tired, José, and I'm going to bed." She hung up and turned her phone off. Hearing the house phone ring, she knew it had to be him. She should have told him not to call, not that it did any good. She crawled under the purple quilt her grandmother had made her. *Grandma, what should I do? How I wish you were here so I could talk with you.* She heard a knock on her door, and her mother put her head in.

"It's José."

"I know, I just talked to him."

"I see." Leah heaved a sigh and backed out, shutting the door behind her.

Kirsten sat up and thumped the pillows into a mound behind her. At least at work she'd not had to think about this for hours at a time. José had called there too. At lunch her aunt Keira had told her about their policy of no cell phone calls at work. She'd felt like crawling under the seat. She'd never call José when he was on lifeguard duty. So why didn't he give her the same courtesy?

She didn't want to talk to him until she knew what she should do. If she had the abortion, she could just tell him she'd miscarried. That all was well now, they could go on the missions trip, work all summer, and go to school in the fall, just like they'd planned. To have it all over with. She laid a hand on her abdomen. Was there really someone growing inside of her? Or was it just an it, a nonviable cluster of cells? Those words kept ringing in her head. Mrs. Nimitz had been so gentle, so sure, so caring. "We can make this easier for you."

Sure, easy. But if this was truly a baby growing in her, that baby would never see the sun, play in the sprinkler, ride a bike. She waited, chewing her lower lip. If only she could turn back the calendar and relive that night, but relive it responsibly, not through a haze of desire. They had known better, but all of a sudden, all sense of right and wrong flew out the window. She'd never felt so out of control in her entire life. Like a steamroller, it started slow and took off when they didn't stop. Why did they have such strong emotions that they couldn't control? Another one of those things that just wasn't fair.

Puffing out a breath, she got up and went to the closet where she had saved some of the antiabortion information. Sorting through the box, she found what she wanted and took the booklets and papers back to her bed. The one she wanted was at the bottom of the box. Turning on another lamp, she clicked on her phone to the calendar and started counting the days since March twenty-seventh. Fifty-four to sixty days was the spread on the page. The black-and-white picture showed a head, a body, the beginning of legs and arms, and the lungs and heart showed plain as her eyes could see. She could almost see the heart beating. She tried to blink away the tears. Flipping back to the beginning, she looked at all the pictures, and the progression was so plain. She reached for a tissue and blew her nose, mopped her eyes, and rolled her lips together, anything to stop the tears.

How could anyone say this was not a baby, a real person growing inside of her? Of course it could not live yet outside the womb, so the argument had to be that. The other side would say these pictures were made up, not real. The picture became seared on her mind. The shape, the heart—was it already beating? The first tears burned, but those that followed drowned the burning and ran rivers down her face. She turned back to the picture but she didn't need to. Would she live with this always? A tissue didn't begin to stem the flow, so she grabbed a handful and sobbed into them. "God, forgive me, please, for even thinking of an abortion. I can't quit crying. I am so sorry."

A while later, Kirsten made her way downstairs, heading to the kitchen for something to eat. She could hear her parents talking in her mother's lair and paused to listen. They were talking about her and the situation.

"Marcus, you don't need to tell them right now. Give us some time. I could take her to another state, or at least far from here to have it done. No one need know." She looked up in time to see Kirsten standing in the doorway, her mouth and eyes wide open.

"I asked you for advice, to tell me what to do. You sound like the woman at the pregnancy center. You think I should murder this baby too?" Kirsten turned and stomped her way up the stairs, before either her mother or father could reply.

Chapter Seventeen

*H*er mother stuck her head in the door. "Are you all right?"

The tears gushed. "No, Mom." The word became a wail. Kirsten rose up on her knees and reached out to her mother. Safe in her mother's arms, the torrent continued, the sobs shaking her entire body, even to the bed.

"I can't have an abortion. You didn't mean that, did you? What I heard, I mean." Sobs and hiccups punctuated her words. "I looked at the pictures again. I can't have an abortion!"

"No, of course you can't. God forgive me, us, for even thinking such a thing. All will be well." While the sobs continued, the worst of the storm had passed. "Easy, sweetheart, cry it out. Let it all go. We'll make it through." The words ran together in a gentle, maternal murmur that eventually penetrated the onslaught. Kirsten lay in her mother's embrace, feeling safe and above all, surrounded by love. Love so deep and high and wide that it had to include the Father's love, soaking through her mother's hands and arms.

When a silence, other than an errant sob, filled the room, Leah asked, "What happened?"

Kirsten, barely able to see out of her swollen eyes, felt

around for the thin book, found it under her seat, and handed it to her mother. "That page."

Leah held the page under the circle of light from the lamp. She reached for tissues, handed one to Kirsten, and used the other. "I see."

"I had forgotten."

"From when we fought so hard?"

"I wonder how many of these booklets I handed out." *And yet, after all the knowledge, I fell into the trap after all. They all warned us. We thought we could handle it, and now I have to grow up and deal with it.* "There is no easy way out."

"No, not really. Those who go through an abortion learn the ramifications of it years later. I've talked with some who say the guilt is probably worse for burying it all those years. Especially now, when things like this are available. Lord, please forgive us for even thinking of such a thing."

A gentle silence, broken only by the cat's purring, comforted the room.

"Mom, I almost went ahead with it. I went to the clinic and Mrs. Nimitz, the lady I talked to, was so nice and gentle and reassuring. She said they were trying to make things easier for girls like me." She looked down at her body, where she could not see any change yet. She heaved a deep sigh and blew it all out. Blinking rapidly, she continued. "So now I have seven months to decide what to do about the baby, right?" She scrunched her eyes closed, her jaw clenched. "Seven months to decide for three lives."

"Right."

"I need to figure out what day the baby will be born."

"You can say the day but this baby will come when it is good and ready. All three of you were two weeks late. For some reason, that was the pattern. Nowadays the doctors don't always let a mother go that long."

"What do they do?"

"They induce the baby. There are medications that cause that to happen."

Kirsten slid down with her head on her mother's lap, Leah stroking her hair. "Will Daddy ever forgive me?"

"Yes."

"When?" Kirsten watched her mother shrug and look down at her hands. Sitting up, she crossed her legs and propped her elbows on her knees. "Have you talked a lot about this?"

"Not a lot." Leah gazed at the upper wall, at least that's what she appeared to be studying, but Kirsten was pretty sure she wasn't seeing much of anything.

Leah turned with one knee up on the bed, swinging her other leg. "So we go on from here." She, too, sniffed back tears, switching into nurse mode. "Your job now is going to be to take care of that precious life inside of you, to do things that are best for him or her, whether you feel like it or not. You have a lot of growing up to do."

Kirsten felt herself stiffen. "I've always thought I was pretty grown up."

"In many ways you are, but now you absolutely have to consider this someone else. And what about José?"

Kirsten studied her ragged cuticle. "I don't want to see him."

"Too bad. You two are in this together. This baby is his too."

"And he thinks getting married will solve everything." The words gushed out. "It won't."

"I know that. Getting married would solve a problem for the baby, and marriages between couples younger than you have survived and even been very happy, but that, sad to say, is not the norm. Most die of divorce sooner rather than later." The silence stretched. "Curt and Gwen are only a year or two older than the two of you and they seem to be happy."

"How could it happen to me from one time, but not for them yet?"

"Many marriages don't have children. God has different plans for different people."

"Do you think this pregnancy was in His plan?"

Leah shook her head. "But I do know that God promises to bring good out of evil for those who love Him."

"And are called according to His purpose. I never understood that last part."

"We are all called, but we have to answer and go with Him."

Kirsten rubbed her eyes and yawned. "I better text José and tell him I'll meet him tomorrow."

"You're not working for Keira tomorrow?"

"Nope, day after." Kirsten shut down her laptop and got up to set it on the desk and plug it in. She texted José and set her cell on the nightstand. "I thought I'd work on a flyer tomorrow."

"Oh, Lindsey called." Leah rose and headed for the door. "A cold washcloth will make your eyes feel better."

"Thanks, Mom."

"You're welcome."

Kirsten changed into her pj's and located a spiral notebook on her bookshelf. She ripped out the pages that had been used and wrote the date at the top of the page.

"Question one: are you a boy or a girl? What do I call you now? I need a name for reference. You cannot be an it because you aren't. You are a person growing inside of me." She reached for her Bible on the shelf above her bed and flipped to Jeremiah 1:5. "Behold, I knew you in your mother's womb." After copying that on the page, she read further.

As she drifted off to sleep, she remembered a sermon of her father's on forgiveness. That God promised to remember her sins no more. How could that possibly work when the product of her sin was growing within? Her father also said you had to forgive yourself. How, when the reminder would be with her every day? She could just hear the gossip when this got out. *How could she do that when she claims to be a Christian? They took the chastity vow, remember?* She clenched her eyes closed and her fists tight. No wonder they used to send the girl away to live somewhere else. She'd read about that in a novel one time, well, more than once.

But things were different now, weren't they? Girls who got pregnant stayed home with their families and... another thought crept in. Did she want to do that? Was she brave enough to ignore the gossip? The looks? More tears leaked into her pillow.

In the morning she called José and asked when they could meet at the park, at their favorite table.

"I have to be at work at noon, so right away or tonight after I get off." His words were dressed in ice.

"Half an hour?"

"You want me to come there instead?"

"No." All she needed was to have her father come home.

Who knew what he would do? "I'll meet you there." Besides, this way she could leave when she wanted or needed to.

Instead of washing her hair, she clipped it up and slipped into shorts and a T-shirt. Since her mother wasn't in the kitchen, she left a note on the table and exited by the back door, in case her father was in his study.

Leah had a basket full of weeds by her side as she knelt in front of a flower bed. She heard the door click and looked up. "You want to come help me?"

"I'm meeting José at the park. I might be right back."

"Did you eat something?"

Kirsten waved a food bar. "I'll be okay." She ripped it open and took a bite as she left the yard. She'd almost asked where her dad was but realized she didn't really want to know. For a change she was almost in a good mood and seeing him would jinx that. She finished the bar, stuffed the wrapper in her pocket, and picked up her pace to a jog. Was this only day three after graduation? It felt like she'd lived a lifetime since then. And here she'd thought that was the beginning of her new life, free from school and classes and homework. Only now the chains were even stronger.

The more she thought, the faster her feet moved and she ran hard the last block and into the park. The mower had just been by and the smell of new grass got her attention. She slowed her pace back to a jog and looked ahead to see José already at their table. She knew she wasn't late, so that meant he was even earlier.

He didn't wave, didn't smile—just sat on the table top, feet on the bench seat, waiting.

The urge to turn and run the other way made her falter.

But only for a moment. She sucked in a deep breath and strode to the table to take a place on the same side, but two people could have sat between them. She was not going to stand in front of him like a little kid called to the principal's office.

He turned his head to look at her. Usually his eyes were warm and full of love. Not this time. Cold, black coal seemed a better description. "Good of you to finally call."

"Sorry. I've been having some heavy stuff to deal with." *And you only made it worse calling all the time.*

"I wanted to help."

"You can't." *No one can.* "I just have to get through this."

"In case you've forgotten, this baby is mine too."

"As if I could forget." She stared straight ahead, her eyes narrowing.

"If we were married, I could be there for you."

"How could you? You'd have to go to work. Where would we live? How would we pay the rent?"

"We would live with my grandma. She said we could."

"That's great. Tell her thank you for me. But what about fall? When college starts?"

"I'll work during the day and go to the community college at night. You can go during the day."

"Until the baby comes. What about your scholarships, my scholarships, med school, all the plans we had? What about all that?" Her voice rose but she swallowed it back down. "Can you support us on lifeguard pay or working at the grocery store?"

"So what do you want to do?" He threw himself off the table to stand in front of her, his eyes flashing.

"I don't know yet! But I know one thing. I do not want

to get married. Not now. Not in two weeks. I need time to work this out myself, without you putting more pressure on me than I am under already." She stood and glared right back at him.

"I thought you loved me."

She rolled her eyes. "Oh great, play the sad card." She wanted to say "I do love you" but the words would not come.

He stiffened and leaned a bit forward. "You want time? Fine, you can have all the time you want. Call me when you get around to it."

She watched him stride toward his car. If this was how he acted when he got mad, so be it. She dashed the tears that blurred the shape of his black car as he roared away. It would serve him right if she never spoke to him again. And here she had wanted to tell him she had made some decisions. Number one—no abortion.

Chapter Eighteen

"Read this for me, please."

Leah looked over her shoulder to see her husband holding out a piece of paper written by hand. "What is it?" She rinsed the flour off in the sink, thinking she would say "how about later," but the stony look on his face stopped her. Frying chicken could wait. She dried her hands and took the paper, sitting down at the kitchen table. For some reason, she felt the need to sit. This did not look to be a pleasure.

> To the elders of Munsford Community Church,
>   It is with great sorrow that I offer my resignation as
> pastor of this community of faith, effective immediately.

Leah laid the paper down and looked up at him, leaning with his rear against the kitchen counter. "Oh, my darling…" She rolled her lips together, shaking her head, and when he said nothing, she went back to reading.

> I love these people and this church with all my heart, but
> there are circumstances beyond my control that obligate
> me to do this. I have always preached the inerrancy
> of the scriptures, therefore I must comply. Since I have

learned of my daughter's out-of-wedlock pregnancy, I
have to concede that I do not have control of my family
and therefore these verses apply to us, to me. I have
wrestled with the Spirit, but the facts remain.

I do not know what tomorrow or the next day holds,
but I know who holds them in His mighty hands. I
cannot be a stumbling block to anyone's faith. I cannot
preach forgiveness and grace when I am fighting with
all that is within me to accept either of those gifts, or to
extend them to the ones I love.

Thank you for your friendships and these years we
have had together.

In Christ's holy service,
Marcus Sorenson

Leah propped her forehead in her hands. "I think you are rushing this." There, she'd said it. She'd been so afraid this was coming and now it lay before her. *Lord, give me wisdom here. Please, I need it right now.* "Don't you think we need to talk this over? I mean, this affects us all." No, those were not the right words. She turned to look at him.

"You think I want to do this? The Bible clearly states that one who cannot control his family and household is not worthy to pastor or serve in a leadership capacity in a church. How can I expect other people to live by the Word if I don't?"

"But this isn't your fault!"

"Before God, I am to blame along with them. I asked you to read it to make sure it is correct. Not to correct my actions but my words." He stared at his crossed arms. "I see no other way."

"Wouldn't it be wise to talk this over with your mentor before you submit it?"

"What good would that do? The Word is the Word. Better this way than somehow it leaks out and someone has to confront me." His head kept shaking. "I cannot be a Pharisee, living above the law while laying it on others."

"Marcus." She rose and turned to wrap her arms around his waist so he was forced to hold her. "Please, can we pray about this, talk some more and—"

"What do you think I have been doing, if not praying, seeking, searching for some other way? There isn't one. I won't send it right this minute, but the meeting of the elders is two nights away and I thought to send it to Jim first, since he's the president, and then pass out copies at the meeting." He rubbed his forehead. "I can't even think what day that would be."

"Thursday." If only she could wipe the sorrow from his face. Having him mad would be better than this. His heart was indeed breaking.

He tipped his head back to stare at the ceiling. After a long pause, he whispered in a broken voice, "I don't know what else to do."

Because he was such a man of action, she knew what a terrible admission this was. When someone needed something, he put the wheels in motion to make it happen, like the tornadoes to the south or the repairs to a decrepit house in town so the old woman living there could continue to do so and not get rained on. He led by example, walking his faith, not just talking it.

"Marcus, I hate to put any more pressure on you, but you have to talk with Kirsten."

"I know. For a while I was too angry but..." His voice trailed off.

"But what? She needs you to at least say you don't hate her."

"I don't hate her. I told you that before." His voice clipped the last words.

At least that sounded better than the despair. "But you need to tell her." Leah paused, letting an idea grow. "If she were one of the other girls in the congregation, and she came to you, what would you say?"

"But Kirsten isn't one of the other girls. She's my daughter."

"I know. And?" She waited without moving or seeming to breathe.

"And..."

She watched the struggle going on in this man she loved so dearly.

"And I guess I expected more from her." He sniffed and touched his forehead to hers. A snort and he shook his head. "I would say to her that abortion is not an option. Giving nine months of your life right now seems insurmountable, but the time will pass quickly and at the end of that time, you can pick up your life again and go on." It sounded so glib. "But what about that baby then? Do we want to raise our grandchild so Kirsten can go on with her planned life? Does she give it away?" He heaved a sigh that came from the soles of his feet. "It sounded so much easier when we were actively supporting the antiabortion programs."

"I know. I've been going over the same things."

"Any answers?"

"No, because the decisions aren't ours to make."

"What direction we encourage her is up to us. Strange, I guess I never dreamed one of our children would do this. I trusted her, and I trusted José, and look where it got us. I'll talk with her soon."

She closed her eyes and leaned against his chest. His heart beat steadily, surprising for a broken one.

Marcus gripped her upper arms and set her back enough so he could move. "I'll let you get back to supper." His businesslike voice was back in place. "I'll go put this in the computer but I won't print it out yet, at least not to send out. Maybe later tonight."

She wrapped her arms around her waist and watched him walk away. *Lord, get us through this and help us still be a family, please.* And hanging over her head was the reunion coming up so quickly. Next year, would they be among the relatives visiting from out of town? How could they stay here when he resigned? Where would he work? What would he do? So many questions needing answers and none of them easy. She heaved a sigh. They couldn't live on her salary, which went to help pay the school bills. She could always get more hours but still that wouldn't be sufficient. She understood the scriptures he referred to, but surely there was another way.

Who felt like making fried chicken for supper now? And here she'd been hoping she could get him to talk to Kirsten tonight, after an early supper so she could have a nap before going to work. Perhaps he would, but she had a feeling he'd said that to put her off. Not like him, but then nothing in this whole thing was like any of them. No matter what happened there tonight, life at the assisted-living facility was far more simple than what was going on under her own roof. She picked up her cell on the first blip.

"You feel like going out to the home place in the morning?" Keira asked.

"I work tonight, remember?"

"Sorry, I forgot. Did you get through any more of those pictures?"

"A few, why?"

"I'm still hoping to find more on *That Man*."

"How about Thursday?" Keira still had to tell Marcus, but now wouldn't work either. This had to stop.

"I might go before then but we'll plan on that. Thanks."

Leah turned the burner on under the cast-iron skillet and poured in oil. As it heated, she dredged the remaining chicken pieces in the seasoned flour and laid them carefully in the hot pan so it all fit. Her mind wandered as she scrubbed and cut up the potatoes. What was going to happen to them in the next weeks?

All because of two kids who let their passion get away from them. A flame of anger shot up, from coals within she was not aware were still alive. Their daughter—right now she didn't even want to say her name. Anger was useless. Screaming would never solve anything. But right now that's all she wanted to do. Here she was, caught in the middle again. Years ago, when there had been any problems with one of the boys, she'd resolved to never be in the middle again. Let the two opposing sides work it out themselves. In this case, sister talk to brothers, daughter talk to father, and father talk to daughter, and mother stand back and pray for them all.

She turned the chicken and forked the potatoes to see if they were done. No one was even here to set the table. Did she have to take care of everything? Where was Kirsten? She'd last seen her working in the south flower bed, pulling

weeds like they were her mortal enemies. She'd not commented on her meeting with José, but being her mother
and knowing how to read body language, Leah knew it had
not gone well. Not that it could, really. They were polar
opposites and there was no middle ground. Or at least there
didn't seem to be. It wasn't like this was a discussion of
where to go for supper or what movie to see.

Leah checked all the kettles one more time, then headed
outside to find her daughter, who wasn't anywhere in the yard.
Back in the house, she called up the stairs. No answer. She
called Kirsten's cell phone and it finally went to voice mail.

"Where are you?" Leah left the message, then sent a
text with the same message and added, "Supper is ready."
Taking the Jell-O salad out of the refrigerator, she set it on
the table and got down the bowls and dishes for serving.
While the chicken drained on paper towels, she made the
milk gravy the way Marcus liked it, and let it simmer while
she went to call him to supper.

"I'll be right there," he answered while he studied the
computer screen.

"I'm putting it on the table now." Her cell blipped with a
text message from Kirsten. "I'm out at the home place. Eat
later. Sorry."

What could she be doing out there? Leah clicked her
cell closed and put it back in its holster on her belt. She set
the food on the table, poured water in two glasses, and took
her seat. When Dagmar was alive, Kirsten often walked out
there to spend time with her grandmother. Or ran, more
often than walked, as she grew older. *She could have let me
know.* But maybe it was better this way. This was not a good
time to spend a meal together, anyway.

Marcus sat down and faked a smile as he looked at the meal. "Thank you. Let's pray." He reached across the table and took both her hands in his. "Father God, thank you for this food and for Leah who fixed it. Amen."

Leah passed the chicken platter first. But while Marcus put the food on his plate, he didn't appear to know what he was doing.

"What are you looking for?"

"My napkin."

"It's in your lap."

"Oh, thanks."

He ate one leg instead of his usual two and half the potatoes and gravy remained on his plate when he pushed it back. "I can't eat any more. Thank you for trying."

When he glanced at Kirsten's chair, Leah said, "She's out at the home place."

"Why?"

"I don't know, but often when she needed to talk she'd go out there and Grandma would make it all better."

"Well, not this time. Mother would be horrified." If Marcus knew what Keira had discovered, would he still think that? Leah wondered. Dagmar had been in the same situation as Kirsten. Because of that, would she have understood?

Marcus dropped his napkin on the table and pushed his chair back. "I'll be in my study and then I'm going for a run later. You want to come?"

"No, I have to work tonight so I'll take a nap." As he left the room, she rose and started putting lids on things to put the extra food in the refrigerator. Kirsten could fix her own plate. It was probably a good thing Kirsten wasn't here right now. She wanted to shake her and yell and—and what?

Tell her to give her dad more time. Dump all her frustrations on a kid who was trying to deal with this and struggling so hard herself? Sure she was supposed to dump all her cares on Jesus, but He let her take them back. Couldn't He hold on to them? She slammed the palm of her hand on the counter. Surely a run would help sort this out, but she needed to take a nap so she would be alert all night. She looked heavenward. "I am sick and tired of being in the middle here, you know? I don't know what to do and you're not speaking clearly, if you are speaking at all." Letting the tears roll, she sucked in a deep breath and felt the anger drain away.

When her cell chimed, she could tell by the Illinois prefix that it was either Curt or Gwen. Her hello sounded almost normal, so well trained was she to sound like a nurse and pastor's wife. Right now broken hearts would have to wait. Kirsten hadn't talked with her brothers yet either. Maybe she would go for a run and just keep on running.

"Hi, Mom," Curt said. "Thought it was about time I called, since you haven't been calling me."

If you only knew. "Things are rather crazy around here. How are you two?"

"Things are always crazy around there. I take it the graduation and party went off as planned?"

"Pretty much. It rained, so they held it in the gym but the sun came out later. We had a houseful and plenty of food."

"And Kirsten is glad it's over? I'm surprised she didn't call me."

"Sorry to hear that, she's had a lot on her mind." *If that's not oversimplifying things!* "Are you done with finals now?"

"Almost. One more to go. Gwen got a raise and likes her job more all the time."

"That's good. When will you be here for the reunion?" If they ever got it going, that is.

"I thought we'd come on Wednesday but we'll have to leave right after. She has to be back to work on Monday morning."

"Well, I was hoping for longer, but we'll be happy with every minute we have with you."

"How's Dad?"

"Out running, I think. He said he was going to."

"Tell him it's his turn to call." He dropped his voice. "Gwen is doing better, Mom, but it seems to come and go. I'm so glad the job is helping."

"Me too."

"Tell Kirsten to give me a call. I want to hear about graduation and her plans for the fall."

"I will. I need to go. Thanks for calling and tell Gwen hello for me." Once they hung up she held the flat cell against her forehead. How to not lie but not give out the information either. How she hated keeping secrets. Especially ones of this magnitude. But it was Kirsten's and Marcus's place to tell the rest of the family. Knowing her sons, they would be really unhappy to know they weren't told right away. As the Bible said, the truth shall set you free. And right now she needed some freedom. And Keira still hadn't told Marcus. *Lord God, what am I going to do?*

Chapter Nineteen

They can't use the house.

Keira sat straight up in bed. She needed to be able to search the house again, armed this time with knowing what she was looking for. Surely Leah would help if only they knew what they were looking for. Which raised the question—what was she looking for? Trinkets, mementos, cards, mention of Dagmar's life in St. Cloud. All that would just take time and perseverance. The important thing: something about the man who was her biological father. Some scrap of information. Anything. Of course she hadn't gone through all the letters yet. Reading letters was on her list for today. Thursday. She'd told Kirsten to work today.

She heaved a sigh that made Bjorn roll over. It wasn't fair to wake him early because she could no longer sleep, so she slipped out of bed and into her robe and slippers. A glance at the red numerals on the clock told her she had a couple of extra hours. Downstairs she changed the timer on the coffee machine so it would start immediately and took out two chocolate crinkle cookies from the tin. The first cup of coffee of the day always tasted better with cookies. When the machine quit gurgling, she poured her mug full and, with plate in hand, ambled over to her chair surrounded by stacks of letters on the various tables. Inhaling the steaming fragrance, she took her first sip of coffee and smiled at the pleasure. Much as she loved tea, there was something special about the first cup of coffee in the morning.

Alternately munching and sipping, she found the stack with the earliest postmarks and set them in her lap to sort according to correspondent. How they had written letters so faithfully when the telephone was so much faster was beyond her. After all, St. Cloud wasn't across the country, not even that far across the state. But thank God they did— she might be able to find some scrap of information.

There were letters from her mother, Keira's grandma Ilse, from her next-up-the-line sister, Helga, and from Elaine, the eldest daughter. There were no letters from her two brothers. They probably used the telephone, or just didn't talk, like many men of the day. Well, many men in general. Keira started with the letters from Ilse. Removing the paper from the envelope she skimmed the cursive on lined note paper. News of the day from Munsford caught her attention but there was no mention of a man. If only she had the letters from Dagmar to her family!

Ilse expressed disappointment that Dagmar was not coming home for Christmas. Her mother offered to send her a train ticket, but Dagmar must have declined. What had happened that sent her away from home?

Another asked, "Are you in some kind of trouble? Your letter sounds so sad and distracted. If you lose your job, you know you are always welcome here. We would love to have you come home again. With harvest coming on there is plenty of work for everyone."

That was the only clue in the stack of twenty or so

letters from Ilse. Keira picked up the calendar and started figuring the timeline. Her mother moved away after high school graduation. Dagmar and Kenneth returned to Munsford two years after she was born, and moved into the farmhouse to help her parents as they added more acreage to the farm so it would support two families. The original farmhouse had burned down in a prairie fire back in the forties. She had pictures of that house, and now Leah had them for the memory book. Marcus was born in Munsford six months or so after they returned to the farm.

Keira started to read Elaine's letters next. She heard Bjorn stirring and then the shower. Time to make breakfast and get ready for work. How she hated stopping already. Someday, she promised herself, she would go back and read the letters again and get them in a scrapbook with pictures or something. Would the younger generation care about these letters and the stories they contained?

"How did the committee meeting go?" she asked as she set a bowl of oatmeal with dried cranberries in front of him. "The muffins will be ready in a moment." She'd taken some from the freezer and was heating them in a brown paper sack in the oven. They stayed moist that way.

"Henry says the truck will roll again on Sunday morning. He's got too much to do to go earlier. They'll be loading on Friday."

"You aren't going this time?" She put the muffins in a tea-towel-lined basket and set them on the table, then sat down.

"No, we'll pass the privilege around. They don't know yet if there will be a family to bring back or not."

"Oh goodness, I forgot to mention that. I've given this a lot of thought and I'd really rather we didn't have a family living out there what with getting ready for the reunion and all." She buttered her muffin carefully so she needn't look at her husband.

"But we offered."

"I know, but...well, I'm concerned about the reunion and some of those coming are planning on staying there. That doesn't give a family much time to move in and then be moved out again." She thought a moment. "Maybe we could rent a house in town if we have a family in need."

"Keira, what is going on?" He laid his spoon down and gave her his full attention.

"Nothing, I'm just feeling overwhelmed. You know I've not been excited about the reunion this year. Leah isn't either, but since some of the relatives have already bought plane tickets, what choice do we have but to go ahead?" She realized she was rattling.

"Does this have anything to do with Kenneth not being your biological father?"

"Why would you ask that?" *Don't lie, you cannot lie.*

"I don't know, this just isn't like you." He went back to eating his breakfast but glanced up at her every once in a while. He checked his watch. "I have an appointment in fifteen minutes so I have to run. You're bringing Kirsten?"

"Yes, at least I guess so." *I better check on that.*

He picked up the briefcase he'd left by the door. "See you in a bit."

"Whew," Keira huffed out as the door closed behind him. Even something like this was not worth telling a lie for. She had been stretching the truth some since he felt she was blowing the father thing out of proportion but not an out-and-out lie. She just wanted to be able to search every inch of that house for more information and she couldn't do that with a family living there. What was so wrong about that?

A couple of hours later, after setting Kirsten down with the birthday card list, Keira picked up her to-do list and set to getting items crossed off. The phone kept ringing, but all the calls were for Bjorn. She transferred them, took messages when he was on the phone already, and kept on trying to get her own work done. At this rate she'd have to stay late today and that definitely wasn't going to raise her happiness scale.

A call from Leah after lunch was a welcome diversion.

"You got a moment?" she asked.

"For you I do. What's up?"

"I have a strange piece of paper here. It fell out from behind the picture in one of those stand-up cardboard frames."

Keira felt her heart leap. "What does it say?"

"Just a man's name. Sam. None of our relatives are named Sam or Samuel, are they?"

"Not that I know of. Probably just some friend. Who is in the picture?"

"It's Dagmar's high school graduation picture. Strange to have it in one of those old-fashioned cardboard frames, though."

"Well, don't throw it away."

"I wouldn't. But I just wondered if you had any idea who it might be."

Keira set the phone back in the charger. Could this be the man? She'd be watching carefully for a mention of a Sam in any letters. *That's a help. I've not thought to look on the backs of any of the framed pictures.* Often she used a frame more than once too, putting a more current picture

on top of an older one, like with her children's school pictures. And so many photos were still on the walls at the
home place. The thought that those fairly current frames
might be a storage place for old secret things never entered
her mind—until now.

If only she had time to go out there, but then Bjorn
would make some comment about her leaving work and
letting this situation take over her life. She did not feel
like arguing right this minute. He just didn't understand
how finding out something about that man was so terribly
important to her. And she didn't really understand why he
didn't understand, so they would have to agree to disagree
on this subject.

Sam. Who was Sam? She pondered for a moment. If she
found out who he was and he was still alive, that would be
one thing, but if he had already passed away, which was a
strong possibility, so what? Did she have half brothers and
sisters? If he had known about her, he could have found a
way to contact Dagmar, couldn't he?

Maybe Bjorn was right, and leaving sleeping dogs lying
in the sun was the better action. But still.

That evening Keira sat back down to peruse more letters,
now looking for any mention of a man named Sam. In the
first of Helga's letters she found a Sam all right, but it was
short for Samantha. So why was the paper in the back of a
picture? She put Ilse's letters together in a manila envelope
and labeled them with a name and dates for beginning to
end. Then she did Elaine's. As a writer of letters, she was
the least prolific. Keira remembered her as the quiet one.
But when she spoke, people listened because she came up

with such profound things. She and her husband, Arnold, had moved back to Munsford when his health started to deteriorate. The other two sisters helped care for him until he died, but Elaine didn't last a long time after he passed away. She always said he took her heart with him.

Keira blinked. Even thinking about her aunt and uncle made her sad. Her mother and Kenneth had such a good family. So many people no longer had family close by. *You better appreciate this family reunion instead of grumbling about it*, she scolded herself. *Another one of those times to count your blessings.*

Bjorn's car had a squeal in what must be the brakes. She'd been hearing it for a while now. Was he ignoring it or did he not hear it? It was about time for both of them to get their hearing checked. She'd noticed the TV control was on a higher volume.

"Close your eyes," he said, after setting his briefcase on a chair.

"What? Why?"

"Keira, just do as I ask for once without questioning."

"Oh, all right."

"Hold out your right hand."

She did and felt something paper laid in her palm. She closed her fingers over it and grinned in anticipation.

"Open your eyes."

She did and stared down at the folder in her hands. "A cruise in Norway? Through the fjords? Oh how wonderful." She threw her arms around his neck. "This trip gets better and better. Now I wish I had made something special so we could celebrate." She kissed his chin. "You are a man of many surprises, Bjorn Johnston." They walked arm in arm into the kitchen and together got the meal on the table. How could she have gotten so distracted by the past that she hadn't thought about their trip lately? *We are going to Norway. We are actually going to Norway and now on a cruise too.* Maybe she should buy a language program so they could brush up on their Norwegian. They'd both learned to speak it as children, but, like many other things, it had been neglected through the years as the Norwegian-speaking relatives passed away.

After supper, she went back to reading the letters while Bjorn worked on the computer in his home office. She made up an envelope for Helga's letters and put the letters in as she read them.

"So you have a new boyfriend," Helga wrote. "Tell me more about him in your next letter. Mor wishes you would write more often. I know that you would rather talk on the phone. But long distance is expensive and you know that our mother squeezes every penny until it squeals like a baby pig.

"I would love to come visit you, but now that the baby is here, travel is far more difficult. At least on the train it would be, and we have only one car between our families. The other died a lingering death and we can't afford to replace it right now. I wish you would come home for Thanksgiving or Christmas this year.

"Well, let me know how you two get along. Be careful about giving your heart away too quickly. Love from your big sister, who isn't quite so big now, Helga."

So Dagmar was dating a new man. Keira slid that letter into the envelope and opened the next one, dated a month later. She read through it quickly down to the final paragraph. "I wish I could come meet this Sam. You make him sound like a real hero. I've heard it said that women are especially susceptible to men wearing a uniform."

Opening the third letter, Keira smiled when she read Sam's name. So that was indeed his name. But this time there was only one line that caught and held her gaze. "You didn't mention Sam. Are you still seeing him?"

Keira was almost afraid to open the next letter. "What is going on with you? What do you mean you are crying all the time? What has happened? Send me your new phone number and I will call you. And no, I will not tell Mor. Your loving sister, Helga."

Chapter Twenty

"Hi, Lindsey."

"Hey, you want to go for hamburgers and catch a movie?"

"I just got home from work." Kirsten slid her feet into her favorite flip-flops and checked the mirror to see if her capris and a tee were okay.

"I know. We haven't even talked since graduation. What's going on with you?"

If you only knew. "Okay, what's playing?"

"Not sure, I'll look it up. Are you sure you don't need to check with José?"

The sarcastic bite made Kirsten flinch. "No. I think he's working late." But then how would she know, she'd not talked with him since their argument in the park. "You driving?"

"Mom said I could use the four-by-four. Will you be ready in an hour?"

"I guess."

"Well, don't get too excited."

Kirsten rolled her eyes. "We're only going for burgers and a movie, what do you expect?"

"I expect a full report on all that's been going on with you. And I'll tell you my good news."

"What good news?"

"Tell you when I see you." A giggle and click.

Kirsten flipped her cell closed and, after brushing both teeth and hair, made her way downstairs. "Mom?"

"In here, working on the book." The reply came from her mother's lair.

After checking the oven to see what smelled so good, she poured a glass of cold water out of the refrigerator pitcher and ambled to find her mother.

Leah turned from her stacks of pictures and almost smiled. "Hi, how was your day?"

"I addressed birthday cards for their clients. Did you know they send everyone a card on birthdays?"

"Sure, yours came in the mail today. Challenging, huh?" Leah arched her back and kneaded her waist. "Sure will be glad when this is finished."

"Guess I just never thought about it. They sure are busy. Uncle Bjorn is on the phone or meeting with people all day and Aunt Keira says she's always running to catch up. I never realized all that it takes to run a business like that."

"That's why many people do internships in the field they're interested in. Gives them a taste of it."

"Well, I don't think it's for me. I want to help make people well again." Kirsten picked up one of the pictures of her and her cousins when they were younger, playing in the orchard at the home place. "We sure had fun."

"That you did, and that's why I'm killing myself putting this book together—to help everyone keep those memories alive."

"Oh." She laid the picture down.

"How come you went out to the home place last night?"

"Guess I was hoping Grandma would still talk to me. Crazy, huh?"

"Not altogether. Any idea yet what you plan to do?"

"I know what I don't want to do." Kirsten clenched her jaw. "I don't need to decide on the baby's future right now, do I?"

"True. But you do need to see the doctor." Leah gave her daughter one of her mother looks. "I know you don't want to do this, but taking good care of yourself and this baby is mandatory. No shirking your duty there."

"Duty, duty. I'll go make an appointment now. You don't have to get mad at me." She stomped out of the room, with a glance over her shoulder to see her mother shake her head and return to her pictures, adding in the stories each of the families had given her.

"Next Monday at ten," Kirsten announced when she returned from the phone call.

"Good."

Kirsten spied the travel brochure on the table and picked it up. "Are you and Dad going with Uncle Bjorn and Auntie Keira to Norway in August?"

"We've talked about it," Leah answered without looking up from what she was doing. "But with all that is happening, I think it's pretty iffy."

"Mom, I don't want you to stay home because of me—and what has gone on." One more thing that was her fault. They just kept piling up. A baby, their trip, her dad, José, and her brothers when she told them. I'm sorry was never enough.

"We'll just have to wait and see." Leah looked up at her daughter. "We'll keep praying about it, all right?"

Kirsten nodded, knowing that when her mom said that,

she really was doing so. They weren't pat words that indicated either a no or a yes.

She swallowed and bit her bottom lip. "Uh, are you praying for me too?" Her voice cracked. "I mean, about what I should do?"

Leah put down the picture she was working with and turned to hug her daughter. "You are at the top of my list, my ongoing, pray-without-ceasing, give-God-the-glory list."

"I know He listens to you better than to me."

"No, He doesn't. He listens to all of us equally. Maybe I listen to Him better because I have many more years of experience. This is one of those times, I think, where..." She put her palms flat against her daughter's cheeks and looked deep into her eyes. "You have to search His Word and believe His promises. Make a list of promises that you can repeat over and over and over."

"But where do I find them?"

"I'd say start with the Psalms. If God promises something to one person, it applies to all of us. When Jesus said to his disciples, 'And lo I am with you always, even to the end of the age,' He meant that promise for you too. And for that baby you are carrying. Start with Psalm 139." She wiped Kirsten's tears away with her thumbs. "Also, 'Be still, and know that I am God.' This is a hard one for you because you are so seldom still. Actually it is a hard one for all of us."

Kirsten blinked and then broke the embrace to reach for a tissue. "Thanks, Mom. Keep reminding me, okay?"

"You are almost eighteen now. Legally an adult. And I will not nag you. But we can search out verses together once a day if you want."

"Thanks. How come I don't feel like an adult?"

"How do you think an adult feels?"

"Oh, sure of herself. Ready to leave home and go to school, or a job, or whatever. I just want to curl up in a ball and wake up with everything back to normal."

"Don't we all at one time or another?"

"I need to tell Curt and Thomas, don't I?" She watched her mother nod. "And I need to work things out with José."

"You do."

"And with Dad, but he doesn't want to talk with me."

"He will."

Kirsten rolled her eyes. "And you say God still has a plan for me." She stared into her mother's eyes. "And you really, really believe that?"

"I do."

"But what if—what if I don't?"

"That's part of growing closer to Him. The more you read and say His Word, the more you will believe it."

"You are sure."

"Yes! Absolutely!"

"And Dad?"

Leah inhaled and rolled her lips together. "You'll have to ask him that. He is struggling too, you know."

"And it's my fault." Kirsten sniffed and swallowed, then stepped back. "Thanks, Mom."

"You're welcome. Because you are an adult, I can't make decisions for you or force you to make them. But if you don't, you'll make a tough situation a whole lot worse and eventually you might be forced into something you didn't want."

"Like being pregnant?"

"There are always consequences for our actions. Always."

Why did her mother always have to be right? Kirsten

kept from giving a smart answer by chewing on her lower lip again. "Lindsey called and asked if I wanted to go out for burgers and a movie. I said yes, okay?"

"I don't care. If you want to."

"I do. Be good to think of something else for a change. Any calls on my flyers for work? I got a few put up."

"Nope, sorry."

"Maybe Lindsey will help me spread more out tomorrow. Where's Dad?"

"At the church. The elders meet tonight and..." Leah stopped and stared down at the picture in her hand.

"And what?"

Leah heaved a sigh and sort of smiled. "Nothing, we'll see."

Kirsten studied her mother for a moment, shrugged, and drained her water glass. "We won't be late." Since Munsford was too small for a theater, besides many other things, they would drive to the mall on the interstate. She kissed her mother's cheek.

"Tell Lindsey to drive safely."

"Oh sure, as if we were into racing or something."

"Just doing my job."

"Bye." Kirsten set her glass in the sink, grabbed her bag, and slung it over her shoulder. When she heard a car stop in the drive, she headed out the back door to slide into the passenger seat.

"Well, I can't believe we are actually doing this," Lindsey, wearing dark glasses and a grin, announced.

"What?"

"Having an evening together, just us. Without José or my little sister. Just us."

Kirsten slid her sunglasses into place and buckled her seat belt. "Yeah, well, let's go. I'm hungry."

"Kirsten, how come you're not returning my calls lately?"

Kirsten heaved a deep sigh. "I've had a lot on my mind."

"What? We can talk about anything, right? I mean, I thought we were best friends."

"We are. I'm sorry." Kirsten puffed out a breath. *Tell her and get it over with. You know you want to.*

"You didn't break up with José, did you?"

"No."

"Uh-oh. You're mad at him?"

"You could say that. Look." Kirsten turned as much as the seat belt would let her. "I'll tell you the whole sad story later. First, I want to know the good news you so nicely teased me with."

Lindsey eased the car out on the main road, after looking both ways. "You ready?"

"More than."

"I have a job."

"Good for you. Where and when?"

"I start Saturday. At the Bar Z."

"Waitress?"

"Yep. Didn't want to do that again, but hey, the money is good and I couldn't find anything else."

Kirsten nodded. "They know it's only for the summer?"

"Unless I decide to go to community college."

"I thought you were thinking of going to State instead." Kirsten shook her head. "What's been going on that I missed out on?"

"First, I didn't get the scholarships you did. Second, I'm

still not sure what I want to do, and my dad said I can figure that out a lot cheaper at CC."

That's where I'll be going too, Kirsten thought.

"Kirsten, what's wrong?"

"Nothing." Kirsten heaved a sigh. "Can we talk about it later? I just want to eat and see a movie and have fun and then we can talk."

"You sure?"

"I'm sure. Where are we going to eat?"

"Burger Barn?"

"Sounds good."

"What are we going to do for your birthday?"

"I have no idea." Her birthday was tomorrow, but not much mention had been made of it at home. Her grand announcement had taken over all their lives, leaving no room for things like birthdays and birthday cake and a party. Not that she wanted a birthday party. But she and José would have planned something. Only she hadn't heard from him since he stormed off, and she had managed to keep from calling him. Even though her fingers itched to hit the number four on her speed dial.

"Maybe I won't have a birthday this year."

"Hey, girlfriend, you don't turn eighteen every day. Only one day in your whole life. You getting too old for birthdays?"

"What movie are we going to and what time?"

"Oh, another thing we can't talk about yet."

Kirsten didn't answer. It wasn't like Lindsey to be sarcastic. Kirsten watched the green fields giving way to houses and more houses as they neared town. They turned on New Main Street, and Lindsey pulled into the parking lot of the red, barn-shaped building. After parking they started to get out, but Kirsten stopped with her seat belt still in place. "I'm sorry, Lindsey."

Lindsey nodded. "Okay. But you better have a good reason." They both applied gloss to their lips and, bags in place, strode to the doorway. Kirsten opened the door. "After you." They slid into a booth and smiled at the girl who waited on them.

"Just think, that could be you," Kirsten said.

"I applied here, but the Bar Z is so much closer. And besides, the tips will be better in a steakhouse than in a place like this."

"They make good burgers and the place is always busy."

"True, so you apply here."

"I'm working for my uncle, remember? And trying to find odd jobs for the other days. I put flyers out. Did you read yours?"

"No, but my mom did and she said she already had someone to do those things, namely me."

"And your brother and sister. They're big enough to do those things too."

"That's what I keep telling her—and them. They help too, Mom makes sure of that."

When their orders arrived, they kept talking while they ate. It felt normal again, like they always had been, not like the last few days. When they walked out of the restaurant, they smiled at each other and Lindsey nodded. "Thanks and welcome back." She glanced at her watch. "We have ten minutes to showtime. Let's drive the car around instead of walking all the way to the other side of the mall."

"What if we didn't go to the movie?" Kirsten replied.

"What would you like to do? Please don't say go home or call José or..." She shrugged. "Whatever."

"No. I told you I'd—"

"How about if we grab some sodas and park somewhere where we can talk?"

"Good."

Once they had their supplies, Kirsten said, "If we go to the church parking lot, someone will see us and ask if we need help."

"If we go home, too many people."

"How about the home place?" Kirsten nodded as she spoke. "We won't go in, but parking in the driveway should be okay."

"Won't one of the neighbors call either your house or your aunt's and ask if they know if someone is out there?"

"No, most of them wouldn't be driving the roads this late."

They talked about general things on the roads back to Munsford and out to the home place. When they parked under the newly leafed maple tree by the garage, Lindsey unscrewed the cap on her cola bottle. "So, what's happening that's got you so down?"

Kirsten stared straight ahead. Might as well get it over with. "I'm pregnant."

"You're what?" Lindsey turned in her seat and leaned against the door. "Are you sure?"

Kirsten nodded. "We—I took the test, then a few days later, I bought another kit and took it again."

"But you two took the chastity vow... and all our anti-abortion work. How could you get pregnant?" She shook her head and raised her hand. "No, TMI."

They were both quiet a moment.

"Where is José in this?"

"He wants to get married right away." Kirsten stared straight ahead, shaking her head at the same time.

"I thought you two planned on getting married. This just speeds it up."

"Yeah, like four years from now. After we graduated from college."

Lindsey turned so she was facing the windshield too and propped her crossed arms on the steering wheel. "So what do your parents say?"

"Say? My dad hasn't spoken to me since that night, other than one comment before graduation." She could hear the anger in her own voice.

"Well, at least he didn't throw you out."

"Thanks for the consolation. Mom and I have been talking, after she got over the shock. I didn't talk to José for a few days either. He called more than you did. Texted. Good thing we have unlimited or my dad would have killed me over the bill."

"Who else knows?"

"No one. I took the test three days before graduation and dropped the bomb on them that night." Kirsten used the tips of her fingers to wipe away the tears leaking through again. "I don't know how we could have been so stupid."

"When?"

"After that dinner when we went out to celebrate José's scholarships and aid package. That's the only time, I swear it. I asked forgiveness and said it would never happen again and please God, don't let me be pregnant, but I missed my period two weeks later. I thought maybe it was accidental—you know, like it used to be—and I prayed a whole lot more and begged God and promised I'd do anything to not be pregnant. And then I missed the next one and I knew. José kept saying everything was gonna be all right, but I knew it wasn't." She dug in her bag for a tissue and when she didn't find one, used a paper napkin to wipe her eyes and blow her nose. "So my dad won't talk to me, my mother is acting like a nurse, making sure I know everything, José and I had a big fight in the park and he's not called since, and now you're the only other one I've told. Oh, besides my aunt Keira."

"And you know I won't tell anyone."

"Right, but pretty soon everyone will figure it out when they see me getting fat. And fatter."

"How will you go to college now?"

"I'll probably be going to the community college. We'll be able to drive together."

"When are you due?"

"Christmastime. And before you ask, no, I am not getting married. José and I are too young to get married."

"So what about the baby?"

Kirsten hunched forward. "I even looked into an abortion without telling anyone." She turned to Lindsey. "But I couldn't do that. The lady at the clinic said it would be easy and this is not a baby but a group of nonviable cells." She shook her head. "How can she say that? What a lie to feed girls." A silence stretched but for her sniffing. "Getting pregnant was bad enough, but I can't kill a baby. He or she deserves to live too. This isn't the baby's fault."

"All your plans and dreams…"

"Are on hold for now."

"So will you keep the baby or put it up for adoption?"

"I don't know. Adoption makes more sense, but I don't have to decide that yet." She turned in the seat again, staring at Lindsey in the deepening dusk. "Everyone will know we broke our vow. What we did."

"Well, at least school's out and if you don't tell anyone, for a while they'll just think you are getting fat."

"I've messed everything up." She took a swallow of her drink. "I know what you're thinking."

"What's that?"

"Should have thought of that earlier?"

"No, I'm just feeling so sorry. I don't know how you can even act normal. Like go to work, get out of bed, not be screaming and crying all the time."

"Already did all that. Didn't help."

"Stop and think. Would getting married be so terrible?"

"José wouldn't be able to go to Northwestern, he'd lose all his scholarships. We'd live with his grandmother. She's a great lady, but... I would go to school during the day and him at night. Or perhaps I would be able to find a full-time job. What would we earn? Minimum wage. Remember that class we took on economics? The budgets we had to work out, baby costs, no insurance unless one of us got a really great job. And how would that be without any kind of training?" She shook her head as she talked, then dropped her voice. "I don't want to give up everything either—school, a career in medicine, a family when I'm old enough to take care of them."

"So you're thinking about giving it up for adoption?"

"I don't think I can. José will hate me if I give our baby away. And I'll hate me too."

"Sondra's parents are taking care of her baby while she's at school and at work."

"Right, and she went on welfare. Tell me how great that is."

"Just telling you what I know." She drained her soda. "So...is that why you didn't order a cola?"

"Yes. My mother told me that my biggest job now is to do everything in my power to have a healthy baby. Caffeine is bad for babies."

Lindsey's cell sang. She flipped it open. "It's my mom." In a minute she clicked it shut. "I'm supposed to stop for ice cream on the way home."

"We better go, huh?"

"Wish I could think of something to help you."

"One thing: don't tell anyone, not even your mother."

"I won't. Some birthday present, huh?"

"Right."

Lindsey started the car and backed around to head out the drive. "I'll be praying for you."

"Thanks. Maybe your prayers will do better than mine. I think God turned off the receiver from me."

When they stopped in her driveway, Kirsten unbuckled her seat belt. "I'll call you in the morning about my birthday."

"'Kay." She paused. "We could go to the pool."

"No thanks. Guess who's the lifeguard?" She slid out and slammed the car door. "Night."

"Night."

She watched Lindsey back out. She really didn't want to go in the house. Her dad's car was in the garage. That used to make her happy.

Chapter Twenty-One

I have to talk with Dad."

Leah looked up from her memory-book table. "I know. He's in his office. Go ask if he's ready."

"What if he says no?" Kirsten fought back the tears that brimmed instantly. *I don't want to talk with him, I want this all to go away.* She couldn't stand the disappointment in his eyes, the shadows that lined his face. Her stomach clenched, leaving the acid-bile taste in her throat. "Will you come too?"

Leah nodded. "Let me put this away so nothing happens to it." She reached down into a hanging-file box and withdrew a file folder, added some pictures to it, and put it away.

Lord, help. Kirsten felt like she was watching a slow-motion movie. Even her mother's words dragged out, making her sound like some kind of monster. *Oh sure, now you pray for help.* The fiend shrieked and cackled in her inner ear, a parody of her own voice. Tonight she didn't have the strength to argue. Her confession to Lindsey had taken every bit of energy she possessed. Maybe now was not the best time. But would there ever be a good time for a talk like this? What was she going to say? "I'm sorry" didn't make much difference at this point.

She forced her feet to carry her to the door of her father's study. Books lined one wall and a window onto the garden took up a good part of another. Her father sat in his recliner, staring out the window. "Daddy."

"Yes."

How could such sorrow, depression, anger—whatever it was—be packed into one word?

"Can we talk?" Never before had she stood at the door and asked. She'd always known he would put down anything he was working on and open his arms to her. She would crawl up in his lap and he would lay his cheek on her hair and say, "I love you, little princess. What can I do for you?"

Now, he only nodded.

Look at me, Daddy, please look at me. She wasn't brave enough to even kneel by the arm of his chair, another favorite place of hers. Instead she pulled the ottoman away from the wall and let her mother have the wingback chair that matched it. *Just do it*, she screamed at herself, the words echoing in the halls of her mind. "Please forgive me."

The silence pounded her into the floor. His sigh ripped at her heart.

"Yes, I forgive you. And if you have asked, Jesus does too."

A tear dripped on her clasped, clenched hands. "Thank you."

"But there is no way to undo what is done." He shook his head slowly as if the action was almost beyond his control. "No way."

"I know." *How well I know.*

"I wrote my letter of resignation. The elders are meeting tonight."

"Oh, Dad, why? You didn't do this. I did. Why should you have to pay for my mistake?"

"Sometimes that's just the way life is."

"But this is your church."

"No, this is not my church, it is God's church. When I read the scriptures, there are clear rules there for pastors, and I must follow them."

"But where?"

"In the book of Timothy."

"It's not fair!" *Why could she not make him understand? Let her pay the price, not her father.* But she knew, deep inside, that when her father believed something and made up his mind, nothing she said or did would change it.

"What will you do?"

"I don't know." The three words lay like a dead body between them. He didn't look up, only at his lap where his hands lay, fingers curved in, not moving. Usually some part of her dad was moving, often one forefinger silently tapping on the other.

Kirsten looked to her mother, who sat perfectly still but for the tears leaking one at a time down her face. "I-I knew I messed up my life and José's, but not yours." *What can I do? An inner snort. Haven't you already done enough?*

"Sin is like that. It never affects just one person." He spoke softly.

Get angry at me, yell at me, something. I can't stand this. How can I pray? God, would you hear me now? Are you listening to my father? I know he's been praying. And Mom. Don't punish them for what I did. Please, the blame is mine, the sin is mine. Not theirs, they did their best. It was me. Me and José. Oh God, it was me. She crumpled into the ottoman, no longer able to remain upright. She looked to her mother, who sat with her face in her hands. Three people, three chairs, the canyons between them wide as the night sky.

How could there ever be any healing for them all?

After a long silence broken only by a stray sigh or sniff, Leah stood. "I'm going to make some tea. Do you want some?"

As Kirsten followed her mother out the door, the house phone rang. Taking a deep breath and blinking away tears, she made sure her voice didn't betray the sorrow pressing down on all of them. "Sorenson residence."

She could hear a woman crying. "P-please, can I talk with Pastor?"

What to do? How could her father talk on the phone right now? "Uh, just a moment." Kirsten covered the receiver. "Someone is crying and wants to talk to Dad."

"Go get him."

"But…" At the look on her mother's face, Kirsten padded back to the study. Keeping the receiver covered, she stopped beside him. "Dad, someone needs you."

He straightened, his eyebrows went up in a question, so she shrugged. "I don't know who, but she's crying."

Marcus closed his eyes, inhaled, and reached for the phone. "Pastor Sorenson."

As she left the room, Kirsten heard him say, "Oh, Virginia, I am so sorry. I'll be right there."

Kirsten joined her mother in the kitchen. "He said he'd be right there. How can he do that?"

"Your father is first and foremost a pastor and he will go where he is needed."

"But he resigned."

"No, he sent in his letter of resignation. The deacons have to accept it before he is officially no longer their pastor."

Kirsten felt hope leap in her heart. "So what if they say no?"

"They will all talk and decide how best to handle this."

"Would it help if I left?"

"Left what? The church? Our family?" Her mother almost smiled. "Sorry, sweetie, but you are stuck with us. And while there will be gossip and possibly rude remarks, you are still part of the family of God and the family of Munsford Community Church."

"But it might be easier on everyone if they didn't have to see me grow bigger and bigger."

"But not easier on you, and you are the most important part of this equation to us." They sat down at the table, tea mugs steaming. "I fixed apple spice, so there's no caffeine." She pushed the plate of peanut butter cookies across the table. "Keira sent these over." She picked up one for herself. "You never told me how the meeting with José went."

"He has things all planned out. We will live with his grandmother and he will work days and go to school nights. I would keep working for Uncle Bjorn and go to school if I'm able."

"Until after the baby is born. Then what?"

"Then his grandmother will take care of the baby while we work and go to school."

"I see."

"He stormed off when I told him no. He's not called since."

"And you will call him...when?"

"I don't know. I want to talk to him and then I think, why bother? He doesn't have to stay around for this. He can go away to school and be just fine. One of us is going to have to have a good education. It'll take me years longer to get my degree now." She circled the rim of the cup with her fingertip. "If I ever do." The pause lengthened. "I told Lindsey."

"So the ones who know are Keira and Lindsey. I'm not sure if Keira has told Bjorn or not. I'd like to invite them over for supper tomorrow night...no, that's your birthday. The next night. Tomorrow night we'll just have cake and ice cream. But maybe I better wait and ask your father if he can handle company."

"They aren't company, they're family."

"True, and we need to act like they are. When are you going to tell your brothers?"

"I thought maybe at the family reunion."

"I think before then, so they can recover from the shock before the others find out."

Kirsten nodded. "Like when they call to wish me happy birthday? That's just great. Thanks for your good wishes and I have a bit of news, I'm pregnant." Shaking her head, she drained her mug and picked up the last cookie. Cuddling Patches, she trudged up the stairs. Now she was wishing José would call. Before she didn't want him to. *Can I never figure out what I want?* She turned and called back down the stairs. "Lindsey and I are going to the pool tomorrow and for ice cream to celebrate my birthday, okay?" She'd made up her mind on one thing.

"Sure, just plan on being home for supper."

"At least she remembered that my birthday is tomor-row," she told the cat in her arms. "I was beginning to won-der. Just think, I'll be eighteen." Dumping the cat on the bed and shaking her head she went to stand in front of the full-length mirror. "Eighteen and pregnant. How can this possibly be a happy birthday?"

Chapter Twenty-Two

At the breakfast table the next morning, Kirsten had toast and tea in front of her when her father came into the kitchen. "What happened last night, Dad?"

"A terrible tragedy. The Winchesters' grandson, you know, little Kirby?"

"Of course." Her stomach was already tying in knots. "What happened?"

"He was riding his bike and a car hit him. The surgeons tried to save him, but he died about two a.m." He rolled his lips to keep back the tears and shook his head. Leah laid her hands on his shoulders and her cheek against her husband's.

"Losing a child is the hardest thing ever. I put it out on the prayer chain first thing this morning." She sniffed back her own tears.

"He was so cute. Like in the Christmas program. Waving to his family and dancing to the music." Kirsten wanted to go hug her father but sat stuck on her chair.

He sat with his head in his hands, propped up by his elbows. He heaved a sigh and scrubbed fingers through his hair. Looking up at his daughter, he blinked. "Kirsten, I have to ask for your forgiveness."

"What?" She shook her head. "Uh-uh."

"No, listen to me. I have been so angry and heartsick, and yes, we have a problem here in our family..." He looked up at Leah. "But we still have our daughter and I am so grateful I can't begin to tell you." He held out his arms. "Please forgive me for the way I've been treating you. Thank you, heavenly Father, we still have our Kirsten."

"Daddy!" She threw herself in his arms. "Of course I forgive you. It was my fault, not yours."

He held her close, his tears mingling with hers and Leah's arms wrapped around them both. "I can't say I won't be angry anymore, but please, God, help us love each other no matter what."

Kirsten sat on his lap, held in her father's arms, something she hadn't done in years, just what she had cried out for. She wiped her eyes and grabbed for a napkin to blow her nose. Leah handed round the tissues. "What about José, Daddy?" How that had leaped into her mind, she didn't know.

"I'll talk with him. I have to keep remembering that God will bring good out of this somehow. He said so." Marcus blew out a breath. "How can that be with little Kirby? Lord, I don't get it." He sniffed again and glanced at the kitchen clock above the window. "I told them I'd come by about ten so I better get a move on." He kissed Kirsten's damp cheek. "I love you, princess, and don't you forget it, no matter what."

She sat up and turned to stare into his eyes, her vow echoing his. "No matter what."

"Bjorn and Keira are coming over tonight for your birthday dinner. Is there anyone else you'd like to invite?"

Kirsten immediately thought of José. But decided not to. She didn't want another argument on her birthday. "Lindsey."

"Okay. Steaks all right?"

"With twice-baked potatoes?"

"If you want."

Kirsten returned to her own chair. "You want me to stay home and help?"

"On your birthday? Not likely. You go have a good time and don't get sunburned. That's not a good way to celebrate."

After Marcus left, the front doorbell rang. Kirsten went to answer it. An elderly man stood on the porch, holding a vase of peach-colored roses.

"Hey, Kirsten, I think you must be one lucky girl. These are for you."

"For me? Thank you, Mr. Olson. It's my eighteenth birthday today."

"Well, that young man must like you a whole lot to send two dozen roses." He handed her the card. "Happy birthday."

She blinked and grinned at the same time. Opening the small envelope, she pulled out the card and read: "I love you. Nothing else matters. José."

She carried the vase into the kitchen. "José sent these."

Leah leaned in to sniff the blooms. "Ah, they even have some fragrance. They certainly are lovely. You want to put them on the table for everyone to enjoy?"

"Yes, and then I need to get ready. I'll text him a thank you so we don't argue."

"Maybe you two need a referee."

Leah smiled as she heard her daughter jogging up the stairs. So many good things happening on Kirsten's birthday. That was as it should be. "Thank you, Lord." Her cell phone sang—a call from Keira.

As soon as she flipped it open, Leah heard, "What would you like me to bring?"

"Good morning to you too."

"Sorry. I'm baking bread, should I turn some into rolls?"

"Sounds wonderful. We're having steak, twice-baked potatoes, and I thought to make that broccoli salad. Kirsten really loves that."

"So do we all. I'll bring that too, then. Angel food cake?"

"You sure know a lot about this family, my friend. The cake is in the oven." A laughing snort was her answer.

"I'm taking bread and a Jell-O salad over to the Winchesters. You want me to take anything for you?"

"Not today. I'm going to wait until after the funeral. They'll need things then too."

"Okay, anything else?"

Leah eyed the steaks thawing on the counter. "You'd better bring a big appetite, the steaks are huge." She paused before continuing. "I bought fresh strawberries yesterday to go on the cake, along with whipped cream. Am I forgetting anything?"

"Not that I know of. See you later."

Leah took the cake from the oven and turned it over while still in the pan. She hulled the strawberries, cut and sugared them. What an easy dinner this was turning out to be. Keira was doing the hard part. While the oven was still hot, she scrubbed the baking potatoes and put them in the oven, and set the timer for an hour. Back in her room, the end of the memory book was in sight, over a rise or two, but still coming closer.

"So is José coming to dinner?" she asked when Kirsten joined her.

"No, but I called and we did better. You might have a good idea with the referee. I'm thinking both you and Mrs. Flores. She said I should call her Betty now, but that still feels strange."

"Work up to it. I still call a teacher I had in high school Mrs. Southworth. I know her name is Jen, but my mouth can't say it."

"You want anything from the store?"

"Nope, all is well."

"Hey, Mrs. S," Lindsey called from the porch. "How come you're inside on a day like today?"

"She's finishing up the memory book for the family reunion. Wait until you see it."

Leah smiled as the two strolled down the walk to the car. They could walk to the pool, so perhaps they planned... that's right, they were going for ice cream. She brought the wrapped packages out from her hiding place and arranged them on the coffee table in the family room. The boys had sent theirs ahead too so they could surprise her. Some of the gifts she'd bought were for Kirsten's dorm room. She heaved a sigh. Oh well, she could use the desk things in her room upstairs. The gift card for the bookstore would be good anywhere.

They had given her a Kindle for Christmas, and the Amazon gift card could be used for books on the e-reader. The kids had tried to talk Leah into using one, but she could see no sense in it. There was something about holding a book in her hand and smelling the printer's ink that was pleasing to her. Or maybe it was because she had always done it that way. Was she getting old enough to get caught in that trap?

Every time she thought of the Winchester family, she

prayed for them again, just like she did for Kirsten and José and the life they had created. Kirsten had to tell her brothers, that was all there was to it. They tended to get more than a little upset when something important happened and they weren't notified.

When supper time arrived, she had set up in the backyard, just like she'd planned. One always took into account that a spring storm could blow in in a matter of minutes. Marcus started the grill and she laid the plastic bags with marinated steaks onto a tray. The potatoes were reheating in the oven, and the sun tea was ready to pour.

"Mom?"

"Out here." When the girls had arrived home several hours earlier, she'd sent them down to the local office supply to scan in and make copies of the last of the pictures. She'd worn their rented machine right out.

"The pictures and the discs are on the table."

"Good. Thanks."

Keira and Bjorn pushed open the gate and came in bearing both food and gifts for the birthday girl. "Smells good out here," Keira said, handing the gaily wrapped packages to Kirsten, along with a kiss.

Marcus waved his long-handled tongs in the air. "Five minutes."

Bjorn ambled over to the grill, and Keira set her bowl and basket on the round glass table. "You need me to do anything?"

"Nope, unless you want to pour the iced tea."

When they sat down for supper, Marcus said grace and then, "Pass your plates. I'm thinking these are all medium, but feel free to swap if you like." He placed a steak and a potato on each plate and passed them around.

After supper, Leah brought out the cake and they sang happy birthday. She served it with the strawberries, a decided hit with all of them. Kirsten brought her presents outside to open and laughed when she opened the package from Curt and Gwen, a bobblehead of her favorite baseball player on the Minnesota Twins. "For your dorm room," the note read. That caused a bit of a pause, but she carried on.

When the breeze picked up the wrapping paper, they brought everything back into the house, then gathered in the family room to let Kirsten finish opening. Most of the presents were for her dorm room in the fall. Kirsten smiled and thanked everyone, but Leah noticed she avoided eye contact with Lindsey. The smile fell from her lips and she shifted uncomfortably, her hand moving instinctively to her belly. Surely she wasn't going to throw up her birthday dinner. Leah saw her swallow. Catching Leah's concerned look, Kirsten gave a nearly imperceptible shrug.

When the phone interrupted, Leah answered, then handed it to Kirsten. "Your oldest brother wants to wish you happy birthday." Kirsten took the phone and, after a deep look into her mother's eyes, carried the phone into Leah's lair.

"Hi, Curt," Leah heard her say, a touch nervously, just as she closed the door.

While the others chatted, Leah busied herself gathering dishes and wrapping paper for a few minutes before going to the door to her lair and tapping softly.

"Come in," Kirsten said. Leah found her pacing.

"I told them. They didn't say much. I think Gwen was crying. I wasn't feeling well, so I said I had to go."

"You'd better call Thomas right away or Curt will call him and then there will be fireworks."

"I know, I just need a few minutes."

Leah turned at the ringing of the phone. "You want to get that or...?"

Kirsten picked up the telephone. "Sorensons'."

"Kirsten?"

"Yes. Hi, Thomas." She seemed to wait for him to start in, but then looked relieved. "Yes, I just finished opening presents. Thanks for the gift certificate."

"You're welcome. Don't spend it all at once," Leah heard him reply.

Kirsten sucked in a deep breath. "Thomas, I have something rather important to tell you." Another breath. "I'm pregnant." She flinched at the expletive echoing in her ear.

"José! I swear I'll beat him into the ground. When are you getting married? Kirsten, how could you?" The questions tumbled loudly over each other.

"Thomas. Thomas! Stop!" Suddenly, she dropped the phone, rushed to the bathroom, and shut the door.

Chapter Twenty-Three

Another cramp hit. Kirsten glanced down to see bright red blood staining her underpants. Was she starting her period? No. Losing the baby? "Oh, please." But she wasn't sure if that expressed horror or relief.

"Kirsten?" Her mother tapped at the closed door to the half bath.

"Come in."

Leah entered the bathroom, the concern on her face changing to alarm. "What is it?"

"I'm bleeding."

Leah stared at the telltale stains. "Oh, dear God. When did this start?"

"I don't know. I felt like I was going to throw up but then it felt more like menstrual cramps. And then I had to go. What does this mean?"

"It means we see the doctor first thing in the morning. Is there more?"

Kirsten shrugged. "I'm afraid to move."

"How do you feel now?"

"Yucky. Crampy. My stomach is heaving."

"Okay, let me go get you a pad and we'll get you up to bed. We'll see how the next few hours go."

Leah fetched the supplies and helped her daughter up to her bedroom where she propped pillows under Kirsten's legs. There was a knock at the door and Leah asked who it was.

"Lindsey. Can I help somehow?"

"Yes, come on in and sit here and talk with Kirsten."

When Lindsey stopped beside the bed, Kirsten gave her a half smile, half grimace. "I started bleeding."

"Your period?" Lindsey glanced to Leah.

"I don't think so." Leah started for the door. "Think I'll call Dr. Youngstrom just to be on the safe side. Just stay down, Kirsten, you need to relax."

When her mother left, Kirsten turned her head. "Sit down on the floor, the bed, whatever."

"Does it hurt?"

"Not much now and it wasn't terrible before. Like cramps, you know."

"So what does it mean?"

"I don't know. Maybe I'm losing the baby. It could mean..." Kirsten chewed on her bottom lip. "If I lose the baby, everything will be so much easier." She sniffed and reached for a tissue. "Am I a wicked person to want such a thing?"

"I don't know, ask your mom."

Kirsten laid a hand on her abdomen. "Poor little baby, not wanted." She heard the phone ringing. Would Thomas call back to see what had happened? Curt would surely be calling. "Are Aunt Keira and Uncle Bjorn still here?"

"I guess."

"What a way to end a perfectly nice birthday."

"Are you going to tell José?" Lindsey wrapped her arms around her bent knees.

"I don't know. All depends on what happens, I guess."

"The roses sure are awesome."

"I know."

"What are you going to do?"

"I don't know yet." Another cramp made her squirm. "Sometimes I feel like this is happening to someone else. It can't be happening to me. I thought my world was perfect and then this came along. One time. One time." She turned her head to look at Lindsey.

Her mother tapped on the door.

"Come in."

"That was Thomas. He and Curt talked. They said they are praying for you."

Kirsten heaved a sigh. "Did you talk to the doctor?"

"Yes. He said he'll see you in the morning and stay flat. If it gets worse, he'll see us at the ER."

"Did you tell the others?"

"I just said you were having female problems."

"Right."

"I'm glad you told Keira. She said to tell you she is praying for you even more."

Leah took her daughter's wrist in her hand to check her pulse. "All normal. How are you feeling?"

"Not the best but not real crampy."

Lindsey's phone rang. She flipped it open and read the text. "I need to get going. I told Mom I wouldn't be late."

"Thanks for coming."

"Happy birthday, girlfriend. You are now as old as I am."

Later, after everyone had left, Kirsten pulled her journal from the drawer of her bedside table and, propping it on her raised knees, tapped her pen against her chin. Today was her eighteenth birthday and most of it was a good day.

She could almost forget that she was pregnant and be herself. She wrote about the pool and Lindsey and the dinner and the roses. José hadn't worked at the pool today after all, so she hadn't seen him. But she had a picture in her cell phone of the roses and left room to put the picture in her journal. "I guess he loves me after all!!!!" Writing about the early morning scene with her father made her wipe her eyes again. That poor family to lose such a cute little boy like that. "My father asked for my forgiveness, can you beat that? I hope that the board of elders refuses his letter of resignation. God, it really isn't fair that my dad should be punished for my mistake. It wasn't his fault at all." She doodled some shapes on the page before heaving a sigh and adding more.

"I was bleeding tonight. When I thought I might be having a miscarriage, I was so happy until I thought about it. The baby would die, my life would be back to normal, and all would be well. Do babies that die before they are born go right back to heaven? Sometimes I think of this that is growing inside of me as only cells but most of the time I see that picture in my mind. This is a real live baby growing inside of me. How can I be the kind of person that would want that baby to die? What kind of freak am I? How can anyone love someone who would wish that? God, how can you love me? You heard me. You know my thoughts. I hate these things that I am doing. This isn't the person I want to be. But I don't know how to be anymore. I just don't know." She slashed a huge line across the bottom of the page.

The next morning at the doctor's office, she thought she would die of embarrassment at the examination and all the questions he asked. Dr. Youngstrom had known her since she was in kindergarten, when he took over his father's practice. She told him that she'd slept through the night and had only a little spotting in the morning. After he finished writing on his laptop, he looked up at her sitting on the examining table. "You get dressed and I'll meet you in my office. Your mom too if you want."

She nodded. "I do want that."

"So, what do you plan to do?" he asked a few minutes later, looking at her over his desk. "You said you explored an abortion?"

"I realized I can't do that."

"But your body might be doing just that."

"Did I do anything to make that happen last night?"

"No, it doesn't sound like it to me. I've known you all your life and I know how you have always wanted to be a doctor."

"I still do."

"So you and the father of this baby need to make some hard decisions in the weeks ahead."

"I know."

"I'll be glad to answer any questions you have." He wrote on a prescription pad and handed the paper to her. "In the meantime, your job is to grow a healthy baby. These are prenatal vitamins, take them as ordered. My nurse will give you a couple of booklets about your months ahead and, of course, you can find lots of information online. And I will see you once a month for the first four months, unless there is something unusual happening. Like this bleeding. If it continues or worsens, I want to hear from you immediately. Okay?"

Kirsten nodded.

"Thank you," Leah said as she stood. "Oh, one other

thing. The kids were to be part of a missions team that leaves for Mexico in about ten days. What do you think of Kirsten going on that?"

"I might have said go with my blessing, but this bleeding episode makes me more dubious. How about passing this one up, just to be on the safe side?"

Kirsten nodded on the outside but inside she was fuming. One more thing to give up. One more thing that wasn't fair. Her life was changing, but José's was pretty much going on as usual.

Chapter Twenty-Four

Leah woke early the next morning. It had been two days since her baby had become an adult, legally at least. Physically she'd been there a while. Her second thought went to the Winchester family. Kirby would never have another birthday, go swimming with his grammy, or fall in love with the new baby that would arrive in the next month or so. *Dear Lord, comfort this family and bring them the peace that only you can give.* She heaved a sigh and Marcus rolled over.

"Are you all right?" he asked.

"Praying for the Winchesters."

He scooted his pillow up and locked his hands behind his head. "Virginia is being so true to trusting God but the sorrow behind her eyes breaks my heart. His mother tried the stiff-upper-lip routine but she fell apart and they sedated her, for overnight."

"What about the car that hit him?"

"A man from out of town, visiting friends here. He is devastated. The bike swerved in front of him before he even realized what was happening and could hit the brakes. Kirby was at Grammy Virginia's house, so she is blaming herself, of course. I pray she will let that go. All these years and I still have trouble coming up with the right words."

"There are no right words in a case like this." She turned on her side so she could see him more clearly. "You slept better than at any time since Kirsten made her announcement."

"I know. Hard to say that Kirby's death set me free, but it did. When I held Kirsten on my lap, I felt this huge load lift, like giant hands were raising it so I could stand straight again."

Leah heaved a sigh that held some strange combination of relief and joy. "I'm glad Kirsten was able to enjoy her birthday, in spite of everything. You should have seen the look on her face when she brought the vase of roses into the kitchen. She was positively beaming. I was beginning to think this whole thing had killed the love she had for José."

"That is childhood love, you know that. Things could change."

"Just don't call it puppy love. They could change, of course, but not always. We'll just have to wait and see."

"Going to be a long, long time."

"You sleep for a while longer, I'm too wide awake." Sitting up, she slipped her arms into her summer robe and after stopping off to brush teeth and hair, meandered downstairs. She loved this time of day. The birds had just broken out in full chorus and the peepers hadn't turned off their night song. Stepping out on the back porch she inhaled summer and hopefully exhaled the last of a long winter. Spring had been shortchanged this year. Two ruby-throated hummingbirds darted to the sugar-water feeder, as if afraid she might take it away, not that they were really afraid of anything. The flat seed feeder now held mealy worms for the bluebirds. The flock of purple martins had finished moving into their condos and were dipping and darting around catching bugs. While the petunia baskets lacked color yet, the backyard was beginning to look and feel like summer. Maybe they should eat out on the patio again tonight. So far she'd not seen any mosquitoes.

The coffeemaker created an aroma that drew her back inside to pour a mug and pick up her Bible. Outside again, she sat down at the table to read her lessons and work on her memory verse. One a week had been her goal every year ever since she and Marcus were married. By the time she finished her reading and her questions, her cup was empty and she could hear Marcus stirring in the kitchen.

She poured herself another cup, seeing that he had already poured his. "Come on outside. It's glorious. We could have breakfast out there."

He nodded, but appeared distant.

"You thinking about the elders?"

"Trying not to. They said they'd make their decision by this morning. I've been telling myself I am trusting God to work this out for everyone's benefit. Have you ever said, 'I trust you, Lord God,' with your teeth clenched?"

"Well, we got bombarded with a lot of stuff here in the last week. Not surprising that we are reeling." Leah thought about Keira's discovery. As much as she hated keeping secrets from Marcus, maybe Keira was right. In a way it may have been best. He had so much to deal with already. But he did need to be told.

"Leave it to you, Leah, always the pragmatic one."

"I know, but has He ever let us down?"

"Felt like it with Mother's death, but it was only selfish to want her to keep fighting when she was suffering so. So no, other than not healing her in the first place, He didn't let us down." He paused and looked up at her. "So, what are you doing today?"

"Getting the memory book to the printer. I work tonight. And you?"

"Preparing for the funeral service tomorrow. This will be one of the hardest I've ever done."

"I know. Is the truck going south again this weekend?"

"Yes, Lars is going with Henry and he'll look into the need for a construction crew to go down there. They're talking about taking self-contained RVs and campers down if a crew decides to go. From what Bjorn said, just repairing the church is going to be a major job, let alone homes and businesses."

The questions she wanted to ask above all others stuck in her throat. *What if the elders let us go? Would we have to move? What could he do for a living? If he couldn't pastor here, he couldn't elsewhere either. Stop it! We are trusting God for the answers here. We are. I am. I am trusting you, Lord.*

Marcus reached over and covered her hand with his. "It will be all right."

She heaved a sigh. "I know."

They had finished breakfast and he was about to go out the door when the phone rang. Marcus picked it up. "Pastor Sorenson here. Good morning, Jim…Yes, it is a glorious one." He glanced over at Leah, who had stopped what she was doing. "I'm on my way, so I'll meet you in my office in ten minutes. Good. Bye." He set the wireless phone back in the charger. "I know it is late to pray for a certain outcome but please pray that I can accept their decision as an edict from God."

"They would all have been praying for guidance and wisdom; you know how faithful they are."

"I know. I believe, Lord, help thou my unbelief." He crossed the room, kissed her, and strode out the back door.

Leah watched him go, knowing that the squaring of his shoulders like that said he was hanging on to his hope for all he was worth. "Just like me, Lord. We need you to intervene here." She closed her eyes, willing herself to trust that God would do the best thing for them all. After one more deep breath to keep her from hyperventilating, she pushed the speed dial for Keira. When she answered, Leah blurted, "Please pray for us, for Marcus; he is meeting with Jim at the church."

"Jim as in the chairman of the elders?"

"Yes." Leah put a hand on her chest to keep her heart from leaping out and running off. "I'm going to go running. Thanks." She clicked shut and within minutes had her running shoes and shorts on and was stretching on the porch steps. *Lord, please* pounded out with her shoes slapping the concrete. When she hit the end of the street and the beginning of the dirt road, she increased her speed, sprinting until her side yelped. She settled into a more consistent pace, reached her turnaround point, and headed back toward home. Sure was easy to tell she'd been a few days without running, more like a week. But her mind had cleared, the panic was driven back once again, and as she slowed, she could hear a praise song drifting through her mind. A children's song, one she hadn't sung for years. "Praise Him, praise Him, all ye little children, God is love, God is love." And children were singing it. She slowed to a jog and then walked the last block to cool down. What a way to celebrate an almost summer, but officially still spring, day.

She'd just entered the backyard when her cell bleeped,

the ring for Marcus. *Open it. Don't open it. God, help me.* "Hi."

"They refused to accept my resignation."

She collapsed on the metal mesh chair she'd occupied earlier. Heaving a "thank you, Lord" sigh and still catching her breath from the run, she waited for him to clear his voice. She knew he was fighting to keep control, so she kept the words bubbling to the surface from exploding from her mouth. All the while her "thank you, Lord" litany danced in her mind.

Marcus cleared his throat again. "I am to take a six-month sabbatical without pay, since that will go to pay someone to fill in. And this will take effect after the funeral. I won't be preaching Sunday. The goal of the sabbatical is so we can get our lives back in order so I can give a hundred percent like I always have before. Jim said they knew something was terribly wrong and were trying to think how to approach me." He stopped and blew his nose. "I think what I will do is go south with the truck, if that is all right with you. That seems to be where God is leading me."

"Will there be an announcement of the circumstances behind this sabbatical?"

"No. Not unless we choose to make our situation public."

"But scuttlebutt will get out."

"I don't know and at this point, I don't care. They are being gracious, God is being gracious, beyond measure." He paused to answer a question from someone in his office and slid from grieving and rejoicing man back into pastor mode. "I'm preparing the funeral and meeting with the family in half an hour. Please put out the word that they don't want flowers but want memorials to be sent to a fund at church to be used for something for children. They're not sure what yet."

"I will. This is such good news. Thank you, Lord." She said out loud what her mind had been singing. Marcus was not being forced to give up the calling of his life, God planned to use him in this capacity for years ahead. She stuffed the whisper that he was leaving her with all the turmoil ahead and reminded herself that God had a plan and this all seemed to be part of it.

When she entered the kitchen, Leah came back to the real world with a thump. Kirsten was sitting at the table, looking green and bleary-eyed.

"Uh-oh. Morning sickness?"

"I ate some crackers like you said, but like an idiot, I didn't buy the Sea-Bands. I will today if they could help. I thought maybe this was over with. I've been feeling so much better since yesterday."

"They say until about month four, and still something can set it off later." Leah filled a glass with water, and after chugging half of it, sipped the rest. "I'm going to get a shower and then finish up a couple of things and take the book to the printer. You want to go along?"

"Not really."

"Okay."

"Where's Dad?"

"Oh my word." Leah thumped her forehead with the heel of her hand. "His news. He called to say the elders would not accept his resignation but they stipulated that he must go on a six-month sabbatical without pay since his salary will be used to pay someone to fill in for him."

Kirsten stared at her mother. "Really?"

"Really. He will do the funeral for Kirby tomorrow and then he said he might go south with the truck. I have a feeling that if a construction crew goes down there, he will be one of them."

"He likes fixing things. He could go on the missions trip in my place since we already paid our money."

"You know, that's not a bad idea." Leah thought a moment. "I'm sure God is going to find plenty for him to do. What are your plans for the day?"

"Put out more flyers. On the windshields of cars in parking lots. Lindsey is going to help. Then we'll go door to door, I guess. I thought I'd get some response by now." Kirsten paused, staring down at her hands on the table. "Then I thought that if José gets off work early, I think he is done at five today, I thought maybe you and Mrs., er, Betty would be our referees so we can really discuss what we are going to do."

"Let me know what you want. I suggest you make a list of the things you want to talk about."

"I haven't mentioned this to José yet. He might get all mad and say no. But he has always liked talking with you and..." Kirsten sighed. "Maybe this isn't such a good idea. At least not yet."

"All right."

"But he has to understand why I don't want to get married right away. And why I can't do his plan." She looked up at her mother. "I wish I knew what was best for all of us."

Leah crossed back to the table and hugged her daughter. "Sweetie, that is our prayer all the time. Lord, give us wisdom and guidance, all that we need and then some."

A few minutes later, Leah realized she hadn't hummed

in the shower for a long time. She just hoped she wasn't getting ahead of herself.

"Please, José, let's give this a try. It can't hurt." Kirsten clutched her cell to her ear. Taking a deep breath, she fought to calm her stomach. Was it morning sickness or stress causing her to feel so rocky? She rested her elbows on her bent knees, sitting on the second-to-the-bottom step of the stairs.

"You want my grandmother and your mother to sit and listen to us fight."

"No, I want to talk and discuss without a fight. We never used to have more than a two-minute argument. I thought I could tell you everything, and if we disagreed, we could always find a compromise. That's one of the things I love about you—and us."

After a pause broken by a heaved sigh, he said, "Let me think about it."

"My mother agreed, do you want me to ask your grandma?"

"You want to go to a movie tonight?"

"No, I want to have a talk tonight." *Easy*, she told herself. *Don't let him get to you.* At least he wanted to see her. She waited out the silence.

"I need to get back on the chair. I'll call you at lunch."

"Okay." She thought a moment. "José, remember in speech class, how we had to have an outline? I'm thinking that might help for both of us. A list maybe."

"I said I'll think about it." He clicked off.

She trudged up the stairs, feeling better with each step. Up in her room, she stared at the bed. It would be so easy to crawl back in and take a nap. Instead she sat down at the desk when the bed would have been more comfortable and, flipping open her journal, started her list, topping it with school. When she'd written all she could think of, she set it aside and showered, dressed, and headed back downstairs. Now she felt ravenous.

"You here?" Lindsey called from the front porch.

"In the kitchen."

"Little bit late for breakfast, isn't it?"

"Not when you wake up with your head in the throne."

"Oh, sorry."

"I'm fine now. How hot is it out there?"

"Just nice. You sure you wouldn't rather go to the pool?"

"Sure I'd rather do that, but I need a job. Money is handy."

Sometime later, they had covered two parking lots with flyers when her cell bleeped José's ring. She leaned against the car she'd just left a flyer on. "Hi."

"I will do it, but not tonight. How about tomorrow night? I'm done at five then too."

She sucked in a deep breath. "Okay. You'll talk with your grandma then?"

"Yes. And I'll make a list."

"Seven?"

They set the time and she clicked shut. What if this didn't work? She shook her head. What did a referee do? Call time out if the argument got brutal?

That night, sitting cross-legged on her bed with her journal in her lap, Kirsten let her mind drift and ponder. Life should have been so simple this summer. Working, hanging out at the pool, getting ready to leave for school in mid-August when freshmen were required to attend orientation. Regular classes didn't start until September.

She, however, would be attending the community college in McGrath. She'd gone to the school library to read the book on procedures and requirements. She'd also discovered she could use two of her scholarships there. If all went right, depending on what they decided, perhaps she could transfer to Northwestern for the winter quarter. Or maybe she would go to the U of M.

José was not going to give up a free ride to Northwestern. Not if there was anything she could do about it.

She read again some of what she had written. Dreams, all of it. The most important thing she needed to concentrate on was taking care of this baby—and deciding what she, or rather they, would do. Keep the baby and figure out a way to raise it and go to school. Or...She swallowed the tears that suddenly burned behind her eyes, making her nose run too. Or give the baby to someone else to adopt and raise. One minute that sounded like the best idea, the next she was horrified at the thought. So many decisions to make. And she was so not ready to make them. How could she and José ever come to an agreement when she couldn't get herself to make decisions?

She started at a rap on her door. "Come in."

Her mom stuck her head in. "Night, I'm heading for bed."

"Are Curt and Thomas still coming to the reunion?"

"Of course. They both called back after you had gone to bed and we talked for quite a while. They're worried about you. But they were terribly disappointed, as you know."

"They're not the only ones. I know Paul and Eric are

going to grill me too, once the guys talk. The first thing
Curt will say when he sees me is 'How could you do such a
thing?'"

"You have to remember you are their baby sister and
little cousin who can—could—do no wrong."

"Yeah, right. I sure took care of that." Kirsten glanced at
the clock by her bed. "I'm surprised they haven't called again
to talk with me. But what can I say? I don't know what we're
going to do yet." She rubbed her forehead. "I really don't
want to talk with them, at least not yet. What's Dad doing?"

"Sleeping, I hope. He came up before you did. Night."

"Night. Wait." When her mother's head reappeared, she
asked, "I don't have to go to the funeral tomorrow, do I?"

"Not if you don't want to."

"And you remember our discussion tomorrow night?"

"Yes."

"Thanks. Night." The head disappeared. Kirsten raised
her voice. "Mom."

Leah reappeared, shaking her head. "Now what? Maybe
I should just come in and sit down."

"No, I don't want to keep you. But tomorrow night—I
will not compromise on José leaving for college in August
and on not getting married. Just thought you should know."

"That kind of blasts his entire plan, doesn't it?"

"Yes, but I will not give on those two points. Someday
he will thank me."

"You realize he wants to make sure this baby has what
he never had, a father and mother that care enough to raise
their child?"

"I-I guess I hadn't thought that through. Why didn't he
say that?"

"He's a man of few words?"

"Not always." *At least not when he's yelling at me about this.*

"But it is possible to put the baby up for adoption and still be able to take part in his life. Or hers. So many choices." She stroked the cat's back and received a hearty purr. "Can I go now?"

Kirsten threw her pillow at the quickly closing door. She got undressed and, standing nude before her full-length mirror, studied her body. While it didn't look any different, the waistband on her shorts was too tight and her breasts were tender, making her bras tight. She heaved a sigh and pulled her nightshirt over her head. According to what she'd been reading in the books her mother gave her, her belly would start to push out pretty soon.

Chapter Twenty-Five

The next afternoon, Leah slumped into the lounger in the shade on the patio. "If I never go to something like that again, it will be too soon. Children should not die, that is all there is to it."

Keira took the adjoining one. "I agree. I was glad I was working in the kitchen." She rolled her lips together. "Just thinking about him and them and I start to cry again."

"I felt so sorry for Marcus, he had such a hard time."

"My brother might try to convince the world that he can handle things but inside he's mushier than a marshmallow." Keira pulled out a tissue and dabbed at her eyes. "With my mascara running, I look like a raccoon. And this is supposed to be waterproof." She held out her tissue to show the black smudges.

"You want some iced tea?"

"Sounds good. You have any peanut butter cookies left? One sure would hit the spot right now." She started to get up but Leah told her to stay put.

She returned in a couple of minutes with two tall glasses of iced tea and a plate of cookies on a tray. "This is Earl Grey with a bag of mint. I really like it." She set a little ceramic container with packets of sweetener on the low, round table between their loungers.

"Somebody asked me what Marcus was going to do, so some kind of word is out. I said I was sure he would announce it when he could."

"Yes, Jim said they are telling those who ask that Marcus is taking a six-month sabbatical or leave of absence. The first reaction is shock and 'is he ill?'"

"Does he know what he is going to do?"

"He's going to the tornado zone with the truck this evening, that's all we know for sure. But I wouldn't be surprised if he takes a construction team down there to help repair that church we've been sending supplies to. Kirsten said he should take her place on the missions trip. I'm glad I didn't have to fight to keep her from going. The water and everything in Mexico? All she needs is some virus or bacteria at this stage."

"One day at a time. Wonder who started that joke that if you want to make God laugh, tell Him your plans?"

"I don't know, but things sure aren't going the way I planned."

"But you got the book to the printer. When are they saying they'll have it done?"

"Next Thursday, the day before the reunion starts."

"If all goes according to plan. Schedule is just a fancy word for plan."

Leah turned at the sound of the gate squeaking. "We're out here!"

"You two sure look comfortable." Marcus was shedding his suit coat and tie as he walked toward them.

"Sit here and I'll bring you some tea."

"No thanks. I need to get my things together. Henry says he hopes to leave by four."

"I fixed the cooler with sandwiches and fruit, some potato salad. Oh and drinks are in it too. Can you think of anything else?"

"Henry says he has a big thermos for coffee. He refills it at truck stops."

When he headed for the back door, Keira smiled at Leah. "I think he's excited to go along."

"True, but he's really happy because he knows what is going to happen to his ministry. The scimitar is no longer hanging over his head. Writing that letter to the board of elders nearly killed him."

"I imagine Kirsten's bombshell about broke him. 'Bout did me. That bleeding episode on her birthday..." Keira shook her head. "I can't believe you didn't tell me right away."

"Me either, but that was Kirsten's job to tell people. Just like I am keeping the secret about Dagmar from Marcus. This is killing me."

"Sorry. I was going to tell him and then all the rest of this happened. I could tell how close he was to the end of his rope. I mean, what if that had been an error on the birth certificate? So I had to wait for the copy. It came a few days ago, same as the one we found. And then I read Helga's letters. Like you said, she is the one with the answers."

"Did you try calling her?"

"Of course, but their answering machine is full and you know how they are about taking phone calls when they're traveling. I couldn't really say this was a life or death necessity." Keira blew out a breath. "I still can't believe I didn't realize this situation with Kirsten was happening when I first saw she was feeling so bad. The shock must have about knocked you out too."

"It did. Dumbfounded is the only way I can describe it. Then I alternated between total fury and hurting for and with my suffering children." Leah sipped her tea and watched a hummingbird at the feeder. "Remember when we vowed to never say, 'Our kids will never...'?"

"Sure, and we haven't."

"Well, I was pretty cocky about this, so sure these two would not make those mistakes. All of our antiabortion participation, discussions, classes, their vows of chastity. Never ever think 'my child will never.' You're setting yourself up for heartbreak."

"So think what a shock it was to find out my mother had been in that same place. My mother, queen of truth, no lies allowed. And you know, she didn't just talk the life, she walked the walk."

"I thought of something."

"What?"

"Remember what Jesus said, something along the lines of him who is forgiven much, will love more. No, that's not right. But maybe the knowledge that she had that huge failing and God forgave her is what helped make her love so unconditionally. She'd found that love and wanted others to have it too. You think?"

"Could be. Oh, the questions I would love to ask her. That's still one of the hardest parts of all this, not being able to ask her questions. I wonder if she debated keeping her baby—me—or putting me up for adoption. What if?" Keira rolled her lips together and looked skyward. "Is Kirsten thinking of putting the baby up for adoption or keeping it?"

"She doesn't know yet, but she sure is adamant that she will not get married."

"Think about it. What if my mother had put me up for adoption?"

The question fell like a pebble in a pond, sending out ripples clear to the banks.

"I cannot comprehend a life without you. That's another thing to put on the 'thank you, Lord' list. I am praying that God gives our daughter wisdom beyond her years and the ability to do what is best for this baby."

"Amen." Keira nodded as she studied the liquid in her cup, then looked up at Leah. "I think it is time to tell Kirsten about her grandmother, what little we do know for sure."

"You should tell her father first."

"But he'll be gone. I can tell him when he gets back, but I think Kirsten needs to know this before she and José make any final plans, not that at this point, plans can't be changed."

"Let's play it by ear. I hate to see Marcus all strung out again when he's just feeling somewhat back together."

Both women waved Marcus off as the big truck stopped on the street in front of the house. He promised to see them in two days, and, after setting his cooler and small duffle behind the seat, climbed in.

"Will he do some of the driving?" Keira asked.

"I have no idea. He has driven a truck before, so who knows. What's Bjorn doing?"

"He had an appointment that he put off until after the service. Then he went to Uppsala to meet these people. He should be back soon."

"I am going to put away all the mess from getting the

book together, and then Kirsten and I will go for burgers. And then Betty and José are coming over."

"Really?"

"Yes. Kirsten has asked us to referee a discussion between her and José so they don't fight. I jokingly suggested a referee and she took me up on it. Then I would like to take a bubble bath, relax, and read a book until the water turns cold."

"Make sure you don't fall asleep and drown the book." That had happened a few years earlier and had been a joke between them ever since.

Keira stopped at the gate. "Guess I'll head on home then. If you need anything, holler."

"Hey, if you need a research assistant, I'm volunteering."

"I'll take you up on it."

Leah had her room back in shape again but for the three plastic containers with all the pictures sorted by year and packets ready of pictures she had sorted out that other family members might want to have. Those were filed in another box. She heard the screen door bang.

"Mom?"

"In my room."

"Are we going out for supper?" Kirsten appeared in the doorway. "You've been busy."

"I thought maybe this would be a cozy room to have our discussion in."

"I guess. I'm hungry."

"Okay, we'll go. Where you been?"

"Got my first job from the flyers. I weeded flower beds for this lady who has a broken foot and hasn't been able to get out much. I go back on Monday to finish it. I'm going to suggest that I can plant some things for her, if she wants. Her yard usually looks so pretty."

"Just think, all those years weeding here is now paying off. We trained you well." Leah slung her bag over her shoulder. "Let's go. You drive."

José's empty car was in the driveway when they returned. They found Betty and José on the loungers on the patio.

"This is so lovely out here, we decided to not sit in the car but enjoy this." Betty made a sweeping gesture to encompass the yard.

"Thank you. I have iced tea in the fridge if you'd like. José, you know where the sodas are kept. Help yourself." Leah smiled at him. "I've missed you around here."

"Thank you." He looked to Kirsten. "You ready?"

She nodded. "In the lair."

When they were settled with drinks and snacks, a silence stretched. Kirsten finally cleared her throat. "Thank you for coming. I guess we could start this like a debate. Flip a coin and see who talks first. Mom and Betty are here to listen and offer advice if they think of something that could help. Is this all right?" This question she directed to José, who nodded.

"Okay. You want to flip or call?"

"You flip, I'll call." He dug a quarter out of his pocket. "Here." Kirsten flipped the coin and he called tails. She lifted her hand. "It's yours. You get to talk first."

"Okay." He reminded her that his idea was to get married immediately, move in with Betty, and both work until school started and then he would go to school whenever he was not working, so his schedule depended on his job. "I want our baby to have two parents who love each other and love our baby too."

Kirsten listened, watching his face and body language. She nodded and made sure she didn't flinch when he said he would work and go to school. "We didn't say if we could ask questions. What do you think?"

José shrugged. "In debate we each talked first and then questions."

"Right. So are you finished?" At his nod, she glanced at her list again. "I want to make something clear right up front. José, I love you and I want what is best for each of us—you, the baby, and me. I have to say I have made no decisions on what to do next except work this summer and go day by day. This is all new and I am asking God to lead us on the right path, which might not be the easy way. No, that's not what I meant. Nothing is easy about this. I want you, José, to go to Northwestern on your scholarship as you have planned and dreamed for years. This way you will be able to provide for your family in the way you want to, not in subsistence jobs. I will go to McGrath to CC and should be able to complete the fall session since this baby is supposed to come at Christmas. I will live here with my parents and when we all decide whether we keep our baby or put it up for adoption, then I will decide what to do next. I think this long-term plan will be better for all of us in the future."

While she was speaking she watched José school his face, like he did on the debate team. But she knew him well enough to recognize his disagreement.

"Now we can call for questions." Leah smiled at both Kirsten and José. "Kirsten, since you listened first, you get to question first."

"I don't have any questions at this point. No, yes, I do." She looked straight into José's eyes. "Do you still want to be a doctor?"

He nodded. "Someday."

"That's all I have."

"You said, 'I will make the decision,' regarding what happens to the baby. This is my baby too, and I think I should have a say in what we do."

"But what if we never agree?"

"I don't know."

"Sometimes you have to compromise," Betty said gently. "Sometimes you have to step back and let God do the leading, the decision making. Life is always best if we do the 'letting God' first."

If only we had done that, we wouldn't be in this situation. Kirsten stilled herself. "José, remember our class on life management? All the things we learned about costs and expenses and managing homes and jobs and family? Remember how she said that more couples divorce over money problems than any other reason? And that education is crucial to becoming the people we would like to be?" Kirsten knew she was pleading and debating didn't allow for that, but she had to make him understand and—please, God—agree.

He nodded, his voice grew clipped, but he paused, took in a deep breath, and continued in a debating tone. "But this is a real baby, not a hardboiled egg, and there are couples who make it." He nodded to his grandmother. "I have a good example right here."

Okay, Lord, what can we agree on? Kirsten glanced at her mother, who nodded, closed her eyes for a second, and put her palms together. Kirsten almost laughed. Her mother was indeed praying, why had she doubted? Taking in a deep breath, she exhaled and started again, feeling her way along as she went.

"José, can we agree that I cannot go away to school right now but you could? This is exploration, okay? Can we agree on that?"

He stared into her eyes and finally answered. "Yes."

"Can we agree that our education is critically important?"

"We have always said that."

"Yes or no?"

"Yes. But I will get my education, it'll just take longer."

"Okay. You have a strong will and a great deal of determination. What if education is your job and this baby is my job?"

"A baby needs both a mother and a father."

"I agree. But there might be other ways of solving this that we have not looked into yet. Things like student housing and college services, that if you were at Northwestern, you could look into. We wouldn't be the first to be in this situation, that's for sure." She paused for a moment, letting an idea germinate. "And besides, there is nothing you can do for this baby until after it is born, right?"

"True."

"Then what if we postpone this discussion until we have more information, and in the meantime, agree to disagree on the parts neither one of us wants to bend on?" Kirsten felt her eyes widen. Where had that idea come from? It sure hadn't been on her list.

He tightened his jaw and stared into her eyes. "So we'd be apart. You'd be here, going through all this alone."

"No, I'll be able to live at home with my parents while

still going to school." Along with growing a baby. And hopefully working part time. Where she would get the energy to do all that was something else she would deal with later. Someone had told her it didn't make a whole lot of difference where one went to school her freshman year. She sure hoped that was correct.

His eyes narrowed, his jaw taut. "Do you promise that you will make no decisions that concern us and the baby without talking with me first? And listening to me too."

Kirsten closed her eyes and clamped her lower lip between her teeth, fighting the flame of anger his stubbornness caused to flare. After all, she was the one who called the meeting, debate, whatever you wanted to call it. Compromise. There had to be compromise. "I promise."

All four of them released held breath at the same time, all in a whoosh.

Gentle applause came from the two women listening so carefully.

Kirsten sank down into a chair, sending José a tentative smile. "I think I saw ice cream in our freezer. The rest of you want to join me in strawberry sundaes? For a change, I'm really hungry." Would that someday soon they'd be able to discuss things again without referees.

The next morning Kirsten was dressed for her gardening job and heading out the door when Keira came through the gate.

After the greeting Keira put a hand on Kirsten's arm. "I know you are off to plant, but can I take a couple of minutes to tell you something?"

Kirsten stared at her aunt. This sounded serious. "Sure.

You want to ride with me to the nursery while I pick up her plants? Or...?"

"That's a good idea. I need some more geraniums. Let me go get my purse."

When they were both in the car, Kirsten turned from buckling her seat belt. "So, what's the secret?" Was that a flinch she saw? This was indeed getting interesting. One did not see Aunt Keira uncomfortable very often.

Keira chewed the inside of her cheek. "You know your mother and I have been doing a lot of research for the family memory book and I had to find my birth certificate to get my passport?"

"Yeah, because of the reunion and all that."

"Right. Well, when I found your father's and my birth certificates, behind the picture of him and me that always hung in the sewing room..."

"Grandma stuck them behind a picture? Why?"

Keira shook her head, a half smile in place. "Who knows, but we have found a lot of things behind pictures and under drawers. Money, important papers, poetry, other pictures, a wealth of stuff. She was a pack rat of the first order, as you well know."

"Drove Daddy nutso."

"I know." Keira paused to take a breath. "Well, when I read my birth certificate, it said 'father unknown.'"

"Wait a minute. Grandpa was your father."

"That's what I thought too." Keira blew out a breath. "I felt like someone had chopped off part of my life."

"So..." Kirsten thought about the conversation for a few long moments. "So who is your real father—or rather, your biological father?"

"I don't know. That's why I've continued searching. We have found a few things that make me think the man's name is Sam. I've read all the letters Mother kept and I've been trying to get ahold of Aunt Helga. She's the last living member of the family, and according to the letters she knew at least some of the facts."

"She'll be here for the reunion."

"Yes."

"So you never knew." She turned to watch her aunt's face. "What if she had given you up for adoption?"

"I know, I've thought about that a lot. I was angry and confused for a while..."

"Why?"

"Because she always said to tell the truth, no matter what, and here she'd been living a lie all those years. And now I can't ask her any questions."

Kirsten shook her head slowly, still watching her aunt, who was now staring straight out the windshield. "All these years she kept the secret. Guess there's been a lot of secret keeping around here lately. What did Daddy say when you told him?"

"I haven't told him yet. With all that went on, I couldn't lay one more shock on him."

"I can't believe Grandma did that." Like her father, she tapped a finger on the steering wheel. "So what if this Sam is still alive?"

"I've thought of that, then decided I would have to cross that bridge if and when I came to it." Keira looked back at Kirsten. "I just thought, since you have so many decisions you have to make, that it was important for you to know this."

"So you'll tell Dad when he gets home?"

"Right."

"But he thought Grandma could walk on water."

"I know, that's why I hate to tell him. But I will. I'm really tired of trying to keep secrets. They can eat you alive."

Kirsten reached a hand to pat her aunt's arm. "I'm sorry you had such a shock. Grandma and Grandpa kept you, but I don't know what to do about this baby yet. I just want what's the very best for him or her."

"And you and José too."

Kirsten turned the key in the ignition. "You know what Mom always says is one bad thing about weeding and planting?" Keira shook her head. "Too much time to think."

That evening, lying on her bed, Kirsten thought back to the conversation with her aunt. So Grandma got pregnant before the wedding too. She would have understood, or had she forgotten all about those early years? The more she thought about it, the more questions danced into her mind. Was Keira born before or after Grandma and Grandpa were married? The way she understood it, the father was another man. Did they just pretend the baby came early, like they did in books?

She closed her eyes and pictured her baby. Boy or girl, it didn't really matter. She would bathe him, and dress him in the cute clothes she saw in stores. Like the babies she played with in the nursery at church. She loved to make them smile and try talking, waving fat little fists. Maybe that's the medical field she really wanted to go into. Pediatrics, helping babies and small children get well again. Her mind ranged to Kirby; she'd known him since he was born.

He'd been a favorite in the nursery and at times she babysat for him. Tears gathered at the edge of her eyes. Babies, little kids, should never die. She and José could help change that. She had to get to school too. She laid her hand on her belly. Was she strong enough to go to school, raise a baby, and help keep food on the table?

Chapter Twenty-Six

One week and one day till the reunion. Keira stared at the calendar. Surely that couldn't be right. She studied her to-do list, which seemed to grow longer day by day no matter how hard they worked.

"Maybe looking at this list where things are checked off would be more encouraging." Leah handed her the list from three days earlier. With all of them working, the yard at the home place now looked ready for company. After Marcus returned from the relief trip, he and Bjorn spent three days mowing, edging, and weeding. Leah and Keira cleaned the house and labeled all the pieces Dagmar had designated be given to certain people. Kirsten and Lindsey washed the windows, along with making and posting signs telling the guests where to camp and park.

Keira handed back the list. "Thanks. What have you heard from the printer?"

"She didn't return my call and then I forgot to call back." Leah dug her cell phone out of her pocket. "Answering machine," she growled after giving her information.

"Maybe you and Marcus ought to go over there."

"Why Marcus?"

"Because sometimes having a man along can help, especially the well-known Marcus Sorenson. Use any clout you can."

"This really makes me crazy. They said they'd be done."

Keira shrugged. There was no need to say the book should have been turned in sooner, Leah had already moaned about that more than once.

Leah's phone rang. "Well hi, Curtis, how soon will you be here?"

Keira turned back to her list. *Tell Marcus*, she had written some time before. She'd have to tell her sons as well, but she wasn't nearly as worried about their reaction. Now she was in another quandary. If she could talk with Helga first, she would have more information to give Marcus. Shame they weren't coming to the reunion early so they could get all the secrets out of the way before everyone else arrived. Maybe she should just get it over with. Of course, that led to one more question. If Helga confirmed what they knew and added more, did they need to tell the rest of the family? If so, the reunion was the ideal place, but she hated to throw a pall over the party. Or...why was there always an *or*? Maybe it wouldn't bother the others as much as it had bothered her. After all, to most of them it was just a story, a true family story, but they weren't the baby.

The longer she waited, the worse the anticipation felt. She hated to make her brother angry. Especially after all he was going through. It was one of those things on the list that she kept putting off: "Tell Marcus."

Wednesday evening, she had Marcus and Leah to her house for supper. Kirsten and Lindsey had pleaded to be released from their slave labor to go to a movie. All day she'd been going back and forth. Tell him. Don't tell him.

One by one, her excuses were taken away. A bit of a breeze kept the mosquito population in abeyance so they were enjoying the respite from their labors and a barbequed chicken supper.

"Are you ready for dessert?" she asked.

Marcus and Bjorn swapped looks. "When aren't we ready for dessert? You didn't make apple pie, did you?"

"I did. I still had one in the freezer. Ice cream?" *Tell him now!* The voice sounded adamant. "I'll be right back." She and Leah carried the plates and things into the house. "How about you dish up the dessert and I'll go get the birth certificate?"

"Good idea."

Keira fetched the envelope with the two copies of her birth certificate and set up the tray. She carried it out while Leah held the door. *Please, Lord, make this as easy as possible.* She set the tray down and handed Marcus the envelope. "I wanted to wait until I'd talked with Aunt Helga but..."

He took the envelope with a puzzled look and drew the papers out. The world seemed to stand still while he read it.

The glare when he looked up made her take a step back. "Where did you find this?"

"Behind that framed picture of you and me that always hung in the sewing room. The one beside the photo of Kenneth."

"Kenneth? You call our father Kenneth now?"

"Well, no. I mean yes. I mean, he's not really my father. Not my biological father anyway."

"Maybe not, but he raised you and loved you."

"I know it. And I adored him." Just the thought of the man who held her on his lap and told her stories brought up tears. Sometimes she wondered if all her searching for information on the man who sired her was really being unfaithful to the man who always said she was his best girl. She'd reply that she was his only girl and they'd both laugh. So why then did he and her mother never tell her the real story behind her conception? Was it the same reason Keira did not tell Marcus right away? Because she didn't want to add more to his hurt burden? She brought her mind back to the conversation. "What did you say?"

"Is this what you've been researching so hard?"

"Yes, I wanted to find out all I could, but all I know is that man's name is Sam. I plan to ask Aunt Helga for more information."

"So Mother made the same mistake Kirsten did."

"I thought of that too. Do you think knowing this will help Kirsten or make her feel worse? She has always idolized her grandmother, ever since she was little. I told her. I thought it might help." She watched her brother process the information. "Do you think we need to tell the others—at the reunion, I mean?"

Marcus shook his head. "I just don't know. I'm never in favor of keeping secrets but…"

"But?"

"How could you have kept this from me? Why?"

"You had so much you were dealing with. To find out I'm not really a Sorenson on top of everything else…"

He stared at his sister. "Whatever made you think you were no longer a member of the Sorenson family? I mean, I just don't get it."

"All I could think was that I have been living a lie, all these years."

"But it isn't your lie, it's theirs."

"So who am I? Inside of me, I mean, what am I made of? From? Mother was always such a stickler for telling the truth. I feel like she let me down."

"What if, instead, you start counting up all that she gave you?"

The urge to kick her brother in the shins made her foot twitch. How could he be so analytical instead of emotional? But now that she thought about it, and had wasted all those hours on a fool's search, she would have to admit that Bjorn had been right all along. What difference did it make to her life right now?

"Well, I sure hope he didn't give me some rogue chromosome that is going to ruin my life at some point."

Marcus tried to keep from laughing, but when he looked at her disgruntled face again, a hoot slid by his restraint and burst out.

The squeak of the gate caught their attention. "Curtis, you made it already!" Marcus took two strides and threw his arms around his eldest son, then turned to the slender woman at his side. She stepped into his embrace like she was his daughter, not his daughter-in-law.

"Hi, Dad. We couldn't wait to get here."

"I hope those are tears of joy." Marcus looked from Gwen to Curtis, who shook his head.

"It's a long story."

"Well, come sit down. Have you eaten? You know we have all the time you need."

Keira hugged the two young people. "We're sharing family secrets and do we ever have some doozies."

"As big as Kirsten being pregnant?" Curtis asked.

Gwen turned her head at his comment. "We can talk

about it later," Keira said quickly. "You didn't answer, have you eaten?"

When the two shook their heads, Keira and Leah brought the supper back outside, where they served memories along with the food and only adjourned to the house when the mosquitoes arrived at dusk.

"We need a full-time telephone answerer," Leah complained after the umpteenth call.

"At least they aren't calling to cancel." Bjorn settled back in his chair.

"No, most to say they are bringing someone extra." Leah made sure everyone had the beverage of their choice before sitting down. "Okay, why the sad faces when you arrived, Curt?"

Curt glanced at his wife, who began. "We've been going through a series of tests and the doctors concluded that I'm diabetic and that's why I have lost three babies. He said we had a choice, me or a baby. He suggested a hysterectomy to remove the possibility of another miscarriage." Her voice broke and Curtis took her hand.

"I want my wife to live, so . . . so that's where we are. We hadn't told you about the other two. This is so sad." He paused and sniffed. "Perhaps I'll have the surgery instead so she doesn't have to deal with the anesthetic and such."

"When did you learn you were diabetic?" Leah asked.

"About six months ago. I've been on insulin and pretty stable."

"Good." Leah reached across the gap between their chairs and took Gwen's hand. "At least there are a lot of good studies, better insulin and things now, and new products to make blood draws easier."

"Why don't you tell us the big secret you mentioned?" Curt asked, finishing his pie.

"I learned from my birth certificate that Kenneth was not my real dad."

"I wish you wouldn't say it that way," Marcus said. "My dad was and is your real dad. That other man, whoever he is, was only your biological father." He turned to his son. "That's all we really know about him at this point. Bjorn and I say, let it drop, but perhaps Aunt Helga will fill in some blanks and your aunt here will be satisfied."

"Does Kirsten know this?"

"I told her the other day. She accepted it much better than I did."

"That's not saying a lot," Bjorn added.

"Thanks, dear, but you have to admit, I am finally letting up on it. That's why I haven't looked up any old records for over a week. Anyone needs to find anything and I can tell you where to search."

"So did you get your passport yet?" Marcus asked.

"I applied but it hasn't come yet."

"I figure any day." Bjorn leaned back in his chair. "Sorry to hear your news, Curtis and Gwen. I know this must be extra hard on you."

She nodded. "I've always looked forward to carrying a baby, feeling it growing inside of me. It's like that was what I was made for." A tear hovered on her eyelashes. "But we'll get through."

As they cleaned up the kitchen together sometime later, Bjorn took his wife's hand. "See, that wasn't nearly as bad as you thought it would be."

"I know. And much as I hate to admit that you were right, you were."

Bjorn squeezed her hand. "I promise not to say I told you so."

"Right."

When he didn't let go of her hand right away, she looked up at him. "What?"

"I've got something I've been needing to say."

"Okay." Now what? Please don't let it be a health issue.

He hesitated again. "Now, please, don't take this wrong."

Serious business. "Bjorn, you're scaring me. What?"

"About our trip to Norway." The words picked up speed. "You know I love your family dearly, but I was hoping the two of us could take this trip with just us. You know, you and me. I know lots of people want a huge party for their twenty-fifth anniversary, but I'd really like the time with you."

"Oh. Well, why didn't you say something earlier?" She stepped close to him and put her arms around his waist. "If you want just us to go, so be it. And thank you."

He tipped her chin up, kissed the tip of her nose and then her mouth. "Thank you." They went arm in arm up the stairs, the warm glow lasting for some time.

The books did not arrive the next morning, or in the afternoon, but many more of the relatives did. Some with RVs or tents camped at the home place. Others took over the bedrooms there and filled those at Bjorn and Keira's too. Their two boys, Paul and Eric, didn't arrive until Friday night, having waited for their cousin Thomas's flight to arrive and driving a rental car up from Minneapolis together. They all stayed up late into the night talking. As she and Bjorn went to bed that night, Keira felt the contentment of having both her boys home with her. Even though she was sad that her daughter-in-law, Laurie, had been unable to come due to an emergency at work.

"I was beginning to think I was going to have to mail them out to everyone," Leah grumbled.

"This is just the way Mother liked it." Marcus turned to his sister on Saturday morning. "You've done well."

"No, we all did well. We made this reunion happen." Keira and Marcus stood on the back porch where they could see the barn and all the outbuildings, the three camping trailers and the two RVs, a volleyball court set up, croquet on the front lawn, and groups of lawn chairs scattered around. They could hear the hum of women's voices from within the house. The men were divided between the horseshoe pits and the three grills set up to help feed the seventy-five people gathered here. More were still coming who lived close enough to drive in for the day. Everyone always arrived with baskets, boxes, and coolers with more food. Running out of food was never a concern.

"Did the books get here?"

"We pick them up in an hour. Just be grateful. You'll have them."

Leah joined them, locking her arms through theirs so they formed a chain. "But only after much heckling."

"All that matters is that they are here today. When are you going to give them out?" Keira asked.

"I thought after dinner. We're eating at one, by the way. Queen Helga has spoken."

"I have the list of all the bequeaths. I'll do that after you hand out the books. You will sign each one, right?"

"Of course. I think you should too." She looked up at her husband. "How's the ice cream coming?" Marcus had volunteered to oversee the ice cream machines, all now on electricity, no more hand cranking.

"They're all set up and running. It's not like the old days, when Dad would break up the ice in a gunnysack, using the flat side of his ax. The guys would take turns cranking, and Dad would feed the rock salt and the ice into the tank. Oh, the stories they told around the ice cream churns."

"Hey, Dad, you're on my team for horseshoes." Thomas stopped beside them. "Always feels so good to come back here."

"When is it my turn?"

"We play the winners of those up now. Most likely right after dinner."

When Helga had the honor of ringing the triangle to call everyone to dinner, she gave it an extra lick. "That's for Dagmar. How she loved to ring this thing." She stepped back from the porch edge. "You say the grace, Marcus."

Keira made sure she sat next to Helga at one of the many picnic tables. "Do you mind if I ask you some questions about Mother while we eat?"

"Not at all. Ask away, I just don't promise to answer them all."

"I have something I'd like you to read." Keira handed her the birth certificate in an envelope. "We found this behind the picture of Marcus and me hanging in the sewing room."

Helga took it, settled her glasses squarely on her nose, and read. "Well, I'll be a monkey's uncle. I didn't think anyone else would ever know." She turned to Keira. "I never did understand why she didn't tell you years ago."

"So you knew about me?"

"Well, a lot of it I surmised by a few of the hints she would drop in her letters. You were a bit large for the age when they moved back here but no one ever said anything. At least not to my knowledge."

Keira gathered up every morsel of courage. "Did you know the name of the man?"

"You mean the rotten son of a...excuse my French. He broke her heart and walked off without a care. I sent Kenneth to find her and bring her home. I didn't expect him to marry her, but in hindsight, I wasn't surprised. He'd had a crush on her for years."

"But did you ever hear his name?"

"Why do you want to know?"

"The main reason is to find out medical history, if I can. But I guess it has become a personal thing for me. So did you?"

"I know she called him 'honeybun,' referred to him as HB in her letters. I thought I would gag. We never told Ma about him. Pa would have taken after him with the fully loaded shotgun, I'm afraid. Anyway, it made me wonder if perhaps HB were really his initials."

"Do you know what town he lived in?"

"He was visiting relatives, I think." She squinted, trying to remember. "I think they met someplace in St. Cloud. She was working at the drugstore there, you know. Had an apartment with two other girls. When she went to the big city, she was so glad to leave the farm behind. Come to think of it, I think she met him at some church event. She wrote to me once, 'I am head over heels in love and I am sure he feels the same way.' Giddy, she was."

"So she lived in St. Cloud?"

"Yes, and after they were married, she and Kenneth lived there too. He got a job in the local lumberyard and then his pa wrote and asked him to come back and help him farm, so they did. You were two or three by then. You were just as cute as a bug's ear. Big, beautiful blue eyes. Dagmar always made sure you had a bow in your hair."

"So you don't know his name, but you do know he was not from St. Cloud."

"Someplace in another state. I remember thinking he couldn't get too far away to suit me. But no, I never knew his real name and I wasn't about to call him honeybun."

"Could his name have been Sam?"

"Could be. Why?"

"Well, I found the name Sam on something and a picture of two couples where the man had been very carefully cut out."

Helga chuckled. "Sounds like Dagmar. Thrifty in all things. Get rid of the bad guy and save the rest."

"You wouldn't have any idea where she might have hidden my adoption papers, would you?"

"Did you look behind all the pictures? She was a great one for storing things 'in a safe place' as she called them, couldn't remember where they were." She chuckled. "Family trait, I think. Don't give any of her books away without checking for money. She always liked to have a private stash at home."

"No, I didn't think to do that with the books, but you

can be certain I will." Keira heaved a sigh and tipped her head back. "I think we've checked all the pictures."

Helga patted her hand. "It's not important, you know, not in the long run. Your mother loved you with such fierceness that I sometimes wondered if she was afraid he might find her and learn he had a daughter." She paused for a moment. "I think she was afraid he might try to take you away from her. I'm sure if he tried she'd have gone after him with the gun herself."

"But Kenneth did adopt me after they were married?"

"I think so." She thought back. "I'm sure he did."

"Well, we are getting closer. I still have more letters to go through."

Helga grinned, her smile so identical to the one Dagmar so often wore that Keira almost felt her mother sitting beside her. Other than that Helga carried a few of the pounds around her hips and middle and Dagmar was always on the whipcord side.

"Can I join you?"

They looked up to smile at Kirsten. "Of course. Sit down."

"I heard you talking about Grandma?"

"True."

"I wanted to ask Grandma's advice about what to do with this baby that I'm carrying. I had no idea she would tell me from her own experience."

"You're pregnant?" Helga stumbled on the word. "You and José."

"Yes. I am nearly three months along and I couldn't tell anyone. I wanted it not to be so terribly. But I am." A tear leaked out.

"So you and José will be getting married?" Helga laid her hand over Kirsten's on the table.

"No. At least not now. We're too young to get married, but I don't know what I, we, are going to do. I only know I am carrying this baby until it is born." She cleared her throat. "Please don't hate me."

"Hate you!" Keira jumped back in the conversation. "How crazy is that. Just think, I was that baby. Not with you but with Dagmar, my mother. Besides, why would we hate you?" She paused. That was what she had feared also. That no one would want her anymore, she wouldn't belong. Shaking her head, she covered the others' hands with her own. "I guess fear like that is what comes from keeping secrets. At least some of the time. Bjorn reminded me again with one of his favorite verses. 'You will know the truth and the truth will set you free.'"

Helga nodded. "Fear and hate and worry, they just wear you out, eat you up. I learned that a long time ago." She put an arm around Kirsten. "Your grandma would tell you to listen to what God's Word says. Let love be your guide."

"I wish God would make things clearer."

"Don't we all? He will guide you, but He won't hurry."

Giving the memory books out brought lots of wry comments and laughter, along with a few wet eyes as people flipped through their books and then their packet of pictures.

"You sure went to a lot of hard work," was the main response. The others were hugs and heartfelt thank-yous.

Keira stood up. "I want you all to turn to page forty-seven." She waited until they were looking back at her. "If you read that page carefully, on the bottom of the birth certificate, it says 'father unknown.' That is how, only a couple of weeks ago, I learned that Kenneth was not my biological father. This really bothered me, because I felt my mother, who always insisted on the truth, lived a lie and thus made my life a lie. As you can guess, I was really angry." She swallowed the tears that were threatening to clog her throat. "But I learned something from my mother that I want to make the center of my life too. Unconditional love. We have all commented on that through the years. She truly accepted and loved each of us, and all those around her, no matter what. Maybe that great crisis in her life, what God forgave her for, made it possible for her to live that way. I don't know. I wish she had told me this story so I could have told her how grateful I am that she was my mom. We don't remember to tell those we love how grateful we are for them often enough and then it gets too late. So let's not make that mistake." She paused to mop her eyes, hearing plenty of other sniffs and noses being blown.

She turned to Leah. "You did a beautiful job, my best friend and sister. But then, that is the way you do everything."

"Okay, knock it off or you're going to have me blubbering all over everybody."

"Right." Keira stood still and waited for the hubbub to die down. "I have here the list of gifts that Mother wanted to give to each of you. She dictated it to me, and we went through the house and put the proper name on each item. I know she planned to do that herself and give them out at the next family reunion, but the cancer got her first." She paused for a moment, fighting the tears that threatened.

"Oh heavens, Keira, just cry like the rest of us and get it over with," someone called. The laughter that followed made her wish for her mother's presence even more. But she read down the list without choking up completely. At the end, she smiled at Aunt Helga. "I have a request to make. For those of you who were given framed pictures, when you take yours down will you please check to see if Mother stashed anything behind it? You might have to check under the backing."

Helga gave her a thumbs-up sign.

When she finished, some of the relatives went searching for their gift, so the house echoed with laughter and voices calling back and forth. Someone found a fifty-dollar bill taped to the bottom of their whatnot table. Leah's younger son, Thomas, discovered an envelope with his name on it. Inside were four savings bonds valued at a hundred dollars each.

"But Mom, she already sent me money for school, every semester a check would appear."

Leah hugged him. "She always dreamed of being able to help her grandchildren get through school. I know she helped Curt too."

"This was deliberate, not her stashing money away."

"I know."

"Was Grandma wealthy so she could do all this?" Kirsten asked, holding her own envelope.

"She saved all her life. If you think your mother and I pinch pennies, your grandma taught us how."

"It's in the genes," Bjorn added.

"Look what I found!" Eric, Keira and Bjorn's younger son, shouted from the parlor. "Mom, come look."

She met them in the hall, the others right behind her. Eric handed her an envelope with a faded piece of paper. "I think this is what you've been looking for."

Keira hesitated. Could this be true? She took the envelope and pulled the certificate the rest of the way out. Sure enough, her formal adoption paper. Keira read swiftly. On the line that listed the father's name, she again read, "Father unknown." Anger flared for a brief moment, then died. Keira shook her head and looked at all her immediate family and then the party going on around them. "Look what the idiot missed out on." Tears streamed down her cheeks. "She was trying to protect me." She read the final page. Kenneth had indeed adopted her. Three days after they were married.

Monday evening after everyone had gone home, the two families were gathered for supper in Leah's backyard. Paul was the only one of the children left, other than Kirsten with José at her side.

"Monday morning quarterbacking?" Marcus asked as he set the platter of grilled chicken on the table.

"You have to admit that other than missing Dagmar, this was the best reunion ever," Leah answered. "And to think we didn't want to have it."

"Aunt Helga hugged me and said that Grandma would understand. And, if she had her way, she would be sending us suggestions on how to figure out what to do," Kirsten said.

"And you know her *suggestions*." Paul rolled his eyes. "I still can't believe all the gifts she gave us."

As the laughter rippled around the table, Keira felt if she turned quickly she would see her mother joining in, the sense of her presence was so strong. "Didn't you just feel her out there all weekend?"

Marcus nodded. "Sometimes I miss her so much that I want to pound on walls or something."

"But instead you pound the pavement," Bjorn said, tongue firmly in cheek.

"I do. But she was there, enjoying every minute." He looked at Kirsten and José. "I had no idea she walked the road you two are walking, but I know she depended on her heavenly Father all her life. Let Him guide you to the way that is best for everyone and then wait to make judgments until you can look back. Looking back is how we best see God in action."

Amen to that, Keira thought. *Lord, you gave me the answers I needed, not necessarily the answer I wanted. But I see now how you took a bad situation and turned it into blessings. And I know you will for these two we love also. I sure don't know how but I know you will. After all, peace comes from you. As Mother always said, "All will be well."*

Epilogue

"I believe we did the right thing." José held Kirsten in the circle of his arms.

"I know, but this hurts so much."

"You suppose this is part of our payment for not keeping our chastity vow?"

"But God forgave us and forgave us." Kirsten pulled back so she could see his face. How could he look so much older? He'd only been gone since August and he'd been home for Thanksgiving. She'd thought giving birth was hard, but that was physical. This ripped at her heart. She'd not realized she had a mother's heart until she held her daughter in the delivery room. Melissa Jean they had named her, and her adoptive parents loved the name too. Curtis and Gwen had taken her home with them from the hospital. The doctor said it would be easier for her and José if they didn't have time to bond with her. How could he say that? She carried that baby under her heart for four days short of nine months. No bond. Obviously he had never been a mother.

"We did what was best for Melissa."

"I know. I've been telling myself that ever since we decided we should do this. One day I know we will be grateful but right now is hard." She hugged him again and stepped back. "What made you agree? I was so sure you wouldn't."

"I don't know." He smiled down at her. "When my grandmother and I were praying about this, it felt like a wave rolled over me. All of a sudden I was absolutely sure. She came to me and said, 'You need to give those two the greatest gift, and they will give your daughter their love as a gift in return.' I told her I felt the same way." He paused, staring at nothing. "She and I, we don't usually agree like that."

"So we will be auntie and uncle, and someday she will learn that we loved her enough to let her go."

The organist started playing, and they wiped their eyes. When the door opened, Curtis and Gwen rushed in, their infant daughter wrapped snugly in a fleece bunting, one sewn by her grandmother Leah.

"Sorry we're late." Curt folded back the pink-and-white fleece to reveal the baby sleeping peacefully. "She wasn't like this a few minutes ago." He smiled at Gwen. "Was she?"

"She was hungry, was all."

"A true Sorenson. If you get hungry, yell and someone will feed you." He grinned at his sister. "Isn't she the most beautiful baby ever?"

"You're saying that to a very biased person."

"I know. I thank God every minute that He told you to give her to us."

"The ultimate gift." Gwen sniffed back tears. "How are we going to get through this ceremony without crying?"

Kirsten handed her a tissue. The joy on her brother's face and Gwen's eased the hurt somewhat. That first night had been the hardest. She'd cried all night, partly from cramping but mostly because she missed the person she'd been closest to. Auntie Kirsten. That would be good. Some-day she would rejoice, something assured her of that.

"Let's go," José said when Leah beckoned them from the doorway. He took Kirsten's hand and walked with her to the second pew from the front. Leah was waiting, smil-ing like the sun on winter snow. Next to her sat his grand-mother, her smile reassuring. Curt and Gwen sidestepped in and then Kirsten and finally José. They looked up to see Pastor Marcus nodding, a slight smile promising peace.

Nothing in the service registered with Kirsten until they were invited to bring Melissa Jean Sorenson to the baptismal font for the ceremony. *Please, Lord, you promised to hold on to me, I need your strong hands. We all do.* She clenched José's hand, almost as hard as when a contraction rolled over her. They repeated the vows to rear this child of God in the faith and teach her the Word. They joined with the congregation in the blessing. Her father dipped water from the bowl and patted it on the baby's head, once for the Father, once for the Son, and once for the Holy Spirit. Then he made the sign of the cross in blessing. Betty Flores brought up the baptismal quilt that the women of the church made for each baby baptized and presented it to Gwen, since Curtis was holding his daughter, who slept through the whole thing.

A line from one of Kirsten's favorite hymns floated through her mind. "When peace like a river attendeth my soul...thou has taught me to say, it is well, it is well with my soul." She stared up at the cross behind the altar and the stained-glass window of Jesus holding a lamb. He was holding her.

Back at the house after the service, she watched her mother rocking the baby in the old family rocker they were sending home with Curt and Gwen too. Now her mother had gotten her wish to turn the spare room into a grand-children's retreat. Right now there was a crib but one day there would be bunk beds with stuffed toys and games and even a rocking horse.

"When do you leave for school?" Gwen asked.

"Tuesday. José will drop me off as he goes on to Chicago."

"I'm surprised you changed your mind on where you wanted to go. I thought you were planning on Northwestern too."

"I was, but something pulled me to the U of M. One of these days I'll probably learn why."

"When we learned you were pregnant, I remember feeling such jealousy. I had no idea our lives would turn this way." The last words caught in her throat and choked out.

"Me either. I thought that after I heard Grandma's story that that was the sign of what we should do, keep our baby. I had no idea how we would manage but I knew I still believed not getting married was the best way." Her tissue was shredding so she reached for another. She caught a smile José sent her. *Will we be married someday? To each other? Can we put this behind us and walk ahead without looking back and getting caught in the if onlys?*

The next morning, Curt hugged her tightly. "Thank you doesn't begin to cover this."

Kirsten only nodded. Smiling wasn't quite possible this frosty January morning. "Drive safely."

"We will." He climbed into the tightly packed car with a rocking chair tied on the roof and waved out the window as they drove off.

Keira and Leah snuggled Kirsten between them, each with an arm around their daughter. Kirsten blew out a breath and hugged them both. "I could not have managed without you." She turned and hugged her aunt, then her mother. "Thank you."

"Someone better have brought another box of tissues." Keira dug in her pocket. "Nada." They sniffed together.

"Our house is sure going to be empty after you leave tomorrow." Leah hooked her arm through her daughter's and the two of them climbed the two steps to the back porch.

"That's 'cause you're sending half your furniture with your kids."

"Half my heart too. We'll pack the car for you this afternoon. Guess I should be grateful that I had you home longer than we expected."

"One more of the good things?"

"Yes. How about a cup of tea? Keira, did you by any chance bring lemon bars?"

"How did you know that? The tin is on the counter. I'll help."

"I'll be right there." Kirsten picked up Patches and went to stand at the dining room window that looked out over the garden, now blanketed with snow. So much had happened in a year. It was probably a good thing they couldn't see into the future. But one thing she knew for sure, God could indeed be trusted to live up to His promises. Her family could be trusted to love each other no matter what. And wasn't that one of His promises, to love His children no matter what? "No matter what" needed to be done in cross-stitch and hung where she could see it every day. Along with "all will be well." She'd ask her mother to add one more project to her to-do list for after the birth announcement sampler she had already started that would have all their names on it: "No more secrets, no matter what."

Afterword

Dear Readers,

   Someone once said that to be a good writer, all you have to do is open a vein and let your lifeblood pour out on the pages. *Reunion* was like that for me. I wasn't planning on writing this book. In fact, I had never told anyone this part of my life. But several years ago I was asked to speak at a mother/daughter luncheon at a friend's church. I had my talk all prepared and that morning was praying that God would use me and my stories to help or encourage others. He said, in the listening part of my heart, tell the story of you and your mother. I, of course, said something along the line of "are you crazy?" or "surely I didn't hear you right." I heard Him chuckle and remind me that He is not crazy and yes, I had heard correctly. Right about that time I felt sick, like the breakfast I had just eaten was not going to stay in my stomach. I was not prepared to give this talk; I totally believed He had been guiding my other presentation, the one that now I cannot even remember.

   So, after a period of panic, I let my fear go, agreed to His wishes, and reminded Him that since this was nearly stage time, He was going to have to take over. Now the Holy Spirit has promised that He will give us the words when needed, but standing up to talk without the notes I usually have prepared was not a way to calm the butterflies that were cavorting in my middle. So I told the guests that day that I had a special story to tell them. My mother's story— and mine.

When my brother, sister, and I were planning a party to celebrate my parents' twenty-fifth wedding anniversary, my mother came to me and said, "It's not really our twenty-fifth." Ah, wait a minute. What was she saying? You see, I was twenty-five years old and their firstborn. She explained to me how she had gotten pregnant out of wedlock and the man blew her off, so she went to stay with her sister in another town. There she met my dad and they fell in love, but she would not marry him until after the baby was born in case he changed his mind. He was in the Navy and due to be sent overseas. (I now have the letters he wrote to her.) My mother, who was trained as a nurse and the first in her family to go on to higher education, went to work at a hospital in Chicago, and when I was born she found a woman through social services to take care of me. God worked it all for good, as He has promised. I was much loved by these two women, my mother and my Auntie Bobbie, who took care of me until my mom and dad could marry.

When I learned of all this, I was so shocked I couldn't even ask questions. Since I am such a curious person, it is amazing to me that I didn't ask more questions then, or through the years. But what I know for sure is that Mom loved me more than herself and did not give me away or abort me. My mother has always been my hero and even more so now that I know all she went through to give me life.

No, I had never guessed anything like this—other than,

like all kids will often do when things aren't going right, I thought that I must be in the wrong home or maybe they adopted me or I want to run away or they don't really love me. For all those years neither Mom nor Daddy ever said a word or hinted at this secret. When Daddy and I were going through my teen years we had some real battles, but never once did he say anything about me not being his biological child like my brother and sister were.

I believe so many things that happen are guided by God's hand, but we don't usually see that kind of behind-the-scenes work that He does, until we look back.

So while I told my story that day, there were many tears shed and I learned later that other families were going through similar circumstances and needed to hear this message. Only God can orchestrate all that. And so He orchestrated this book too.

When writers call on some deeply emotional part of their lives to use in a novel, it hurts. And no one wants to deliberately cause themselves pain. But thanks to faithful friends who prayed for me, an editor who kept pushing for my best and encouraged me to dig deep and work through my characters, and the perseverance taught to me by my mother's and father's examples, *Reunion* is now for you. My mother learned through the years how to love unconditionally, and I want to love like that. In my mind, that is the greatest legacy she had to give me. I would hope that reading *Reunion* will help you learn that same lesson. To love like God loves, unconditionally, and to pray for those you love. You have no idea how God will use this desire, but I can promise you this, He will.

Thank you for joining me on this journey, and may we

all learn to listen and love without judging. And no, I never learned the name of my biological father, but I thank him for the parts of me that are from him and for never causing difficulties for my mom and dad. I hope he's had a good life.

Blessings,
Lauraine

Reading Group Guide

1. Which character in the story did you identify with most and why?
2. Why do you think Dagmar never told Keira about her birth?
3. What advice would you give to a friend who found herself in Keira's situation?
4. Do you think it was right for Keira not to tell Marcus about what she learned? Why do you think she wanted to keep it a secret?
5. Have you ever been asked to keep a secret when you were not comfortable doing so, as Leah was? What would you have done in that situation?
6. Is it ever right for someone to keep secrets from his or her spouse? What about other family members?
7. Do you think Kirsten handled her situation well? Should she have let José be more involved?
8. Do you agree with Marcus's decision to resign? Do you think the response from the elders was fair?
9. Did Kirsten and José make the right decision about the baby?

10. Dagmar kept her secret her whole life, while her grand-
    daughter told her parents immediately and was able to
    be more open. Given the era in which she lived, did
    Dagmar make the right choice? Do you think it is easier
    in today's society to be open about personal secrets?
    Why do you think that is?

More contemporary novels that celebrate love and family by Lauraine Snelling

Heaven Sent Rain

Scientist Dinah Taylor's life is upended when she meets seven-year-old Jonah Morgan. A mysterious child faced with a series of trying events, he may need more help than Dinah can give.

Wake the Dawn

When the small clinic run by Esther Hanson is cut off during a devastating storm, she will find strength in unlikely people—a border patrolman in mourning and the abandoned baby he finds.

On Hummingbird Wings

Gillian Ormsby is called from her successful career to care for her ailing mother. As she tends her mother's garden with the help of a handsome neighbor, she begins to question if her life is on the right path.

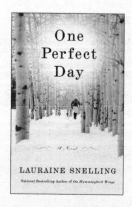

One Perfect Day

Only days before Christmas, the tragic loss of a child devastates one mother but offers another the miracle she's been praying for. With the gift of second chances made bittersweet, can hope be found in knowing that the spirit of each child lives on?

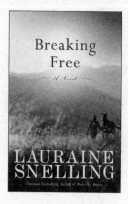

Breaking Free

Maggie Roberts gains a renewed sense of purpose through working to keep a horse from being discarded. But her reason for living is threatened when a local businessman offers the horse a permanent home.

Available in trade paperback and eBook formats
wherever books are sold.